STAR TREK®

MORE BEAUTIFUL
THAN DEATH

DAVID MACK

BASED UPON *STAR TREK*
CREATED BY GENE RODDENBERRY

GALLERY BOOKS
NEW YORK   LONDON   TORONTO   SYDNEY   NEW DELHI   AKIRON

Gallery Books
An Imprint of Simon & Schuster, Inc.
1230 Avenue of the Americas
New York, NY 10020

TM, ® and © 2020 by CBS Studios Inc. All Rights Reserved.
STAR TREK and related marks and logos are trademarks of CBS Studios Inc.

This book is published by Gallery Books, a division of Simon & Schuster, Inc., under exclusive license from CBS Studios Inc.

First Gallery Books trade paperback edition August 2020

GALLERY BOOKS and colophon are registered trademarks of
Simon & Schuster, Inc.

For information about special discounts for bulk purchases, please contact Simon & Schuster Special Sales at 1-866-506-1949 or business@simonandschuster.com.

The Simon & Schuster Speakers Bureau can bring authors to your live event. For more information or to book an event, contact the Simon & Schuster Speakers Bureau at 1-866-248-3049 or visit our website at www.simonspeakers.com.

Manufactured in the United States of America

10 9 8 7 6 5 4 3 2 1

Library of Congress Cataloging-in-Publication Data

Names: Mack, David, 1969– author.
Title: More beautiful than death / David Mack ; based upon Star Trek
    created by Gene Roddenberry.
Other titles: At head of title Star Trek
Description: New York : Gallery Books, [2020] | Series: Star trek
Identifiers: LCCN 2020008147 (print) | LCCN 2020008148 (ebook) | ISBN
    9781982140625 (trade paperback) | ISBN 9781982140632 (ebook)
Subjects: GSAFD: Science fiction.
Classification: LCC PS3613.A272545 M67 2020 (print) | LCC PS3613.A272545
    (ebook) | DDC 813/.6—dc23
LC record available at https://lccn.loc.gov/2020008147
LC ebook record available at https://lccn.loc.gov/2020008148

ISBN 978-1-9821-4062-5
ISBN 978-1-9821-4063-2 (ebook)

"RUN!"

It wasn't the most dignified order Jim Kirk had ever issued, but in terms of its words-to-results ratio, it felt like the right one.

The landing party sprinted back toward the tunnel. All around them, plumes of dark vapor took shape and pressed inward. One of the wights enveloped Petty Officer Kress, who screamed and lurched to a halt. Snared in the creature's smoky grasp, he convulsed, his voice suddenly choked off into a pained gurgle.

Kirk saw the gruesome spectacle, stopped, and shouted, "Kress!"

Beamon turned and aimed his phaser into the approaching swarm of shadows. "Open fire! Wide dispersal! Cover me!"

"Belay that!" Spock said, but it was too late. The security officers had already spun and opened fire, unleashing swaths of electric-blue phaser energy into the wights' swelling ranks. Beamon, perhaps hoping the barrage would clear him a path back to his snared subordinate, charged headlong into the creatures' midst.

Three pairs of vaporous tendrils seized Beamon and lifted him off the ground, then dozens of the entities converged upon him and Kress. As Kirk watched in mute horror, the two security personnel were reduced to twisted, pale caricatures of their former selves and cast aside.

Spock grabbed Kirk's arm. "Captain! We must retreat!"

Kirk pulled free of Spock's grip. "We can't just desert them, Spock!"

The half-Vulcan first officer spun Kirk around so that they stood face-to-face. "If we do not leave now, we will *all* die."

for K

HISTORIAN'S NOTE

The principal events of this story take place shortly after stardate 2258.42, in a parallel reality in which the *Starship Kelvin* was destroyed in 2233 by a Romulan invader (*Star Trek*, 2009).

*And I will show that nothing can happen
more beautiful than death.*

—Walt Whitman
Leaves of Grass, "Proto-Leaf" (1860)

STAR TREK®

MORE BEAUTIFUL THAN DEATH

1

Spock awoke to chaos and agony—the wail of a red alert and a wave of excruciating pain. His limbs were numb and paralyzed, but he was plagued by a profound burning sensation across much of his back. His pulse throbbed in his temples, aggravating the crushing sensation gripping his skull.

Where am I? What has happened?

He forced open one eye. His view of the compartment was sideways and blurry. At first he saw nothing but varying degrees of shadow. Then an alert panel on a bulkhead pulsed, filling the room for a moment with crimson light.

I am on the Enterprise. *These are guest quarters.*

Everything went dark again. Spock concentrated on overcoming the shock caused by whatever trauma his body had suffered. He drew a slow, deep breath and noted the acrid bite of smoke from a plasma fire mingled with the musky scent of traditional Vulcan incense, the kind used for sacred rituals.

Pain is an illusion. He summoned the mental discipline of his half-Vulcan heritage to overcome the physical limitations of his human half. *It is a construct of the mind. I must master my mind and control my pain.*

Another flash of red light bathed the compartment. He blinked and saw two more people sprawled on the deck a few meters from him.

One was his father, the famed Vulcan diplomat Ambassador Sarek. The other was the *Enterprise*'s senior communications officer and Spock's human lover, Lieutenant Nyota Uhura. Both lay unconscious, their faces bruised and bloody.

Darkness fell, and between the wails of the alert siren Spock heard a woman's voice begin a monotonal chant in an ancient dialect of High Vulcan. It was not a ceremony he had ever heard spoken before. Some of its phrases were so obscure that he could not translate them.

He labored to turn his head. It took all his strength to lift his chin from the deck and roll his head from left to right. A weak gasp of effort escaped his lips.

The chanting woman was Vulcan and slight of frame, and she wore her long hair gathered atop her head in a complicated coiffure. She was garbed in the ceremonial vestments of a Mount Seleya priestess, but even dim, fleeting glances in the ruddy half-light made it obvious the woman was far too young to have earned such a lofty status among Vulcan's most revered philosophers.

Though he could not see what the woman held in her hands, he noted the Starfleet phaser lying on the deck by her feet, and a fragment of memory returned to him: *She shot me as I entered.* Another off-key howl of the alert klaxon drowned out the woman's chanting, and Spock struggled to focus his eyes on her profile.

In a bloodred flash he saw her face.

She was L'Nel, his father's chief aide-de-camp.

He rasped, "Why?"

She fixed him with a stare of cold fire. "One must die for the other to live."

Spock's mind was a flurry of questions, but his mouth—dry and filled with a sour taste—refused to form words. All he could do was watch L'Nel turn her back on him and continue intoning her eldritch chants to the smoky darkness.

He turned his head away from her, hoping to see that either Sarek or Uhura had been roused to consciousness. Neither had stirred. As his eyes adjusted to the dim illumination, he became aware of the severity of Uhura's injuries. The young human woman had been savagely beaten, and Spock grew concerned that she might be in urgent need of medical attention.

I must try to reach my communicator.

He closed his eyes and concentrated on moving his hand to his belt. When that proved too difficult, he tried instead to move his fingers, even if only a little, just to confirm for himself that he had not been rendered a quadriplegic by whatever L'Nel had done to him after stunning him with the phaser blast. He felt a very human wave of frustration as his hand refused to obey his mind's commands.

Another whoop of the alarm was cut short, and the flashing red signal on the bulkhead dimmed and went out. From outside the room's door, Spock heard the muffled voice of Mister Sulu over the intraship comm. He wondered for a moment why he had not heard the announcement inside the guest quarters, and then he deduced that the compartment's comm system had been disabled.

Which means its internal sensors are likely offline, as well.

With great effort he turned his head to look again at the Vulcan woman. All her attention seemed to be focused on the object in her hands, and she maintained a hypnotic cadence with her chanting. Then she turned, faced Spock, and strode toward him, focused and purposeful. As she knelt beside him, he was able at last to see clearly the object she bore with such reverence.

It was an urn whose color betrayed its composition of Vulcan clay, and the inscriptions carved in concentric rings on its exterior and lid marked it as a product of the reclusive *Kolinahr* masters on Mount Seleya. The skull-sized container was nearly identical to others Spock had seen in his youth, in the Halls of Ancient Thought on Vulcan—in the days before his homeworld had been obliterated in an act of irrational vengeance by Nero, a criminal from the future.

L'Nel was holding a *katric* ark. The Vulcan artifact had one express purpose: to capture the *katra*—the living essence of a Vulcan's identity, all of one's knowledge and memories—at the moment of death and store it forever among those of its deceased kith and kin.

Despite his mental training, Spock felt alarm as the woman reached one hand toward his face to initiate a mind-meld. His alarm became fear as he discerned an icy gleam of malice in her dark eyes.

"Please," Spock whispered, "do not do this."

"The time for mercy is past."

She pressed her fingers roughly against the side of his face.

Unable to flee, fight, or call for aid, all Spock could do was meet the stare of a madwoman and bear witness to his own murder.

36 HOURS EARLIER . . .

2

Captain James Kirk skulked through the brightly lit passageways of the *Enterprise*, feeling like a schoolboy hiding from the principal while cutting classes. At each corridor junction, he paused and stole furtive glances around the corners, scouting the path ahead—and ignoring the curious stares of his crew, who strolled nonchalantly past him and looked as if they were trying not to let on that they suspected their newly minted young captain had gone off the deep end.

Almost there. He slipped around a corner on his way to the bridge. *Just a minute more and I'll be home free.*

Though the *Enterprise* was now under Kirk's command, the enormous starship still didn't feel like home to him. The vast spaces of its lower decks and shuttlebay intimidated Kirk, and its extensive labyrinth of corridors and crawl spaces often left him feeling like a rat in a maze. And the sheer power of the vessel was daunting; sitting in its captain's chair when the ship jumped to warp speed still reminded Kirk of the primal thrill he got from driving his stepfather's vintage Corvette off a cliff when he was a boy.

He darted across another T-shaped junction and paused. A curvaceous blonde with an angel's smile, a devil's leer, and an ensign's insignia passed him. He nodded and smiled in return, then reconnoitered the next leg of his journey.

All clear. The entrance to the bridge was in sight. He strode into the corridor and quickened his step. He froze as a Scottish voice called out from behind him, "What's with the sneakin' and crouchin', Cap'n?"

"I wasn't *sneaking*, Scotty." Kirk turned to face Lieutenant Commander Montgomery Scott, the ship's chief engineer. "Just being discreet." Scott wasn't the person Kirk had been laboring to avoid, but being intercepted by the fast-talking man certainly wasn't going to help matters.

Scott shook his head. "I've seen a fair bit o' sneakin' in my day, sir, and that definitely looked like sneaking."

Trying not to sound impatient but failing miserably, Kirk asked, "Is there something I can do for you, Scotty?"

"For me? No, sir. Well, not exactly." He scratched his head and squinted. "I mean, I wanted to see how you felt about letting me run a few experiments to see if I could recrystallize old dilithium inside the—"

"Proceed at your own discretion, Mister Scott." Kirk resumed his hurried pace toward the bridge.

Scott fell in barely half a step behind Kirk. "Really? Thank you, Cap'n! I shouldn't need to take the warp drive offline for more than ten or twelve hours if all goes well."

Kirk stopped, turned, and snapped, "Ten or twelve *hours*?"

"Aye. Can't very well go smashing high-energy particles through the warp core while we're chuggin' along through subspace, can we? Not unless you want to put on the galaxy's biggest fireworks show."

Shaking his head, Kirk continued walking. "Does Spock know about this little experiment of yours?"

"Aye, sir! He's the one who suggested it!"

Kirk rolled his eyes. "Of course he did."

"Does that mean I'm clear to proceed?"

Kirk turned and slapped a hand on the engineer's shoulder. "Scotty, as soon as you can find me a twelve-hour window during which we can't *possibly* have any need for warp drive, be my guest." The reply left Scott momentarily at a loss for words, and Kirk chose to walk away from the conversation while he still could.

Pivoting on his heel, Kirk came face-to-face with the one person he hadn't wanted to see: Doctor Leonard McCoy, the *Enterprise*'s chief medical officer, stood between Kirk and the doors to the bridge with his arms crossed. "Good morning, Captain."

"Bones." Kirk shifted his weight from one foot to the other.

"You know why I'm here, Jim."

Kirk tapped the side of his head and adopted a put-upon frown. "Yeah, I know, and I'd love to get that done, but I'm on duty right now, and I—"

McCoy lifted one eyebrow in a mild rebuke. "Your next duty cycle doesn't start for another forty-six minutes."

He grimaced at McCoy's arched eyebrow. "You know I *hate* it when you do that. Did Spock teach you that?"

"Don't try to change the subject. You were due in sickbay a week ago."

Kirk looked over his shoulder, hoping to rope Scott into the discussion as a diversion, but the wily engineer had already slipped away. He turned back toward McCoy. "I know, but it doesn't make any sense, Bones."

"What doesn't make sense? It's an annual physical, mandated by Starfleet regulations for all starship personnel— especially the commanding officer."

The captain raised his hands as if in frustrated supplication to an uncaring deity. "But I just *had* a physical *seven months* ago!"

"As a *cadet*. It doesn't count."

"Why not?"

"Because the regulations say it doesn't." The doctor sighed. "You know I'm supposed to relieve you from duty if you don't comply, right?"

Kirk recoiled from the implied threat. "You wouldn't do that. . . . Would you?"

"I don't want to, but you're not leaving me much choice."

"Oh, this is such a pain in the—"

"Captain Kirk, please report to the bridge," interrupted Spock's voice over the intraship comm.

Kirk smiled. "Sorry, Bones. Duty calls."

Before the surgeon could protest, Kirk darted past him

and through the doors to the bridge. McCoy followed closely behind him.

The oval command deck was defined by pristine surfaces, gleaming metal, and state-of-the-art holographic and touchscreen interfaces. As Kirk entered, Spock stood from the center seat and turned to face him. "Captain," said the first officer, "we have received new priority orders from Starfleet Command."

A red-haired female yeoman stepped toward Kirk and handed him a data tablet. He glanced at the top-level summary of the *Enterprise*'s new orders. "Not another mapping survey, I hope."

"No, sir," Spock said. "A planetary distress signal, from a world called Akiron."

Tapping at the tablet's interface, Kirk found his new orders curiously lacking in details. "Did they happen to say what their emergency *is*?"

"They did not."

"Of course not. That'd be too easy."

Spock hesitated before adding, "There is one additional component of our orders, which specifies—"

"Starfleet Command wants us to rendezvous with a civilian transport in five hours," Kirk cut in, reading from the text on the device, "and ferry its VIP passenger to Akiron at maximum warp." He gave a disgruntled sigh. "Apparently, we have priority orders to turn the *Enterprise* into a taxi."

Kirk handed the data tablet to Spock and settled into the command chair. "Sulu, plot an intercept course to our rendezvous with the transport, and prepare a flight plan from the rendezvous to Akiron at maximum warp." He swiveled his chair toward the duty stations along the aft bulkhead. "Uhura, let the transport know we're on our way." Rotating his chair forward again, Kirk looked over at his first officer. "Spock, see if there's anything in the memory banks about Akiron—the planet, the people, anything we might need to know before we escort a Federation VIP to its surface."

As the bridge crew snapped into action, and Ensign Chekov activated the intraship comm to issue a shipwide mission briefing, Kirk leaned forward and watched the stars twist past on the main viewscreen.

McCoy leaned over Kirk's shoulder and said sotto voce, "I don't suppose you could make time now for that physical."

"Not *now*, Bones. Can't you see I'm working?"

Spock stood between Captain Kirk and Doctor McCoy and watched five people materialize on the transporter platform in twists of light and a wash of white noise. Behind the three senior officers, Commander Scott sat at the transporter console and monitored the beam-over.

"Here they come," Scott said, to no one in particular.

Less than halfway through the materialization sequence, Spock recognized at least one of the visiting dignitaries as his father, Sarek. Beside him was a youthful Vulcan woman; she and Sarek were both attired in traditional Vulcan garb. Behind them appeared a middle-aged, balding male human, a tall young Andorian with long white hair, and a brawny, red-maned male Tellarite.

The transporter effect dissipated. Kirk nodded at Sarek. "Welcome back aboard, Mister Ambassador."

Sarek stepped down off the pad and stood in front of Kirk. "Thank you, Captain." He gestured at the members of his entourage, starting with the Vulcan woman. "Allow me to introduce my aide-de-camp, L'Nel." Continuing, he singled out the Tellarite, Andorian, and human. "My economic adviser, Tog chim Lesh; my legal counsel, Ferron th'Noor; and my scientific adviser, Amadou Sangare."

Kirk acknowledged the other four visitors with a curt nod that did little to conceal his impatience with the proceeding. "Welcome aboard." He quickly introduced Spock, McCoy, and Scott to the entourage, then turned his attention back to Sarek. "Ambassador, we're prepared to get under way to Akiron, so if you'd like to settle into your quarters for the—"

"With all respect, Captain, that can wait. The situation on Akiron is critical, and my team and I require your help." Sarek turned toward L'Nel, who handed him a data card. In turn, Sarek presented the card to Kirk. "We wish to brief you and your officers in detail as soon as possible."

Kirk accepted the data card from Sarek and passed it to Spock. "Have it your way, Ambassador." He turned toward his first officer. "Spock, tell the team to huddle up."

"Yes, Captain." Spock chose not to comment on his young captain's glib metaphor. He hesitated a moment before executing the order because he found himself transfixed by L'Nel's intense, confrontational stare. As soon as Spock met her gaze, L'Nel broke eye contact and turned her head.

Most unusual. Spock stepped away to a wall panel and opened an intraship channel. "Attention, all decks." His voice issued from the overhead speakers and echoed in the corridors. "This is the first officer. Senior personnel assemble in briefing room one immediately. Spock out."

When Spock rejoined the group, they were already leaving the transporter room and proceeding at a lively pace down the corridor, following Kirk to the briefing room. McCoy had lingered as the others departed, and he fell into step beside Spock as they trailed the others down the corridor.

"Must be a nice surprise for you," the doctor said quietly.

His remark puzzled Spock. "To what do you refer, Doctor?"

McCoy lifted his chin in Sarek's direction. "Seeing your father."

"I find it neither agreeable nor disagreeable."

McCoy harrumphed. "Some son you are."

"If you hold paternal visits in such high esteem, perhaps you should invite your own father to the *Enterprise.*"

The surgeon's expression hardened, and the muscles in his jaw tensed. "My father died while I was in medical school."

Spock felt a twinge of regret for the accidental offense he had inflicted. "My apologies, Doctor. I was not aware of your family history."

"Forget it, Spock. I'm just saying don't take your father's visit for granted."

There was no politic way for Spock to explain that every

time he saw his father, he relived the annihilation of Vulcan and the death of his mother. Instead he replied, "I assure you, Doctor, I take *nothing* for granted. . . . Not anymore."

Kirk sat at the briefing room table and listened attentively while Sarek addressed him and the *Enterprise*'s other senior officers— Spock, McCoy, Scott, and Uhura. The ambassador's aide-de-camp, L'Nel, stood behind Sarek, transcribing the meeting for the official diplomatic record of the mission.

"Starfleet Command and the Federation Council view the situation on Akiron as an opportunity to be capitalized upon," Sarek said. "The planet has vast reserves of high-quality dilithium crystals, which were discovered recently by a private mining consortium known as the Lexam Group. When approached, Akiron's dominant indigenous species, the Kathikar, proved amenable to interstellar trade. However, the recent disturbances on Akiron have caused the Lexam Group's board of directors to withdraw their personnel for safety reasons. From a legal standpoint, they have abandoned their claim, creating an opportunity for the Federation to negotiate with Akiron's government for the right to develop and administrate the planet's dilithium mines."

Uhura leaned forward and shot an accusatory look at Sarek. "Aren't the Kathikar a pre-warp culture?"

Sarek raised his eyebrows. "Yes, they are."

"Then why doesn't the Prime Directive apply?"

The ambassador replied in a cool, calm baritone. "The purpose of the Prime Directive is to prevent interference by *Starfleet* in the development of cultures that have no knowledge of warp propulsion or the starfaring civilizations of the galaxy. However, the Kathikar were made aware of the Federation's existence by the Lexam Group, a civilian entity not bound by the Prime Directive. Also, the miners provided the Akiron government with subspace radio technology to facilitate their business transactions. Lastly, that government has specifically requested the aid of Starfleet—thereby negating any possibility of a Prime Directive violation."

Kirk hoped Uhura would accept Sarek's long-winded answer and sit back so the briefing could continue. Instead, the feisty communications officer narrowed her eyes and sharpened her tone. "The Kathikar have a history of sentients' rights abuses, don't they, Mister Ambassador? A quick review of their file in the Starfleet database shows their culture is rife with gender inequalities, ethnically based caste systems, and such barbarisms as capital punishment."

A deathly hush fell upon the room while Sarek considered his answer—and Spock and Kirk both glared at Uhura as if telepathically willing her to be silent.

Sarek folded his hands at his waist. "Starfleet Command, the Federation Council, and I are all well aware of the Kathikar's sociopolitical proclivities. Though the details you have mentioned would preclude Akiron from becoming a member world of the Federation, none of them is sufficient justification for refusing to render aid to a planet in crisis."

Uhura's poise was not shaken by Sarek's answer or by Spock's and Kirk's baleful stares. "Apparently, its people's offenses against sentient rights aren't a barrier to *trade* negotiations, either."

"No, they are not. The Federation does not refrain from trade or interaction with cultures who embrace philosophies different from its own, or even with those whose belief systems are antithetical to ours. It is not our place to pass moral judgment, Lieutenant."

"So we'll just turn a blind eye when it suits our needs?"

"We will set the best example of which we are capable," Sarek said. "If worlds like Akiron someday aspire to share the bounties and protections of our civilization, they will be guided on a more benign path. But they must first desire change for their own sake. We have no authority to thrust it upon them, either by economic coercion in the form of tariffs or embargoes, or by force of arms."

Kirk sat forward and clapped his hands once to draw attention away from the heated exchange. "If we're done with today's civics lesson, let's get back to business. Ambassador Sarek, we'll be arriving at Akiron within the hour, so let's talk about the details. What do you need from us?"

Sarek looked at Kirk. "I have been authorized to negotiate on behalf of the Federation with Vellesh-ka, the elected chief minister of Akiron. Your orders from Starfleet Command are to provide any and all assistance required and possible to the people of Akiron. To that end, Captain, I would like to ask that you and a team of your choosing accompany me to the planet's surface when I beam down to begin negotiations."

"You got it. But before you beam anywhere, I want Spock and Scotty to analyze the situation from orbit, and I'll need to talk with Vellesh-ka."

A slow nod from Sarek. "If you think that is the most prudent course, Captain, I will defer to your judgment."

"Thank you." *Why does talking to Spock's dad always make me feel like I'm just a kid playing at being a starship captain?* "One last question: Do we have any idea what the planet's big emergency actually is?"

The Vulcan diplomat's face slackened with what Kirk took to be mild chagrin. "Unfortunately, no. Even in his original message, Vellesh-ka neglected to offer any details regarding the nature of the crisis."

"Great." Kirk cracked a sarcastic smile. "That always makes a mission like this *so* much more fun."

3

Sarek moved with calm authority through the cool, overlit corridors of the *Enterprise*, following the bulkhead markings to his assigned guest quarters. He pondered what was causing such profound distraction to his aide, L'Nel. The woman kept pace with him, but had not responded to his question of a moment earlier. "L'Nel," he said, repeating himself, "do you have my advisers' summary briefings ready for review?"

L'Nel blinked and cast a wide-eyed, self-conscious look at Sarek. "Yes, Ambassador." She lifted the data tablet in her hand. "The summaries are ready, complete with your earlier annotations."

"Very good." Sarek glanced sidelong at L'Nel. "You seem preoccupied. Is there something you wish to discuss?"

She lowered the tablet. "Yes, Your Excellency. However, it is a matter of some delicacy, and I am reluctant to broach the topic." Her posture straightened as she mustered her confidence. "May I make a personal inquiry regarding your son?"

They turned right at an intersection. "You may."

"Is Spock mated?"

Unable to help himself, Sarek lifted one eyebrow. "As with many queries regarding Spock, the answer is, 'It is complicated.' Technically, he is not mated—his betrothed was among those lost on Vulcan during the cataclysm."

L'Nel looked away, her mien thoughtful. "Does he mourn her?"

"I do not think so. They had been estranged for more than two decades. To the best of my knowledge, they had not seen each other since they were both children." He suppressed an urge to betray his feelings with a frown. "Though I doubt Spock would have sought to consummate that marriage vow in any case."

"Why did you doubt Spock's commitment to the betrothal?"

Sarek lowered his voice. "The human woman who argued with me in the briefing earlier—"

"Lieutenant Uhura?"

"Yes. She and Spock are—" The word *lovers* left Sarek discomfited. Instead he finished his sentence with the euphemism ". . . *involved.*"

His aide failed to mask her disappointment. "I see."

They entered his quarters. While Sarek busied himself selecting his attire for the first audience with Chief Minister Vellesh-ka, L'Nel prepared the room for Sarek's midday meditation by dimming the lights, increasing the temperature, and igniting some mild heather-scented incense cones.

Changed into his formal robes, Sarek joined L'Nel beside the table where the tiny cones filled the air with gray twists of smoke and a pleasing fragrance. "This is satisfactory, L'Nel." He stood waiting for her to leave so he could begin his meditation, but she remained at his side. "Speak your mind."

"Forgive me for interfering in familial matters, but with the procreation of the Vulcan species jeopardized by the loss of our homeworld, permitting your son to carry on his dalliance with that emotional human seems inexcusably *indulgent*. Would it not be logical to counsel Spock to end that relationship in favor of a union more beneficial to Vulcan society?"

Sarek cast a probing stare at L'Nel. In the month since she had come to work for him, she had proved herself to be intelligent and capable. On this occasion, however, she was revealing her naïveté in personal matters. "It might appear logical, but I think it would ultimately be self-defeating. In my dealings with Spock, I have found that the most certain way to encourage him to entrench his opinion is to take a contrary position."

"Then you do not believe Spock will be receptive to a logical argument?"

"Spock has long struggled to balance his emotions and his logic. In this matter, especially, I fear his logic might fail him."

L'Nel stepped around the table to stand opposite Sarek. "Perhaps your son's long association with humans—in particular, this Uhura—has eroded his emotional control. If he were to form a close association with another Vulcan, it might serve to reinforce the foundations of his logic."

Sarek saw merit in L'Nel's proposition. "A reasonable hypothesis. Regardless, I remain reluctant to meddle in my son's private affairs."

"I respect your desire to honor Spock's privacy. However, his privilege comes at the expense of our people's greater good. Logic dictates that the needs of the many outweigh the needs of the few—"

"Or the one." Sarek creased his brow at the old homily. "You do not even *know* my son. Does the proposition of this match mean so much to you?"

L'Nel bowed her head. "I would be most grateful to you for your intercession, Mister Ambassador."

He sighed. "Very well. I shall reflect on the matter while I meditate, and then I will discuss it with Spock. Leave me now."

"Yes, Your Excellency." She bowed again, from the waist this time, and then she turned and walked in graceful strides out of Sarek's quarters.

Alone at last, Sarek inhaled the soothing fragrance of incense and began the process of imposing order on the chaos of his thoughts. He did not know why L'Nel had developed such a fixation on Spock, but he suspected it might be a reaction to the cultural trauma inflicted on the survivors of Vulcan. In any event, as long as her interest in Spock did not compromise the performance of her duties to Sarek or hinder him in his mission to aid the people of Akiron, he saw no harm in making a subtle inquiry to Spock on L'Nel's behalf.

And if arranging a bond with L'Nel served to steer Spock back toward the path of logic and Vulcan tradition, all the better.

Spock stood in his quarters, facing Uhura. They clasped each other's hands at their sides; their eyes were shut, and he leaned forward slightly until their foreheads barely made contact. They would have only a few minutes of privacy before they needed to return to duty, but Spock valued such moments with Uhura.

Often they said nothing, and the silence was as great a comfort to Spock's troubled mind as Uhura's presence. That was not to be the case this time; he sensed words taking shape in her thoughts, felt the incremental shift in the tension of her fingers around his, heard her slow drawing of breath. When she opened her eyes and broke their silence, it came as no surprise.

"I can tell something's bothering you," she said. "Is it the mission?"

"No," he lied. The news of a planetary distress signal had provoked troubling associations for Spock, but he was loath to admit to such obvious sentimentality. A number of factors had contributed to his current unease, however, and since it would be inaccurate to attribute his state of mind to one element alone, he rationalized his lie as one of omission.

Undeterred, Uhura asked, "Is it because of your father?"

He lied again, this time for the sake of courtesy. "It is not."

She broke eye contact. Her voice was heavy with contrition. "You're upset with me for making a scene during his briefing." Looking up at him, she added accusatorily, "You're embarrassed because I argued with him."

"My father is a diplomat. It is part of his profession to listen to people who disagree with him, and the concerns you raised were valid."

Uhura shook her head and cracked a rueful smile. "You say that now, but I saw the look you gave me during the briefing."

"I admit I was surprised by your line of inquiry."

She let go of his hands, stepped away, and turned her back. "Right." Her tone conveyed anything but agreement. "*Surprised.* Sure."

Though Spock had been drawn in by Uhura's fiery passions, her moments of smoldering anger still left him bewildered. "If my reaction in the—"

His door signal buzzed, cutting off his reply. Spock and Uhura both turned toward the door, and he called out, "Enter."

The portal slid open with a soft hush, and Sarek walked in. He stopped a few steps inside the room and took note first of Spock and then of Uhura. "Forgive me if I am interrupting."

Spock looked at Uhura, who responded with an angry stare, a lift of her eyebrows, and a dismissive shrug. Uncertain how to interpret Uhura's somatic cues, Spock said to Sarek, "No, Father. You are not interrupting."

Uhura sighed and folded her arms, giving Spock the impression he had once again misread her mood and desires.

Sarek took a few more steps toward Spock, stopped, and looked at Uhura. "If it would not be too great an imposition, I wish to speak privately with my son."

"It's no trouble at all." Uhura glared at Spock, and then she walked to the door, which opened ahead of her. As she left she added, "Take as long as you want." The door closed as she stormed away down the corridor.

Sarek asked rhetorically, "Emotional, isn't she?"

"I do not wish to discuss it. Nor do I intend to let you meddle in the details of my relationship with Nyota."

Sarek affected a bemused expression. "Why do you assume I intend to interfere in your personal life, my son?"

"Because if you had come to discuss matters relevant to the mission on Akiron, Captain Kirk would be with you."

The vaguest hint of a frown darkened Sarek's face. "A logical observation," he said, implicitly conceding Spock's point. "Now that the topic is broached—"

"I have already said I do not wish to discuss it."

Sarek nodded. "You cannot avoid it indefinitely. Your refusal to consider taking a new Vulcan mate is no longer a matter of mere personal preference. It could have significant repercussions for the Vulcan race."

"I doubt that. I am only one among many thousands of survivors from Vulcan, and there are millions of others residing on colonies both within and beyond the Federation. My individual decision regarding procreation is, statistically speaking, insignificant." He recalled a conversation he'd had with an elderly version of himself from an alternate timeline. "And, for reasons I am not at liberty to divulge, I consider my obligation in this matter to be . . . fulfilled."

Sarek stepped forward to take a confrontational stance. "I do not. You are a scion of Vulcan, Spock, and its people need you. Even I am expected to take a Vulcan woman as my new mate, after my period of mourning ends. Why should you be exempt from this duty to your people?"

He stood his ground even as his father loomed over him. "I will not be lectured on this matter by you of all people. You had the choice to marry a human woman, and you did so. It seems the height of hypocrisy for you now to argue against my right to do the same."

Sarek looked taken aback. "Do you intend to *marry* this woman?"

Realizing he had rhetorically overextended himself, Spock broke eye contact. "Not at this time." Looking up, he added, "But I will not give up my prerogative to do so—not for you, and not out of some ill-defined racial duty."

"Listen to yourself, Spock. Do you not realize how selfish you sound?"

"Selfishness is not always wrong, Father."

"True, all things must be judged in context. But I think in this matter your logic is flawed, Spock. Your evaluation is far from impartial."

Spock nodded. "Perhaps. But it is my judgment to make, not yours."

Sarek held apart his upturned palms. "As you wish, my son." He turned and walked to the door, which slid open, and then he paused on its threshold. "For your sake as well as our people's, I urge you to reconsider."

"I will see you on the bridge shortly."

Sarek grimaced at Spock's implied dismissal and then departed. Spock watched the door shut, leaving him in shadowy solitude.

For a man who prizes logic above emotion, my father excels at making appeals to guilt.

4

Kirk sat in his chair and watched the planet on the bridge's viewscreen grow larger by slow degrees with each passing second. He was impatient to get the mission started, but events seemed to be conspiring against him.

"Uhura," Kirk said, swiveling his chair to look over his shoulder toward the communications officer, "do you have an ETA on Ambassador Sarek?"

Uhura shook her head. "No updates since the last time we checked, sir. His aide assures me the ambassador's on his way."

Turning forward, Kirk caught the eye of Spock, who stood a few meters away at a science console. "Spock, are we within sensor range of Akiron?"

"Yes, Captain."

"Good. Since we have to wait for Sarek, let's make use of the time. Give me a full sensor sweep of the planet. Try and get a look at what we're stepping into down there. Uhura, see if you can tap into their communications."

A vibration in the deck plates alerted Kirk to an increase in power output from the impulse engines half a second before Sulu said, "Getting our first taste of Akiron's gravitational field, Captain."

"Compensate and put us in a high orbit, Mister Sulu, but keep us within transporter range."

"Aye, sir." Sulu coordinated with Chekov as they guided the *Enterprise* into orbit above Akiron's northern hemisphere. The illuminated half of the planet slipped from sight as Akiron's terminator transited the main viewscreen.

Uhura was the first to report. "Captain, I'm picking up panicked chatter on most of the planet's radio frequencies. All of its satellites are overloaded with emergency news reports and private communications." Turning her chair toward Kirk, she added, "It sounds like Akiron's entire population is terrified."

Kirk nodded at Uhura, then looked at his first officer. "Spock?"

"There are major power failures occurring in the electrical grids on all four of Akiron's major continents. Its air traffic control system seems to be overloaded, and all its principal ground transit systems are congested."

An increasingly dire picture formed in Kirk's imagination. "Is there a pattern to the disturbances? Any discernible trigger?"

"They appear to be more pronounced in areas that are currently in the dark," Spock said, "and in those where darkness is about to fall."

In a Slavic-accented whisper just loud enough for Kirk to overhear, Chekov muttered to Sulu, "*Dat's* not ominous."

"Sulu," Kirk said, "adjust our orbit to keep us over the dark half of the planet. Spock, keep scanning the surface. Look for any strange energy readings, unlikely concentrations of exotic compounds, anything unusual."

Spock's reaction was subtle but tangibly dubious. "Captain, we are not yet aware of the reason for Akiron's planetary distress signal. This might be a political crisis, or perhaps a medical emergency."

"Call it a hunch, Spock. You just told me everyone on the planet's acting like they're afraid of the dark, and that makes the hair on the back of my neck stand up. So keep collecting data. Even if I'm wrong, the more info we have, the better we'll be able to help those people."

Spock nodded. "Logical." He resumed his scans.

The starboard door slid open, and Ambassador Sarek stepped onto the bridge, trailed by his aide and three advisers. Kirk declared, "Ambassador Sarek, how nice of you to join us. Hope you don't mind—we started without you."

"I apologize for the delay, Captain." Sarek appeared unfazed by Kirk's acerbic greeting. "My advisers and I needed time to confer before opening discussions with the Akiron government. We are ready now to proceed."

"It's your show, Ambassador. Tell us what you need."

"Please open a channel to Chief Minister Vellesh-ka's office."

Kirk nodded at Uhura, signaling her to carry out the order.

She worked quickly at her console and then looked up at Sarek. "I'm hailing the chief minister's subspace channel, but no one is answering."

"Please keep trying, Lieutenant," Sarek said.

"Yes, sir." Uhura spent several seconds entering commands and listening for responses before her expression shifted to one of keen attention. "I have a response on the main frequency."

Sarek replied, "Please put it on-screen, Lieutenant."

"Patching it in now."

The viewscreen flickered for a moment, and then it became hashed with static and wild interference. Off-key howls of noise oscillated in volume, occasionally drowning out the transmission's synchronous audio. After a few seconds the image on-screen resolved to show a spacious office, with a broad window behind a majestic desk flanked by colorful flags on poles. No one from the planet's government was visible, but from off-screen Kirk heard voices shouting *"Where are the guards?"* and *"Barricade the windows, now!"*

"Well, *this* is encouraging." Kirk looked at Sarek. "Ideas?"

"I must admit: for the moment, I am at a loss."

"Let me see what I can do." Kirk got up from his chair, stepped toward the *Enterprise*'s wide, deck-to-overhead viewscreen, and started shouting. "Hey! Anybody listening? You called for help, here it is! You want it, you better pick up the damned line!" No reply. Outside the window of the minister's office, an explosion bloomed amid the cityscape in the distance. "Last chance! I'm counting to ten, and then we're leaving!"

Sarek interjected, "Captain, I do not think that is—"

"One! . . . Two!"

"—the most diplomatic course of—"

"Three! . . . Four!"

"—action for us to undertake—"

"Five! . . . Six!"

"—at this pivotal—"

A disheveled humanoid with a murine visage stumbled into view on the screen, as if he had been at a full run until a moment before his appearance. He held out a four-digit paw toward Kirk and Sarek. *"Please! Don't go! I am Chief Minister Vellesh-ka. Thank you for coming! We need your help."*

"Calm down, Chief Minister. I'm Captain James T. Kirk of the *Starship Enterprise*, and this is Federation Ambassador Sarek. We're here to help."

Vellesh-ka pressed his paws together. *"Thank you, Captain! And our greetings and felicitations unto you, as well, Mister Ambassador."*

"And the same to you, Chief Minister."

Kirk clapped his hands together. "Okay, let's get down to it, Chief Minister. What, precisely, is the nature of your planetary emergency?"

Vellesh-ka shrank in a fearful cringe: *"Demons."*

5

Kirk blinked, and then he asked Vellesh-ka, "Did you just say *demons?*"

"*Yes, Captain,*" the Kathikar minister replied over the subspace channel. "*That's what we're calling them, for lack of a better term.*"

Sarek stepped forward to Kirk's side, to address Vellesh-ka. "Chief Minister, is it possible these 'demons' are an alien lifeform brought accidentally to your planet by the Lexam Group mining consortium?"

Vellesh-ka nodded. "*My science advisers asked the same question, Mister Ambassador, but we have no technology capable of making that determination. If it helps, the first incidents occurred in proximity to the dilithium mines.*"

"Okay," Kirk said. "For now, let's just call them 'demons' and move on. Chief Minister, how much can you and your people tell us about these demons? The more we know, the better we can assist you."

"*I understand, Captain. Unfortunately, we have very little data to share.*" The minister searched through the clutter of papers on his desk and plucked out a thin folder. He opened it and pulled out its top sheet. "*The entities appear as if made of smoke, and their presence chills the air. Their touch can kill a healthy adult within seconds, and none of our weapons seem to have any effect on them. So far they seem to fear only sunlight.*"

"Good to know." Kirk glanced at Spock. "We'll try to work that into our tactical response." Spock nodded and turned to begin working at his science console. Kirk looked back at Vellesh-ka. "Can you estimate the number of casualties inflicted by these demons?"

"*Thousands are dead already, and dozens more are dying every hour. Wherever night falls, no one is safe.*"

Sarek nodded. "We understand the gravity of the matter, Chief Minister, and we will act with all due haste. However, the *Enterprise*'s sensors have detected signs of widespread public disturbances in your cities. Can your government maintain order while Captain Kirk and his crew seek to contain the threat?"

The minister shrugged. "*We're doing all we can, Mister Ambassador, but panic is spreading faster than we can contain it—mostly because the news media hyped the threat to drive up their ratings and ended up inciting mass hysteria, looting, and riots. Just trying to manage the traffic caused by mass evacuations from the cities has badly overextended our police and military forces.*"

"I understand," Sarek said.

"I'm afraid you don't. The situation has been made worse by a religious sect that is spreading lies in a bid to destabilize this government and establish a theocracy. They're marching in the streets and hijacking broadcast stations to spread the rumor that the entities are creatures out of our world's ancient mythology—the Wights of the Underdark."

Noting the incredulous looks being exchanged by members of his bridge crew, Kirk asked Vellesh-ka, "Underdark? Care to define that for us, Minister?"

"The Underdark is a vast network of natural caverns deep under the planet's surface. One of its deeper levels was recently exposed by the Lexam Group's mining operations, shortly before the attacks began."

Kirk asked Sarek in a subdued voice, "Coincidence?"

Sarek kept his tone free of judgment. "Possibly."

"But not likely. Minister, based on what you've told us, it sounds like the best place for us to start our investigation will be in the mining tunnels that lead to the Underdark. Can you relay those coordinates to us?"

Vellesh-ka nodded. *"I will have my staff do so at once."*

"Thanks." Kirk added to Sarek, "If you and your staff still want to go down there, I'd suggest you take an armed escort, strictly as a precaution."

"A wise recommendation, Captain. For the moment, however, it would seem more prudent for me to continue my negotiations with the chief minister from the *Enterprise*." He looked at Vellesh-ka. "With your permission."

"Certainly. I wouldn't come down here, either, if I were you."

"That makes two of us," Kirk quipped under his breath. "Mister Ambassador, Chief Minister, I'll have my people set up a dedicated channel for you so you can speak in private. In the meantime, my crew and I will start analyzing the situation. As soon as we have a plan, we'll let you know."

"Thank you, Captain. I beg you, please work quickly—I fear my people don't have much time left."

"Just hang tight. We're on the job. *Enterprise* out." Kirk cued Uhura to close the channel as he moved toward the starboard exit. "Spock, I want you, Scotty, and Bones in the briefing room in five minutes. Uhura, set up a secure channel to Vellesh-ka from Ambassador Sarek's quarters. Sulu, you have the conn."

"They don't need a starship crew," McCoy said, "they need an exorcist."

"Aye," Scott said. "Since when are we in the business of chasin' ghosts?"

Spock wore a look of disapproval. "Gentlemen, regardless of the Kathikar's unfortunate choice of words, the danger these entities represent is real."

Kirk interjected, "Spock's right. People are dying down there. This is no time for jokes." McCoy and Scott's gallows humor turned to chastened frowns. He regarded his first officer. "Spock, what've you got so far?"

Spock entered commands on a data tablet, activating the wide display screen on the bulkhead at the far end of the con-

ference table. "Based on Chief Minister Vellesh-ka's description of the entities, I ran a sensor sweep for concentrations of
negatively charged ions, phase-distortion fields, and other phenomena known to be lethal to living organisms." A detailed
map of Akiron's surface appeared on the display. A moment
later it was overlaid with clusters of bright red dots. "These
points represent areas in which I detected unusually intense
pockets of negative energy." He pressed another key, and over
almost every red circle was superimposed a bright yellow one.
"These represent all documented incidents involving the entities, as reported to us by Akiron's government."

Scott pointed at the largest cluster. "That's right on top of
the mine!"

"Indeed it is, Mister Scott," Spock replied. "And all the
other major clusters are in close proximity to ancillary mining
sites, or to natural geological formations that provide access to
the planet's network of subterranean caverns."

McCoy folded his arms. "Which suggests the appearance
of the demons is related to the dilithium mining operation."

"There does appear to be a strong correlation," Spock said.

Kirk stood and paced while he eyed the display screen. "So
what's the connection? Why are these things attracted to the
dilithium? Do they eat it?"

Scott shook his head. "I dinnae think so, sir. If these buggers are made of negatively charged particles, dilithium ought
to be the last thing they'd like."

"We do not know if the dilithium itself is of importance to
the creatures," Spock said. "Until we conduct an investigation

of the mine shafts, it will not be possible to draw an informed conclusion regarding any such connection."

"Scotty," Kirk said, "how detailed a scan of the mine shaft can we make from orbit, using the ship's sensors?"

The chief engineer shrugged. "I can give you a clear picture of the top levels. Anything below that's gonna look a wee bit fuzzy."

"Do the best you can. Focus on the main site. We need as clear a picture of it as we can get. Spock, I want to be ready to beam down to the main entrance of the mine in ten minutes. Bring any experts you need, but I want at least four armed security officers down there with us."

McCoy asked with obvious alarm, "Excuse me, did you just say, 'Down there with *us*'?" Reacting to Kirk's sidelong glance, he continued, "You're not really planning on going down to that lunatic asylum, are you?"

"Damn right I am, Bones—and you're coming with me." McCoy grimaced. Noting a pall of horror crossing the chief engineer's face, Kirk added, "Relax, Scotty, you'll be staying here. I want you standing by at the transporter while Spock and I are on the planet."

Scotty sighed as the color returned to his cheeks. "Well, *that's* a relief."

"For *you*," McCoy snapped.

Kirk turned off the display and marched toward the door. "Meeting's over. Scotty, go run those scans. Everyone else, let's get ready to beam down."

6

"I apologize for the delay, Ambassador," Uhura said over the intraship comm. "I'm having some difficulty reestablishing the connection to Chief Minister Vellesh-ka's office. As soon as he responds, I'll patch him through to you."

"Thank you, Lieutenant." Sarek sat in front of the currently dark comm terminal on the desk in his guest quarters. He muted the channel and turned to ask L'Nel, "Have you downloaded Spock's sensor analysis of the planet?"

L'Nel nodded and handed a data tablet to Sarek. "Yes, Your Excellency."

He perused the tablet's contents. "Please let Mister Sangare know that I would like his input on this data as soon as possible."

"He has already begun his evaluation," L'Nel said. "He expects to submit his report within the next fifteen minutes."

Sarek drew a deep, relaxing breath and noticed that the ship's environmental system, despite leaving his cabin's increased temperature and dimmed lighting intact, had filtered all traces of his meditative incense from its air. "Please light another cone of incense," he said to his aide.

L'Nel bowed her head to acknowledge the request, then set herself to the task with grace and efficiency. Less than a minute later, she fanned a snaking wisp of lavender-scented gray smoke in Sarek's direction, sweetening the air.

"Most satisfactory." Sarek looked up from his reading. He noticed that L'Nel's countenance seemed taut. When she realized he was looking at her, she turned away. He asked, "Do you harbor concerns about our assignment, L'Nel?"

She folded her fingers together at her waist. "Not as such."

He set down the tablet on his desk. "About what, then?"

"I question the logic of Captain Kirk's tactical decisions in this matter."

"I see. Be that as it may, I must ask you to keep confidential any reservations you might have regarding the military aspects of this mission. Our purview extends only to its legal, economic, and political ramifications. Any and all decisions pertaining to the operation of this ship and the disposition of its crew fall under the absolute authority of its commanding officer."

I'Nel aimed a challenging stare at Sarek. "Even if Captain Kirk's orders place our political objectives in jeopardy? Or violate Federation law?"

"Do you believe such a conflict of interests has occurred?"

She averted her gaze slightly. "Not yet."

"Then what, specifically, are your misgivings regarding Kirk's command?"

"He is impetuous. And reckless."

His curiosity piqued, Sarek probed further. "In what regard?"

"Given the high probability of encountering a lethal confrontation on the planet's surface, why is Kirk taking nearly all the ship's senior officers with him in his landing party? Why is he, the ship's commanding officer, leading such an obviously perilous ground assignment?"

"As a starship captain, Kirk is privileged with significant autonomy in such matters. Though his decision to lead the mission on the planet is certainly unorthodox, it is fully within his command prerogative."

L'Nel appeared vexed. "Be that as it may, including his ship's only Vulcan crew member—"

"Half-Vulcan," corrected Sarek.

"—as part of such a high-risk assignment," L'Nel continued, ignoring the interruption, "is careless to the point of negligence."

Sarek regarded her with mild surprise. "A serious charge."

She cocked her head, striking an arrogant pose. "Do you disagree?"

"Whether I concur or dissent is irrelevant. Spock chose this career of his own free will. He could resign his commission at any time, but he elects not to do so. He serves in Starfleet and aboard this ship knowing full well the risks his duties entail, and it is not for anyone else—not even myself, and certainly not you—to question his logic. As for Captain Kirk, you would do well to remember that starships are self-contained societies—and they are, by necessity, *not* democracies. Kirk is the captain of this vessel, and there can be grave consequences for publicly second-guessing his orders."

L'Nel softened her tone. "I made no public objection to the captain's decisions. Any objections I voice to you in private—about this or other matters—should be considered as offered in strictest confidence."

"Most prudent. Consider my advice preemptive, then."

"Yes, Ambassador."

Sarek nodded. "Very well. If this topic is resolved to your satisfaction, I require my handwritten notes for the negotiation. They are in my traveling case."

"I will retrieve them at once." L'Nel stepped away to Sarek's sleep alcove to search his luggage for the missing journal.

Staring at the still-dark and silent viewscreen atop his desk, Sarek pondered the uncharacteristic vehemence and negativity of L'Nel's remarks regarding Kirk and Spock. *Her desire to insinuate herself into Spock's life as his new mate is likely an ulterior motive. Any action that seems to pose an unnecessary risk to Spock might serve to provoke her.* The more he considered the situation, however, the more deeply it troubled him. Her objections appeared logical on their face, but her manner suggested a more emotional imperative. Might she be suffering from a post-traumatic emotional disorder, as so many survivors of the great calamity did? *If she suffers from a mental infirmity, my first duty to her is to help her seek treatment—not arrange her marriage to my son.*

L'Nel returned carrying Sarek's journal, a thick book of unbleached parchment bound inside a creased cover of flexible hemp inlaid with thin planks of strong but lightweight wood. She handed the well-worn tome to Sarek. "Will there be anything else at this time, Mister Ambassador?"

"No, L'Nel. You may retire until I call for you."

She bowed her head, turned, and left his quarters.

Sarek perused the pages of his journal, refreshing his memory with passages he intended to recite in his discussion with Vellesh-ka and the senior members of Akiron's government. He was halfway through the first paragraph of his reading when Lieutenant Sulu's voice resounded from the overhead comm.

"Bridge to Ambassador Sarek."

"I am here. Have you reached the chief minister?"

"Yes, but I'm afraid your negotiations will have to wait."

"May I ask why?"

"Because we have a new problem."

Kirk stood on the transporter pad and checked every item of equipment on his belt for what felt like the tenth time: communicator, check; phaser, check; flashlight, check; tricorder, check. The backpack he was wearing was heavier than he would have liked, but even with all of Starfleet's technological advances, it still was unable to make rappelling gear and sub-space signal boosters that didn't weigh a ton.

McCoy scowled as he fumbled with the straps of his own backpack, alternately tightening and loosening them. From Kirk's vantage point, the problem seemed to be that McCoy's pack straps were entangled with that of his medical tricorder, which he wore with its strap diagonally across his chest.

The surgeon was sullen as he faced Kirk. "Tell me, Captain: What in blazes makes you think beaming down to a mine full of creatures that can kill carbon-based life-forms on contact is a good idea?"

"I never said it was a good idea, Bones. It's just our job."

"Really? Last time I checked my job description, it included practicing medicine and performing surgery. Random acts of suicide weren't covered."

Spock, who seemed perfectly comfortable with his own fully loaded pack, cut in, "Actually, Doctor, according to Starfleet regulations regarding the requirement for medical service personnel on hazardous landing missions—"

"Don't make me sedate you, Spock."

The door slid open, and four security personnel in red uniforms entered, followed by a man and a woman who both wore blue tunics. All six new arrivals wore backpacks and sported the same array of equipment on their belts that Kirk, Spock, and McCoy carried. Surveying the group, Kirk asked rhetorically, "Am I really the only one in this group wearing gold?"

"You can still back out," McCoy said. "Would that I could say the same."

Spock nodded at the two blue-shirted officers. "Captain, these are the specialists I selected for this mission: Lieutenant Jessica Sowards and Ensign Robert Upton." The two junior officers nodded their greetings at Kirk.

"Welcome to the team," Kirk said. "What are your fields of expertise?"

Sowards replied, "Geology, with a focus on dilithium."

"Exobiology, sir," answered Upton.

"Well, those both ought to come in handy." Kirk turned his attention to the four-man security detail. "Which one of you has seniority?"

"I do, sir," said a man of average height and impressive musculature.

"And you are . . . ?"

"Lieutenant Beamon."

"Introduce me to your team, Lieutenant."

Gesturing quickly at his three subordinates, Beamon said, "These are Ensigns Ewen and Willens, and Petty Officer Kress."

Looking over the group, Kirk asked Beamon, "Your best people?"

"Not really. Just their turn on the roster."

McCoy looked up, his focus sharp. "Wait, is there supposed to be a *rotation* for this?"

"Nice try, Bones. Just get on the platform."

"Hang on," McCoy said, "don't we have to wait for—"

The door opened again, and Scotty walked in. "All set, Captain!"

"Good work, Scotty." Kirk shooed McCoy onto the platform. "Let's get this show on the road."

"Not so fast," Scott said. "I just want to make sure you lads know what you're doing with those subspace signal boosters."

Spock cocked an eyebrow at the chief engineer. "I am well aware of the optimal deployment pattern for the boosters, Mister Scott."

"Aye." Scott gestured at the other members of the landing party. "But are they?" He noted the sudden surfeit of dubious glances. "That's what I thought."

Kirk rolled his eyes as Scott opened Ensign Ewen's backpack and pulled out one of the small, circular devices. "Space these no more than a hundred meters apart. Normally the range on these is a lot longer, but there's all kinds of stuff in those mines to bollix up your signals." He flipped over the device. "This li'l toggle's the on-off switch. Flip it, drop it, and forget it."

"Thank you, Mister Scott," McCoy deadpanned. "I'm sure we *never* would have figured that out without your sage advice."

Scott recoiled in indignation. "No need to be all snippy when I'm tryin' to help save your life!" He looked at Kirk. "Can you *believe* some people?"

Choosing to stay above the fray, Kirk asked, "Do you have the beam-down coordinates locked in, Scotty?"

"Aye, sir. Ready when you are."

Kirk stepped onto the platform. "Believe me, I'm ready." He beckoned the rest of the landing party. "Let's go, folks. Every second matters."

Beamon led the security detail onto the dais, and they spread out between the energizer pads. Kirk positioned himself near the front of the platform. Spock took his place beside Kirk as Sowards and Upton found spaces near the rear of the group. McCoy stood on the deck, frowning.

Kirk stared impatiently at the doctor. "Coming, Bones?"

"I don't suppose you have a plan in case the locals turn out to be not so happy to see us."

Kirk hooked a thumb at the crimson-shirted men behind him. "That's what these guys are for." He waved the doctor forward. "Come on, Bones, you're holding up the show."

McCoy glowered as he stepped onto the transporter platform. "You couldn't just send me a postcard?"

Kirk smiled. "Why should I *wish* you were here when I can *order* you here?" He nodded at Scotty. "Mister Scott, en—"

"*Bridge to Captain Kirk,*" Sulu said over the shipwide comm channel.

Kirk bounded down off the platform and hurried to a nearby companel. Keying open a secure channel to the bridge, he said, "Kirk here. Go ahead."

"*Captain, we need to postpone the landing party.*"

Kirk blinked, then looked over at his team. "Because . . . ?"

"*There's been a coup on Akiron. Chief Minister Vellesh-ka appears to be on the run with his subspace transmitter and is now sending out his own personal distress signal. It sounds like he's requesting amnesty, sir.*"

"Okay, so beam him up. What does that have to do with postponing the landing mission?"

"Perhaps you should ask Ambassador Sarek, sir. He made the call."

"Did he?" Feeling his pulse quickening and his temper rising, Kirk struggled not to grind his teeth as he clenched his jaw in anger. He drew a slow, calming breath. "Inform Ambassador Sarek I'll be there shortly. Kirk out."

Kirk closed the channel, shrugged off his backpack, masked his fury with a smile, and moved at a quick step toward the door. "Spock, with me. Everyone else, stay where you are. We'll be right back."

Sarek cleared his thoughts and readied himself for the emotional barrage that he was certain would ensue at the moment of Captain Kirk's return.

The doors leading from the bridge to the corridor parted, and Kirk strode in, followed closely by Spock. They could not have presented a starker contrast, in Sarek's opinion. The fair-haired Kirk was a living portrait of barely contained emotion, while Sarek's sable-haired son comported himself as if he were the very paragon of dignity and control.

Kirk demanded in a raised voice, "What's going on, Sarek?"

"Lieutenant Sulu summarized the situation quite ably," Sarek replied as Kirk confronted him and Spock returned to his duty station. "The government of Akiron has been overthrown, and no viable replacement has emerged."

The young captain's face and hands were animated with

confusion and frustration. "With all due respect, Ambassador, *so what?*"

"In accordance with the letter of Federation law, if no legitimate government exists to sanction our intervention on the planet's surface, then it becomes illegal for us to insinuate ourselves into a strictly local matter."

From the communications console, Uhura said, "Reports of attacks by wights on civilians are becoming more frequent, Captain."

Spock added, "Night will fall on the mining site in forty-eight minutes. If that is the origin of the threat, it will soon become exponentially worse."

Kirk's hands curled into fists, and his eyes narrowed as he looked at Sarek. "People are dying down there, Ambassador. Those aren't just legal abstractions, they're flesh and blood and bone, and you're asking me to turn my back on them."

"To be precise, Captain, I am *ordering* you to break orbit. The law demands you respect the sovereignty of the Kathikar in this matter."

Just as Kirk cocked his arm to point his index finger at Sarek, he was interrupted by a voice over the comm. *"Transporter room to bridge,"* said Lieutenant Commander Scott. *"I've got a lock on the chief minister."*

"Fine," Kirk said, "beam him up. Bridge out." Kirk closed the comm with a push of his thumb against a button on his chair's armrest, then he turned back toward Sarek. "I think the Kathikar have bigger problems right now than worrying about the finer points of their national sovereignty. They're completely out of their league against these things, whatever they are. We have to help them."

Sarek shook his head. "Forgive me, Captain, but I cannot permit it."

"Last time I checked, I was still the captain of this ship."

"I do not dispute that fact. However, your superiors at Starfleet Command have granted me authority over the diplomatic facets of this mission, and I am the final arbiter of what constitutes an acceptable degree of engagement with the Kathikar and their government."

Kirk stepped forward to intrude upon Sarek's personal space. "You want to deal with their government? Fine. Chief Minister Vellesh-ka is probably on board by now. Go greet him and talk politics while I work on saving his people from being slaughtered in the dark by ghosts."

Chekov said over his shoulder, "Demons."

"Whatever."

Sarek insisted, "You must not go to the planet, Captain."

"The word *must* is not used to princes or starship captains."

Sarek labored to conceal his waning patience. "Semantics will not change the facts of the situation, Captain."

"No, they won't. The *fact* is, we were invited here, and the Kathikar asked us for help. I'm not gonna take away that help just because the person who asked for it became a victim of the very mess he wants us to fix."

"But in the absence of a sovereign national authority—"

"It's a no-man's-land. Spare me the legal mumbo jumbo, Ambassador. If no one's in charge, there's no one to complain.

And until there is, I have a job to do." He held up his hands to stave off Sarek's rebuttal. "It's like hearing a man call for help because a wild animal's attacking him and his family in the middle of a storm. If the storm forces him to leave his wife and kids, do we turn our back on them? No—we *finish the mission*, Ambassador. We *save lives*."

The intraship comm squawked again from overhead. *"Transporter room to bridge. The chief minister's aboard—safe and sound, Captain."*

"Good work, Scotty," Kirk said. "Reset the transporter for the landing party. Spock and I are on our way. Be ready to energize as soon as we're on the pad."

"Aye, sir. Coordinates are in, pads are charged."

"Perfect. Bridge out." He snapped orders on the move. "Spock, with me. Uhura, keep an open channel to the landing party. Sulu, you have the conn. And if Sarek tries to countermand my orders again, put him in the brig."

7

Kirk watched the mad swirl of the transporter beam fade from his sight, revealing the twilight landscape that surrounded him and the landing party. Majestic towers of jagged red rock stood in tight clusters on a muddy plain. The night was sultry and thick with the odors of sulfur and ozone. Gray plumes of water vapor drifted from bubbling hot springs less than fifty meters from the *Enterprise* team.

"Don't tell me," McCoy groused. "This must be the garden spot of Akiron."

Spock pointed away from the flats, toward a steep and rocky slope. "The entrance to the mine is one hundred eleven meters in that direction."

Kirk started up the hill, taking point for the hike. "Let's get moving. It's getting dark." Spock, McCoy, Sowards, and

Upton fell in behind him. Beamon and the rest of the security detail fanned out on either side of the marching file.

"Here's a stupid question," McCoy said. "If the entrance to the mine is more than a hundred meters up the hill, why didn't we beam in up there?"

"Because interference caused by waste products of the mining operation would have scrambled our transporter signals beyond all recovery," Spock said.

Ostensibly at a loss for a smart-aleck reply, McCoy said, "Oh."

The effort of climbing the sharp incline while hefting a loaded pack proved more arduous than Kirk had expected. Sweat trickled from his forehead and dampened his hair, and within a few minutes his undershirt was soaked through. At the first sign of level ground he paused to catch his breath, and then he looked back to see how his team was doing. All of them except Spock seemed to be struggling against the heat and humidity.

Stopping beside him, Spock asked, "Shall I take point, Captain?"

"No, Spock. I doubt the rest of us could keep up with you." Spock nodded. "True."

McCoy halted beside them. "That's what we love about you, Spock: your modesty." He bent forward and pressed his hands on his knees to support himself. "My God, this pack feels heavier than when I put it on."

"As well it should," Spock said. "Akiron's gravity is roughly four point six percent greater than the Earth-standard gravity used on most Starfleet vessels."

McCoy glared at Spock. "Must you have an answer for *everything*?"

"I merely have a command of the facts, Doctor."

"Both of you, give it a rest." Kirk nodded at the dusk horizon, which was strewn with brilliant flickers and streaked with ragged black plumes. Cities and towns were burning like beacons in the gathering night. "These people are counting on us. Remember that." He resumed trudging up the slope, and the landing party fell into step behind him. Several minutes later they reached the top, which let out onto a vast, artificially leveled area cut into the mountain's face.

High-tech mining equipment and vehicles stood abandoned, some with their doors left open, others torched and reduced to husks. Handheld tools lay scattered on the ground amid scores of desiccated corpses. The entrance to the dilithium mine was at the far side of the plateau from the slope Kirk and his team had ascended. It appeared to be a natural opening in the rocky gray face of the mountain, but its crooked shape made it look to Kirk like a raw wound.

"Stay sharp," Kirk said. He nodded over his shoulder at Beamon, who drew his phaser. The other security officers did likewise.

The landing party moved with speed and caution through the wreckage-littered killing field, their footfalls crunching on the thin layer of gravel covering the ground. The security officers seemed especially alert. Keeping their backs to Kirk and the others, they sidestepped or backpedaled while watching for danger.

Spock, Upton, and Sowards activated their tricorders, whose high-frequency oscillations cut through the low, atonal moans of the wind.

"These workers have been dead for several days," Spock said.

McCoy stopped and kneeled beside one of the Kathikar bodies. "Looks like he died *ages* ago." The landing party gathered around McCoy as he activated his tricorder. "Severe molecular disruption. Signs of massive hemorrhaging. Damage consistent with a rapid crystallization of tissue." He switched off the tricorder and looked up at Kirk. "Jim, if I didn't know better, I'd say he was flash-frozen."

"Great. If the heat doesn't kill us, the wights'll freeze-dry us."

McCoy slung his tricorder as he stood. "You're the one who wanted to come down here."

Beamon looked worried as he stepped to Kirk's side. "Sir?" He nodded at the darkening sky. "We're losing the light. We need to keep moving."

Kirk nodded. "Spock, are you reading any life-forms near us?"

Spock made a final check of his tricorder. "None, Captain."

"Okay, then. Let's move."

The landing party quick-timed across the open ground to the mine's entrance. "Hold here," Spock said as they gathered in the jagged fissure. He removed his backpack, opened it, and took out a pack of six subspace signal boosters. "The first booster should be placed here, at the entrance." He removed one from the pack. As he activated the device and set it on the ground, he said to Upton, "Monitor our forward progress." Handing the exobiologist the rest of the pack, he added, "Every one hundred meters, deploy another booster. When these have been placed, retrieve the set from your own backpack."

The security officers activated their compact flashlights and proceeded inside the mine, scouting ahead for threats. Kirk and the others followed them. Once he was inside, Kirk felt dwarfed by the titanic cavern. It looked as if the mountain's peak had been hollowed out and its base honeycombed with tunnels.

The sulfur odor became stronger, and Kirk caught other stenches mixed with it—ammonia, hydrocarbon fuels, and a sharp stink of scorched hair.

Roughly a hundred meters from the entrance, the floor ended at a sheer drop into the bowels of the mountain. Layers of red, yellow, and black rock had been revealed by whatever had cut away the stone to plunder this world's crust of its riches. Where an elevator system had been mounted, there remained now only fractures in the rock wall. Debris from the elevator's frame and motor housing was spread out on various small ledges and outcroppings of rock far below.

"This is where the fun begins," Kirk said, taking off his pack. "We'll have to rappel down to the bottom. In theory, we should be able to continue on foot once we reach the lowest level of tunnels." He opened his pack and started pulling out his climbing harness and rappelling equipment, including the motorized winch that was intended to help him make a fast return ascent.

Upton placed a signal booster at the edge of the abyss, then joined the rest of the landing party in donning his gear for the descent.

Kirk was the first one suited up and ready to go, and Spock finished his preparations only a moment later. Within a minute, they, the specialists, and the security detail were watching McCoy fumble with his harness's fasteners.

"And to think," Kirk said, "those are the hands of a surgeon."

Spock added, "Mister Scott did say the harnesses were *foolproof*."

"Shut up," McCoy snapped. "I'm a doctor, not a mountain climber!"

Kirk gestured at McCoy. "Spock, give him a hand."

McCoy backed away as Spock approached him. "No! I'll figure it out myself! Keep your hands off me, you greenblooded hobgoblin."

Spock directed a questioning look at Kirk, who shrugged as if to say, *It's his call*. The landing party watched in embarrassed silence as McCoy wrestled with the clasps and straps of his rappelling harness.

Kirk checked his wrist chrono. "Bones, I don't mean to rush you, but—"

McCoy flung up his hands in surrender. "Just leave me here."

I don't have time for this. Kirk walked to McCoy and held the physician by his shoulders. "Bones, I'm telling you this not as a friend, but as your commanding officer: one way or another, you're gonna end up at the bottom of this mine. If you'd like to do it as something other than a pile of chunky salsa, let Spock help you put the harness on."

Kirk released McCoy and beckoned Spock, who stepped forward. As the first officer secured the doctor's rappelling harness, McCoy frowned at Kirk. "This is because I tried to make you take your physical, isn't it?"

"Of course not." Kirk flashed a cocky smile. "This is just one of the many perks that comes with being a starship captain."

A crash of noise shattered the reverie of Gveter-ren. Startled out of his meditative vision, he lifted his eyes toward his cloister's tiny window. Outside the Oernachta monastery, the sky burned with lightning and the world echoed with thunder.

He planted his old, gray forepaws on the floor and pushed himself upright. His muscles felt like dull aches braided around brittle bones. Each shuffling step he took scraped on the rough stone floor. Another flash of lightning slashed the wall opposite the window with blue light, illuminating his walking stick. The gem-capped shaft of black wood was as old and gnarled as Gveter-ren himself, but unlike the old mystic, it was still as strong as if it had been cast from iron.

Hobbling through the darkness to the door, Gveter-ren held the images of his revelation in the forefront of his thoughts, replaying the vision and committing its myriad details to his memory. Though age had enfeebled his body, his mind remained as clear as spring water and as sharp as a *skirpa*'s deadly sting. Even as pain flared in his ankles, knees, and hips with each step he took, he etched the shapes of the aliens' faces, the sounds of their voices, and their surges of emotion into the pages of his memory.

The door creaked open at his touch. He stepped out onto the covered promenade and looked over the waist-high wall to the garden below. Sheets of rain scoured the carefully tended trees and flowers and the handmade wooden furniture. The reflecting pools were dotted with ephemeral raindrop craters.

Wind roared through the jungle outside the monastery's walls, and Gveter-ren heard an explosive crack as a tree trunk snapped near its base and fell beside the lone road that led to the nearest town, half a day's walk away. This was the most fearsome tropical storm he had seen in years. For a moment he considered waiting until morning before starting his journey, in the hope that the storm might abate sometime after dawn. Then he thought better of it.

He descended the stairs from the promenade to the ground level and overcame the urge to pause in the doorway. Pushing on, he doddered into the storm, fighting for balance against the merciless to-and-fro pushing of the wind. His feet sank into the mud and slipped every which way, forcing him to rely on his walking stick for support. A brutal gale stung his face with rain. Within seconds his clothing was utterly soaked through and clinging heavily to him.

Amid the howl and crash of the tempest, he barely heard

the voice calling out to him from behind: "Elder! Stop! Where are you going?"

Gveter-ren turned to see Kalac-sul, a beige-furred young adept who was new to the jungle retreat. "I am walking to town."

The youth huddled in the open doorway, shrinking from the downpour as he gazed out at Gveter-ren with desperate eyes. "You can't! It's too dangerous!"

"I must. Return to your cloister."

With weary resignation, Gveter-ren turned and continued walking toward the rain-swept dirt road.

Rapid footfalls slapped across the muddy ground behind him, growing closer. Within moments Kalac-sul was at his side, one paw gently grasping Gveter-ren's arm. "Why must you brave the storm? What is so important?"

Refusing to stop, Gveter-ren trudged onward, forcing Kalac-sul to walk with him. "I have had a vision, Brother. A revelation I must share to save our world."

White fire arced across the sky and then was gone. Kalac-sul tugged on the sleeve of Gveter-ren's robe. "Please come back inside. We can radio a message to town if it's that urgent."

"Our transmitter failed yesterday—I suspect the storm is to blame. And considering our government's current state of disarray, I do not expect service to be restored any time soon—or perhaps ever, if I do not convey my message."

Kalac-sul cast a worried glance back at the monastery. "The others will ask after you when they awaken. What should I tell them?"

"The truth: that I have made an urgent journey into town so that I can use the transmitter at the observatory." He gently pried the adept's claws from his sleeve.

"The observatory? Who are you trying to contact?"

"The ship in orbit. I must tell its captain what I have seen, because if my vision is true—and I am certain it is—he alone can save us."

8

Where the machine-drilled mine tunnel ended, the Under-dark began. Kirk stood in the smooth-sided opening at the end of the tunnel. On the other side of a narrow rock bridge that traversed a yawning chasm belching sulfuric fumes, there loomed a titanic cliff face honeycombed with natural caves.

McCoy inched up behind Kirk and looked over the captain's shoulder. "I know what you're thinking, Jim. Please don't say it."

Ignoring his chief medical officer, Kirk looked at his first officer. "Spock, lead us across the bridge. We need to check out those caves."

"Yes, Captain." Spock moved ahead without delay. Ensigns Ewen and Willens followed close behind him. Beamon and Kress gestured for the two specialists to proceed, and then Beamon placed another subspace signal booster and nodded at Kirk and McCoy.

The doctor cast a grumpy frown at Kirk. "I even asked nicely."

"Nice guys finish last, Bones." He motioned toward the bridge.

McCoy parroted Kirk's gesture. "After you, sir."

Kirk shook his head and led McCoy, Beamon, and Kress onto the long bridge, which was barely wide enough for them to walk across single-file. Faint echoes of their footsteps reverberated from high overhead, and stray pebbles kicked off the path vanished into the fathomless pit of shadow beneath them.

No one had to remind Kirk not to look down; his natural instinct for self-preservation told him that much. He kept his eyes on Sowards's back as he quickened his pace to catch up to her and the others ahead of her.

Between one step and the next, everything changed.

A wave of vertigo washed over Kirk, and he inhaled sharply as his eyes lost focus. Then he blinked. Instead of seeing the landing party lit by flashlights, Kirk found himself surrounded by roughly two dozen bipedal reptilians, all of them barrel-chested and thickly muscled. Most disorienting of all, he was seeing them as beacons of heat in a vast, cold space—a crater with a yawning pit in its center.

I'm seeing in infrared? What the hell's going on?

Icy darkness descended on the assemblage of reptilian humanoids, and one by one their heat signatures faltered and went out, snuffed like tapers in a gale. Weapons were being fired, and the energy rifle in Kirk's hand was raised and discharged. He was a spectator, seeing a battle through one soldier's eyes but unable to take part in the fight—feeling his host's fear but powerless to help.

A cold black shadow engulfed Kirk, and he heard his body roar in pain and alarm as it collapsed to the rocky ground, its weapon blazing but having no effect.

He blinked again and felt himself falling. A hand grasped his shirtsleeve, and he heard McCoy shouting, "Beamon, help me!" Kirk felt as if he were spinning; he was dizzy and nauseated as McCoy sat him down on the rock bridge.

"Jim! Are you all right?"

Confused, Kirk fought to regain his focus. "What happened?"

"That's what I'd like to know," McCoy said. "One minute you were walking, the next you were getting ready to take a swan dive off the bridge."

Kirk's vision cleared as an excruciating headache raged inside his skull. "I feel like I'm reliving every hangover I've ever had, all at the same time."

McCoy lifted his medical tricorder and made a quick scan. "Heart rate's up, blood pressure's through the roof, synaptic activity's off the chart." He turned off the device. "Do you remember what you felt during the dizzy spell?"

Kirk nodded. "I was someplace else."

McCoy's brow furrowed with concern. "Where?"

Summoning the images and sounds from his memory worsened Kirk's pain. "I can't remember now. Dammit! It was so *clear*, Bones, but now I can't see it. It's like it was wiped from my mind as soon as it ended."

"I'd better get you back to the ship." McCoy waved over Beamon. "Help me get the captain back on his feet."

Beamon and McCoy each took one of Kirk's arms and hoisted him upright. The captain brushed the dirt from his uniform. "Thanks for your concern, Bones, but we're not going back, not yet." He turned and looked ahead to the rest of the landing party, who were waiting at the far end of the bridge. "We're going forward."

McCoy grasped Kirk's shoulder. "Do you have a death wish, Captain?"

"No, I have a job to do—and so do you. Let's go." Kirk willed himself back into motion despite the crushing pain in his head. He took several deep breaths as he walked, and by the time he reached the far side the pain had abated slightly. He looked at Spock, who was studying his tricorder readout. "Where to next?"

"Down this passage." Spock gestured at a wide tunnel that sloped down at a steep angle. "The negative-energy readings appear to originate approximately two hundred nine meters from here."

Eager to stay one step ahead of McCoy's nagging, Kirk led the way into the tunnel. "Beamon, Kress, stay close on my flanks. Spock, keep an eye on the specialists, and have them keep running tricorder scans."

The walls and floor of the tunnel were festooned with large, jagged chunks of crystal. Some clusters acted like prisms, scattering the flashlight beams into prismatic flashes. Others glowed with intense hues of ruby, emerald, sapphire, and topaz. As the landing party pressed deeper underground, many of the crystals began to take on a smoky quality, until some were as gray as volcanic ash.

Sowards called out, "Mister Spock?" Her voice echoed several times in the passage. Kirk looked back to see Spock move to the young woman's side. Behind them, Petty Officer Kress activated another subspace booster and set it in the middle of the tunnel. Walking with Spock, Sowards lifted her tricorder and angled its screen toward him. They conversed in whispers for several seconds.

Curious, Kirk asked, "What is it, Spock?"

Spock hurried forward to Kirk's side. "The gray crystal formations in this passage are most unusual. Their molecular lattices appear to be identical to that of dilithium, but another element has become entangled in their matrix—one that our tricorders are unable to identify."

"Do you think it has something to do with the wights?"

"Unknown. But it would seem to merit further scrutiny."

"Take a sample. We can study it when we get back to the ship."

Spock nodded at Kirk, and then he turned and gave a thumbs-up to Sowards, who stopped to pry free a loose chunk of crystal and put it in her backpack.

The end of the passage was in sight, and a vast space seemed to lie beyond it. Kirk quickened his pace, sensing he was on the cusp of a major discovery.

Another wave of vertigo dropped him to his knees. He winced and forced himself to push through the pain. He opened his eyes and was somewhere else.

He stood in a brightly lit room that was packed with high-tech computers. Displays updated in rapid flashes with data, graphs, and oscillating waveforms. Manning the terminals were stooped, bipedal figures whose heads made Kirk think of vultures. Their long, bony digits worked the consoles' buttons and touchscreen interfaces with surprising dexterity.

Panic filled the room, a current of fear so palpable Kirk feared it would drown him. He knew, as if by instinct, that these unusual creatures were his friends and colleagues, his collaborators in some grand endeavor gone terribly wrong.

Once more he was a spectator, trapped behind another being's eyes, looking out upon events he couldn't affect. He felt his host body's graceful fingers move with speed and confidence across a computer's touchscreen, but he couldn't read any of its symbols. Then the computers flickered and went off-line, and he felt a blast of frigid air as the room was plunged into darkness. Then he felt only terror.

Back inside his own body, he gasped for air—and was embarrassed to find himself down on all fours in the entrance to the massive cavern, surrounded by the other members of the landing party. He lifted his head, struggled to his feet, and shot a stern look at McCoy. "Don't say it, Bones."

"Say what?" He paused long enough to fool Kirk into thinking the matter was dropped before he added, "That you've collapsed twice in fifteen minutes? Jim, any competent medical officer would relieve you of duty right here and now."

"Luckily for me, I brought you." Kirk slapped the dust off his trousers. He turned and looked out across the cavern, which was dotted with large pits that roiled with black vapors. "Spock, report. What's coming out of those craters?"

"Unknown." Spock checked his tricorder. "Something is impeding my scans." He turned and looked at Sowards and Upton, whose own efforts to elicit useful data from their tricorders also yielded only failure.

Kirk drew his sidearm and looked at Beamon. "I want a quick recon of the area. Set phasers for heavy stun and fan out."

The group split up and moved with wary steps between the smoking craters. The floor sparkled as Kirk's flashlight beam swept back and forth across his path. Tiny shards of pulverized dark crystal crunched under his boots.

"Anybody seeing any movement?"

"Negative," Spock said. "We appear to be alone."

McCoy eyed the ceiling. "Thank heaven for small mercies."

"Okay," Kirk said. "Sowards, Upton: try to collect some of this vapor for analysis, and see if it's emanating from a liquid or—" His next words caught in his throat as the air around him turned bitterly cold in an instant. His skin prickled with gooseflesh, and his exhaled breath formed a white plume as he spun and aimed his flashlight beam on the nearest crater.

Black mist snaked up from the pit and coalesced into a wavering shape that vaguely resembled the top half of a humanoid. It had no face, but it had hands—with long fingers of smoke that evoked the talons of a raptor.

Kirk backed away from the entity. "Spock? I think we have a problem."

9

"Run!" It wasn't the most dignified order Jim Kirk had ever issued, but in terms of its words-to-results ratio, it felt like the right one.

The landing party sprinted back toward the tunnel. All around them, plumes of dark vapor took shape and pressed inward. One of the wights enveloped Petty Officer Kress, who screamed and lurched to a halt. Snared in the creature's smoky grasp, he convulsed, his voice suddenly choked off into a pained gurgle.

Kirk saw the gruesome spectacle, stopped, and shouted, "Kress!"

Beamon turned and aimed his phaser into the approaching swarm of shadows. "Open fire! Wide dispersal! Cover me!"

"Belay that!" Spock said, but it was too late. The security

officers had already spun and opened fire, unleashing swaths of electric-blue phaser energy into the wights' swelling ranks. Beamon, perhaps hoping the barrage would clear him a path back to his snared subordinate, charged headlong into the creatures' midst.

Three pairs of vaporous tendrils seized Beamon and lifted him off the ground, then dozens of the entities converged upon him and Kress. As Kirk watched in mute horror, the two security personnel were reduced to twisted, pale caricatures of their former selves and cast aside.

Spock grabbed Kirk's arm. "Captain! We must retreat!"

Kirk pulled free of Spock's grip. "We can't just desert them, Spock!"

The half-Vulcan first officer spun Kirk around so that they stood face-to-face. "If we do not leave now, we will *all* die."

McCoy seized Kirk's arm and showed him his tricorder's display. "Jim, those men are still alive!"

That was all Kirk needed to hear. "Bones, with me!" He pointed toward the tunnel and commanded the rest of the team, "Go!"

With McCoy at his side, Kirk charged through and past the growing cluster of smoky demons. He reached Beamon and hefted him over his shoulders in a fireman's carry. McCoy did the same for Kress—and then they began their retreat.

Misty talons swiped at McCoy and Kirk as they dodged and ducked back the way they had come. Even running as hard as he was able, Kirk barely stayed ahead of the advancing wights, who seemed to multiply in number every few seconds.

A dozen specters dropped like a black gate, blocking the tunnel. The landing party stumbled to a halt, slamming into a dense knot. Spock glanced at his tricorder, pointed to his right, and ran. "This way!" Everyone fell in behind him.

Kirk shouted, "Spock! Where are we going?"

"The only way we can. We need to hail the ship."

Keeping pace with the team, Kirk held Beamon with one hand as he pulled his communicator from his belt and flipped it open. "Kirk to *Enterprise*! Do you read me, *Enterprise*?"

Sulu replied over the subspace channel, *"Yes, Captain, we read you. Is everything all right, sir?"*

"Do I *sound* like everything's all right? Our escape route's been cut off! Tell Scotty to beam us up, on the double!"

The delay before Sulu's response was brief, but to Kirk's adrenaline-charged mind it felt like an eternity. *"We can't, sir, you're too far underground."*

Kirk's voice shook both from the vibrations of his running steps and his mounting frustration. "Can't you just lock onto my signal?"

Spock interjected, "Without the boosters, we would not be able to contact *Enterprise* at all. The devices do not have enough power or bandwidth to relay a transporter beam." Tapping at his tricorder, he added, "Fortunately, I have an alternative." He raised his voice. "Can you hear me, Mister Sulu?"

"Aye, sir."

"Inform Mister Scott it is time for Plan B."

• • •

Sulu felt as if he were sitting in the glare of a spotlight as the bridge crew reported in from every direction, bombarding him with information.

Chekov silenced a cascade of alerts on his console. "We're receiving multiple distress signals on radio frequencies from the planet's surface."

At the science station, Ensign sh'Vetha, an Andorian, spoke while keeping her eyes on the sensor display. "The negative-energy reading near the mine is increasing, sir. It is dampening the subspace radio signal."

Uhura looked over her shoulder at Sulu. "Spock is sending up data from his tricorder over the captain's communicator channel."

"Route that data stream to Mister Scott," Sulu said.

Over the open intraship comm, Scott replied, *"Already gettin' it, mate. Stand by—I'll send up a firing solution in a few seconds."*

Sulu's eyes widened. "Did you say *firing solution?*"

"Aye! Charge the phasers to full power while I finish my calculations." In an absent-minded mumble he added, *"Carry the one . . ."*

Targeting data appeared on the main viewscreen. It was accompanied by an overlay of crosshairs that began roaming across the planet's surface. The image on the screen magnified a few times in quick succession until it displayed a detailed overhead view of the entrance to the dilithium mine. The crosshairs fixed on a position several hundred yards from the entrance, in untrammeled wilderness.

Ensign Katuscha, a young red-haired human woman who

was at the helm while Sulu had the conn, swiveled her chair around to face him. "Sir? Mister Scott is requesting a change in our orbital pattern."

"Do it." In a slightly less confident tone of voice, Sulu asked, "Scotty? What's going on?"

"No time to explain!"

Sulu and Uhura exchanged worried looks, and then Kirk's shouting voice crackled over the comm: *"How're you guys doin' on Plan B?"*

"Almost ready, sir," Sulu said. "We're working as fast as we can."

The screeching of phasers over the channel drowned out Kirk's reply.

Fighting to make himself heard over the whine of phaser blasts in the enclosed tunnel, Kirk shouted at his communicator, "Well, work faster!"

Ewen and Willens raked the passage behind the landing party with a steady fusillade of phaser fire. Brilliant blasts of energy tore chunks of rock from the walls and ceiling and filled the air with acrid gray smoke. Every other shot passed through one or more wights but seemed to have no effect—the creatures continued their relentless pursuit of Kirk and his team into the planet's depths. Part of the passage caved in, but the wights slipped through the tiniest gaps between the rocks.

McCoy rounded a bend in the passage just ahead of Kirk

and collided with Spock, who stopped him from going forward. "We must remain here," Spock said.

The doctor strained to break free of Spock's hold. "Are you out of your Vulcan mind? Those things are right behind us!"

Kirk craned his neck and looked over Spock's shoulder. Beyond the turn in the passage lay another cavern of inestimable size, but instead of a rocky floor it housed a placid sea of black water. "Spock, what the hell's going—"

Spock flipped open his communicator. "Now, Mister Scott."

Scott replied, *"Fire in the hole!"*

"Duck," Spock told the landing party.

Everyone dived behind the corner, the attacking wights be damned.

The world turned white, and thunder shook the planet to its core.

A scalding plume of water vapor surged into the passage, and the landing team howled in pain and surprise as it billowed over them.

Spock's voice broke through the rumbling of aftershocks. "Forward!"

Kirk ushered the rest of his team ahead of him. He was determined not to leave any of his people behind. Ewen and Willens backpedaled around the corner, and then Kirk took up rear-guard duty, firing blindly into the blistering fog as he retreated with the team toward the Underdark sea. Within seconds he and his team had waded into knee-deep shallows that were as warm as bathwater.

The mist began to dissipate, and Kirk saw a battalion of wights emerging from the walls above him.

Scott's voice squawked from Spock's communicator. *"Transporter locked!"*

Kirk shouted, "Energize!"

A wave of darkness surged over the landing party as the transporter beam took hold. For half a second James Kirk didn't know whether he would live or die.

Then the bright haze of the transporter beam faded, and he and the rest of the landing party found themselves standing on the transporter platform aboard the *Enterprise*. Ewen and Willens breathed sighs of relief. Sowards and Upton looked shaken. Spock stepped off the platform and compared notes with Scotty as if nothing unusual had occurred.

But Kirk knew better, and so did McCoy.

They set down the men they had carried out of the caverns. McCoy scanned Beamon and then Kress. He looked at Kirk, his expression grave. "They're alive. But they're both paralyzed, with barely any brain activity."

"Maybe the wights' touch is only instantly fatal to the Kathikar."

"Maybe. But this isn't much better."

"Can you help them, Bones?"

"I won't know until I get them to sickbay." McCoy looked at the stricken men and frowned. "And maybe not even then."

10

Filing into the *Enterprise*'s briefing room, the landing party—minus Beamon and Kress—looked shell-shocked, and Leonard McCoy didn't blame them one bit. His trousers were still soaked from the knees down, and dirty water squished inside his boots with each step he took. He and the rest of the team stank of sulfur, and the normally vibrant hues of their uniform tunics were dulled by patinas of soot.

Kirk sank into his chair at the head of the table, his youthful face darkened with grim emotions. Seeing two of his crew struck down had robbed the young captain of his cocksure manner and left him looking sullen and haunted.

Sowards and Upton sat together, as did Ewen and Willens. McCoy took the seat to Kirk's left, while Spock moved to the control panel for the viewscreen on the bulkhead. As he activated the screen the door slid open, and Ambassador Sarek strode into the room and sat down at the far end of the table from Captain Kirk. Spock paid his father no attention and remained focused on his duties.

"Scans made in the caves beneath the mine confirm they are a major source of the negative-energy readings we detected on the planet's surface," Spock said. He began a quick review of several screens of data uploaded from his tricorder. "Now that Mister Scott has opened a passage to the Underdark using the ship's phasers, I have directed him to make detailed sensor sweeps of the caves at that depth. We should have a full-spectrum scan ready for analysis within the hour."

Feeling his temper rising, McCoy asked accusatorily, "Might I inquire why we didn't do that in the first place, rather than risk an entire landing party?"

Spock looked at McCoy. "Prior to our excursion, Doctor, we had no accurate charts of the planet's subterranean regions, and mineral compounds in the bedrock impeded our sensors. While we were underground, I used ultrasonic echolocation to map the cave complex. I then relayed that data back to Mister Scott, who used it to drill through the surface, creating a line-of-sight aperture for our extraction. That same aperture now provides us with a means of direct observation."

As McCoy pondered the first officer's long-winded explanation, he glanced with glum disapproval at Sarek. *Like father, like son.*

Kirk turned his intense stare toward the two science specialists. "Sowards, what can you tell me about those crystals you collected in the tunnel?"

The lithe geologist sat forward. "The gray dilithium, as I'm calling it for now, exhibits odd behavior at the subatomic level. Unlike regular dilithium, these crystals capture changelets in their matrix, which causes them to emit microphasic distortion fields."

The captain closed his eyes for a moment and made a fist. "First of all, what the hell's a 'changelet'?"

Spock answered, "A nine-dimensional, five-two-spin variant on the quark strangelet." Reacting to Kirk's expression of pained confusion, he added, "It is an extremely rare subatomic particle associated with spatial disruptions."

"Thank you. And the microdistorter-thing . . . ?"

Sowards replied, "Tiny pockets of bent reality, like blisters in spacetime."

"Got it. What do those have to do with the wights?"

The geologist looked at Spock, who said, "It might suggest an extradimensional origin."

Kirk nodded. "Upton, can you tell me anything useful about those creatures? What they're made of? Why our phasers didn't hurt them?"

"Not yet," said the exobiologist. "I couldn't get a clear reading with all the interference on my tricorder—probably from those crystals."

A moment of silence settled over the group, and then Sarek spoke. "I trust, Captain, that you now see the error of your decision to go to the planet's surface."

There was fury in Jim Kirk's gaze. "What I see, Mister Ambassador, is that two of my crew are in critical condition and billions of innocent Kathikar are still at risk. So if you came here just to say 'I told you so,' do me a favor and get out."

"And if I choose to remain?"

"Then you'd better be ready to help us start finding a solution to this mess, because we're not leaving this planet 'til we find one."

11

Sarek pressed the door signal outside L'Nel's guest quarters, and then he waited for her response. A few seconds later he heard her voice over the door's comm: *"Just a moment, please."* He stood with his chin up and his countenance serene, the very portrait of quiet patience until the door opened, revealing L'Nel.

"Come in." She stepped to her left and beckoned him inside.

He strode in, nodding at her as he passed by. "Most kind."

L'Nel had adjusted the environmental settings of her quarters in much the same manner as Sarek had altered his. The artificial gravity was higher, the illumination softer and tinted crimson, the air drier and warmer. It was still thicker than the atmosphere on Vulcan had been because air pressure was not a user-accessible variable aboard Starfleet vessels. As the door shut behind him, Sarek caught the scent of sage incense, and he noticed a small meditation table against one bulkhead. On the table, a vaguely cylindrical object approximately thirty centimeters tall had been hastily covered with a large square of wheat-colored linen intricately embroidered with ancient Vulcan ideograms.

"I did not realize you observed the ancient rituals," Sarek said.

"They were important to my family. I had not given them much consideration until—" She paused, clearly struggling to maintain her emotional discipline. With effort she finished her sentence: "Until recently."

Sarek nodded. "I see." He strolled slowly through her cabin, and she remained close behind him, interposing herself between him and the table.

"Is your visit social in nature, Mister Ambassador?"

He turned to face her. "Not entirely. Captain Kirk's behavior during this crisis has become increasingly willful and stubborn. He has defied my orders and taken action on the planet's surface in the absence of any legal authority to do so. Furthermore, he has threatened to incarcerate me if I gainsay his command again."

His remarks seemed to make L'Nel pensive. "Is there no reasonable chance of persuading the captain to change his decisions regarding the Kathikar?"

"I do not think so. He seems quite resolute on the matter."

L'Nel met his gaze. "How may I be of assistance?"

He stepped toward the table of meditation-enhancing incense and artifacts. "If we wish to overturn Captain Kirk's decisions, we will need to make our appeal to a higher authority. We must ask Starfleet Command to intervene."

She flanked him in hesitant steps. "All communications off the ship are monitored by Lieutenant Uhura. In order to contact Starfleet's admiralty without alerting Captain Kirk to our intentions, we will need to bypass the usual channels and conceal our efforts."

"Correct. Can it be done with dispatch?"

"I possess the requisite skills. Do you wish me to proceed?"

"I do." Sarek felt the pressure of L'Nel's stare as he looked down at the linen-covered object on the table before him. He modulated his voice to remove any intimation of a threat. "What lies beneath this cloth, L'Nel?"

"An item of personal significance. A memento of Vulcan."

He reached toward the cloth and stopped before he touched it. "May I?" L'Nel gave a small nod of assent. Sarek plucked away the square of linen to reveal a slender receptacle of baked clay, painstakingly shaped and carved, meticulously fired and glazed. A rare and hallowed treasure of Mount Seleya—a *katric* ark.

Sarek regarded the ancient urn with reverence. In a hushed voice, he asked, "Has this ark been consecrated?"

"Yes. It was salvaged from the Halls of Ancient Thought before they were destroyed, and entrusted to me for safekeeping."

Sarek placed his hand on L'Nel's shoulder. "Why did you hide this from me? Do you think I would report you to the Council for Antiquities?"

She shook her head. "No, Ambassador. My trust in you is absolute." Casting her eyes downward, she added, "I was ashamed of myself. Of my sentimentality."

"There is no shame in honoring the memories of the dead."

"I know. And I do grieve for those who perished on Vulcan. But I mourn one person in particular, and I did not want you to think less of me."

Sarek shook his head. "Be not ashamed. We all have someone to mourn. It is both proper and necessary for us to do so—as individuals and as a civilization."

"You are most gracious in your understanding, Ambassador." Composing herself, she added, "I will begin work at once on opening a clandestine channel to Starfleet Command for you. When it is ready, I will contact you."

"Very well. I shall await you in my quarters." He walked to the door, which sighed open ahead of him. Pausing on its threshold, he looked back at his chief aide. "If there is anything else I can do to help you find peace—"

L'Nel raised her hand. "Thank you, Ambassador, but that will not be necessary." She looked down at the *katric* ark. "I have already chosen my path."

Spock stripped off his dirt-dusted tunic while Uhura stood in the doorway of his sleep alcove and watched him disrobe. She asked, "Are you sure you're okay?"

"I assure you, Nyota, I am unharmed." He tossed aside

the blue tunic and removed his black undershirt. "I appreciate your concern, however."

She crossed her arms. "I'd have less reason to be concerned if our hotshot of a captain would learn how to send scouting parties instead of senior officers."

Spock sat on his bed and pulled off one boot. "The selection of landing-party personnel is the captain's prerogative."

"Really?" Uhura confronted Spock. "I thought decisions regarding crew assignments were the province of the first officer."

"They are." Spock took off his other boot and set it aside. "With deference to the commanding officer."

Uhura rolled her eyes at him and drifted back toward the doorway, shaking her head. "It just seems so reckless, that's all."

"I agree." Spock stood and stepped out of his still-damp trousers. "My father was right to tell the captain not to intervene on Akiron. Protocol, however, requires me to support the orders of my captain."

Uhura held up her palms. "Wait. That's not what I was saying at all. I think the captain is right to help the Kathikar. I just don't think he should've gone down there in person—or taken you and Doctor McCoy with him."

Spock opened a clothes drawer and selected a clean uniform. "So, you have no objection to the captain defying diplomatic authority and issuing illegal orders, as long as he assigns them to junior personnel."

"That's not what I said, and you know it. And frankly, I'd expect a bit more honesty in debating tactics from you, of all people." She watched him pull on his pants. "Do you *really* think the captain's order to help the Kathikar is illegal?"

He sat down and pulled on one boot. "I admit, there is a degree of ambiguity to the situation." He continued as he reached for the other boot and pulled it on. "The captain posed a reasonable counterargument to Sarek's position. Regardless, the safer course of action was the one my father proposed."

"Safer?" The word seemed to rile Uhura. "For who? Us? The Kathikar?"

"I meant safer in the legal sense, with regard to our compliance with Starfleet regulations and the Federation Charter."

In a breath Uhura went from riled to enraged. "The *legal* sense? Who gives a damn about that when innocent people are dying?"

"We must not let ourselves be governed by our passions in times of crisis. The law exists to ensure we act out of reason and logic."

Uhura narrowed her eyes. "An ironic statement, coming from you."

Spock stood and pulled on a clean black undershirt. "Hardly. I have learned from experience the dangers of indulging my emotions."

"Your *negative* emotions. Of course we shouldn't base our decisions on fear and anger, but what's so wrong with acting out of compassion?"

He tucked his undershirt into his trousers. "Compassionate acts are not inherently wrong, but even noble actions can be detrimental to discipline if they are engaged in, in direct defiance of legal orders from one's superior."

Flinging her arms over her head, Uhura let out a roar of frustration. "Give me a break, Spock! I'm talking about saving innocent lives, and all you can think about is how it might affect discipline? After all you've been through, why do you still find it so hard to defy authority in order to do what you know is right?"

While Spock was formulating a reply, his door signal buzzed.

"Come," he called out, and then he quickly pulled on a fresh blue tunic.

The door opened, and Sarek stepped into the room. Uhura rolled her eyes. "Naturally." She walked away from Spock, toward the open door. As she shouldered past Sarek, she said to him, "Your timing's impeccable, as always." Then she was out the door and gone without a backward glance.

Sarek stepped away from the door, which slid closed. Gesturing toward it, he asked, "Did you and Lieutenant Uhura have an argument, my son?"

"We were having a discussion. One I hope to resume at a more convenient time in the near future." Spock walked out of his bedroom to join Sarek in the main room of his quarters. "What is the purpose of your visit, Father?"

"First and foremost, I seek to confirm that you were not harmed during the mission to the planet's surface."

Spock clasped his hands behind his back and stood at ease. "I was not injured. Had I been, Doctor McCoy would have insisted I be treated and possibly quarantined in sickbay." Expressing his incredulity with a sly arch of one eyebrow, he added, "Father, it seems unlikely you would come here to ask after my well-being when you had seen me less than half an hour ago at the post-mission briefing. Logic suggests your visit is the product of an ulterior motive."

Sarek reacted with a mixture of what Spock took to be exasperation and filial pride. "You always were an astute observer, Spock." He gestured to a pair of chairs situated in a corner beside a small table. Spock nodded and followed his father to the chairs. They sat facing each other. Lowering his voice, Sarek continued. "Your captain has behaved in a most irregular fashion, as I am certain you are aware. He has endangered himself, his crew, and his ship in pursuit of a course of action proscribed by law."

Spock sensed that his loyalty was being measured by his reply. "Outside of Federation space, a starship captain has significant latitude to interpret and apply the law, Sarek—a fact of which I am certain *you* are well aware."

"Do you think Captain Kirk has applied the law correctly in this case?"

"I think the situation evolved in a way that rendered your diplomatic authority moot and required the captain to make a command decision, and he has done so. I understand your objections to his decisions, but I believe he has chosen this course not for the sake of being insubordinate but in good faith as a Starfleet officer. In the absence of a contravening order from a superior officer, Captain Kirk's decision to render aid to the Kathikar is legal."

Sarek nodded gravely. "And if you were to receive a contravening order from an admiral at Starfleet Command . . . ?"

"Then the chain of command would require us to obey."

"What if Captain Kirk then continued to defy orders?"

Spock stiffened. "I do not wish to discuss such a scenario."

"As you wish, my son." Awkward silence filled the moment, and then Sarek said, "If your relationship with Lieutenant Uhura is at an end, would—"

"It is not over," Spock said, sounding more defensive than he had intended.

"Are you quite certain? She sounded agitated as she left."

"Our discussions are often intense, but never rancorous."

Sarek looked unconvinced and seemed poised to argue the matter when Doctor McCoy's voice sounded over the intraship comm: *"Captain Kirk and Mister Spock, please report to sickbay on the double."*

12

Kirk arrived in sickbay to find McCoy, Spock, and Scott waiting for him. The chief engineer and first officer stood beside a biobed, on which lay the comatose Lieutenant Beamon. Between that bed and the next, where Petty Officer Kress lay unconscious, McCoy stood holding his medical tricorder.

Fearing the worst, Kirk asked, "Bones, what's going on? Are we losing them?"

McCoy held up a hand. "It's okay, Jim, they're stable. I've just finished my first set of tests. The wights did a number on their nervous systems, but we should be able to work up a treatment plan in a day or so."

Kirk regarded McCoy with a questioning look. "Were they just lucky?"

"Preliminary data suggests humans have a better chance than the Kathikar of surviving the wights' disrupting effects.

I suspect Andorians and Vulcans might prove even more resistant—but there's no way to know for sure until it's too late."

It felt to Kirk as if relief and regret were engaged in a tug-of-war inside his chest. *If they had died down there, it would have been my fault.* Kirk gave McCoy's shoulder an appreciative grasp. "Thanks, Bones. Well done."

"The least I could do."

Forcing himself back into a semblance of discipline, Kirk asked, "You said you'd run some tests? What'd you find?"

"Massive tissue damage." McCoy pointed out details on the display above the biobed. "Some of it consistent with neuroelectric shock, some with desiccation, some with molecular disruption." He frowned. "I've never seen anything like it. It's like they were frozen, burned, and electrocuted all at once."

Spock interjected, "I have compared Doctor McCoy's findings to all known biological and energy-based attacks in the computer's memory banks. This pattern of tissue damage appears to be unique in Federation history."

It was just bad news heaped on top of more of the same. Kirk fixed McCoy with a determined look. "Did you find anything that might indicate how the wights did this? Or how to defend ourselves against it?"

"Maybe." McCoy held out his arm as if to ward off a stampede of optimism. "I don't want to get your hopes up, though."

Kirk glared at the surgeon. "Not much chance of that, Bones."

"Point taken." McCoy punched up some data on the screen above the bed. "Here's what I've got so far. All the tissue damage in both men's bodies shows traces of a particular energy signature. Even as the damaged organic molecules break down, the energy signature remains consistent, though it loses strength. I think the wights attack by infusing victims with a negative charge."

"A crude metaphor," Spock said, "but an apt one. The wights harm biological entities with which they make contact by infusing their victims' tissues with their energy signature. Then the victims' own environment attacks them the way antibodies might destroy foreign tissue or viruses inside a host organism."

Scott's brow wrinkled in confusion. "If our environment is so hostile to people marked with the wights' energy signatures, why doesn't it kill the wights?"

"I suspect it is because they remain connected to their native plane," Spock said. "Our universe is harmful to the wights, but as long as they retain a link to their home dimension they are able to survive. Their victims lack this connection and therefore die once 'infected' by the wights' unique bioelectrical signature."

Kirk nodded. "How do we use this? Can we protect ourselves from getting 'infected' by the wights?"

McCoy shrugged. "Beats me. I don't even know how they do it."

"Well, find out. Spock, can you think of a way to inoculate us against the wights?"

Spock responded with a dubious expression. "Not without a more detailed knowledge of the creatures' physiology and native plane of existence."

"How about a weapon?" Kirk asked. He turned toward his chief engineer. "Scotty? Can you take the energy signature Bones found and use it to work up some kind of energy that'll hurt the wights? Because our phasers sure didn't."

"Aye, I'll do what I can. The first thing we have to do is teach our sensors how to see them. Then we need to make sure they don't change energy frequencies or exist on more than one at a time." Scott looked at the first officer. "I could use a hand tweakin' the sensors, Mister Spock. I can jimmy the hardware, but no one knows that software like you do."

"I am at your service, Mister Scott."

"Good," Kirk said. "Keep me informed of any progress. As soon as we have some way of fighting these things, I'm gonna want a field test."

"Understood," Spock said.

An electronic boatswain's whistle sounded over the comm and was followed by Lieutenant Sulu's voice. *"Bridge to Captain Kirk."*

Kirk stepped over to a companel on a nearby bulkhead and opened a channel with the press of a thumb. "Kirk here. Go ahead."

"Sir, we're receiving a message from the planet's surface. One of the Kathikar has been hailing us on a UHF radio frequency."

The captain threw a quizzical look back at Scott, McCoy, and Spock before he replied, "Give him an A for effort. What does he want?"

"He's asking to speak to you, sir."

Kirk imagined the chaos engulfing Akiron. "I'm sure he is."

"No, sir, I mean he's asking for you by name."

That caught Kirk's attention. "Did he say what he wants?"

"Yes, sir. He says only you can stop the wights, but he insists he'll share his information only when he talks to you in person."

Kirk's wide-eyed stare at his comrades was returned in kind by McCoy and Scott, while Spock remained as dispassionate as ever. With a devil-may-care shrug, Kirk turned back toward the companel. "Okay, beam him up."

A whorl of golden light shone and a musical drone resonated in the close quarters of the transporter room as a new visitor from Akiron took shape on its platform.

Kirk squinted against the flare that preceded the final materialization sequence. Spock stood to his right and McCoy to his left. Mister Scott was operating the transporter controls. Though there had been concern that the new visitor might represent one of Akiron's violent insurgent factions, his comm signal had originated from a settlement on the planet's surface near an observatory, on an island remote from any of the ongoing struggles. He also had asked to beam up to the *Enterprise* alone, which had served to reassure Kirk and his crew that the petitioner meant no harm.

As the last remnants of the transporter effect faded away, Kirk studied the Kathikar standing before him. The being was hunched in a way that suggested he suffered from osteoporosis. His mouselike face and large ears were tufted with thick locks of white fur. His broad, drooping whiskers were the color of ivory, and the irises of his large, innocent-looking eyes were silvery gray. One was trained on Kirk with a focus as sharp as a serpent's tooth, but the other appeared to be clouded with age and illness.

In one hand he clutched a gnarled black walking stick topped with a translucent gemstone. His simple, drab robes appeared to have been woven of natural fibers, and they were soaking wet, just like his leather sandals. He gave off an odor that reminded Kirk of the time his favorite pet dog had gotten caught outside in a summer storm.

Kirk stepped forward to greet the elderly Kathikar. "Welcome to the *Enterprise*. I'm Captain James T. Kirk. This is my first officer, Lieutenant Commander Spock; our chief surgeon, Doctor McCoy; and our chief engineer, Lieutenant Commander Montgomery Scott."

"My name is Gveter-ren. Thank you for granting me this audience, Captain. My people and I owe you our deepest gratitude."

"Well, I don't know about *that*. Not yet, anyway." Kirk noted the confused look on Gveter-ren's face. "You said you had information that could help us stop the wights. Care to tell us what that is?"

"Of course." The alien visitor took a few halting steps forward and paused at the edge of the transporter platform to test the step down with his walking stick. McCoy and Spock exchanged put-upon looks and then moved forward to assist the doddering Kathikar off the transporter platform.

Gveter-ren mustered a weak smile for Spock and McCoy. "Thank you." He shuffled toward Kirk until he and the young captain stood face-to-chest. "I am here because the only one who can stop the wights is you, James Kirk."

"So you said. Look, your pitch was good enough to get you beamed up for five minutes of face time, but if I don't hear something useful in the next sixty seconds, you're on your way back to the surface. So, why don't you tell me what branch of science you specialize in?"

The Kathikar recoiled as if mildly offended. "I never claimed to represent any of the scientific disciplines, Captain."

Kirk closed his eyes to hide his frustration. *I don't need this, not today.* He simultaneously suspected and dreaded what the Kathikar would say in response to his next question. "What, precisely, *is* your field of expertise?"

"I am a holy man. The Venerated Elder of the Mystic Order of Oernachta, and I came here because I've had a vision of your struggle against the Wights of the Underdark."

Kirk's taut smile was belied by his wrathful stare. "Of course you did." He turned on his heel to face Scott. "Send him home."

As Kirk, Spock, and McCoy strode toward the exit, Scott and a pair of armed security officers herded Gveter-ren back toward the transporter platform. Then the old Kathikar mystic called out in a confident voice, "I know about your visions, Kirk! Your flashes of sight in the cave! I can tell you what they mean and how they can help you stop the wights!"

Kirk spun around. "Stop!" He marched back, grabbed hold

of Gveter-ren's robe, and nearly lifted the fragile old monk off the deck. "How do you know what I saw in the cave? Did you cause my visions? Is this some kind of trick?"

Gveter-ren made no effort to defend himself. He let himself hang limp in Kirk's grasp. "It is no trick. As I meditated I became attuned to your energy, to your struggle with the wights. I believe you have come to my world not by chance, Captain, but in fulfillment of a long destiny. Your visions in the cave are part of that summons."

The captain remained suspicious. "Do you know what I saw?"

"Yes."

"Describe it."

The mystic's whiskers twitched slightly, and then he said in a low voice, "First, you saw as if heat were your only light. Then came cold and darkness. Next, you perceived emotions as temperatures. It was a moment of tragic failure." Gently closing his paws around Kirk's forearms, he added, "I understand that these visions caused you distress. They caused you to question your sanity. But if you wish to save my world—and your crew—you will need to trust me, Captain."

McCoy and Spock pressed in close behind Kirk, and Scott stood close by with the two security guards. Everyone was looking at Kirk, waiting for him to decide what was going to happen next. He loosened his grip on Gveter-ren's robe and shook the frazzled old alien's paw.

"Welcome aboard," Kirk said.

13

"What you saw in the caves, Captain, were two of your past lives."

Kirk faced Gveter-ren across a corner of the conference table in the briefing room. Spock sat beside the Kathikar mystic, and McCoy and Scott sat on the opposite side of the table.

The captain felt torn between curiosity and skepticism. "With all due respect, I don't really believe in that hocus-pocus, past-lives stuff."

"I understand. You prefer to imagine that we live in a rational universe, one in which cause always precedes effect, and nature is governed exclusively by impersonal forces rather than by intelligent powers."

"Yes and no," Kirk said. "I mean, I stayed awake in enough of my physics classes to know that causes can follow effects in some quantum models, but in general, yes, I believe in a rational universe. I believe in reason."

Gveter-ren folded his hands on the tabletop. "I respect your point of view. And it is not necessary for you to embrace mine; I believe I can make my appeal for aid strictly on your terms."

McCoy mumbled, "This ought to be good."

Kirk looked at the doctor. "Let's hear him out, Bones."

"Thank you, Captain," said Gveter-ren. "In my meditations, I believe I have witnessed glimpses of history from worlds far away—perhaps not even in this galaxy—that have suffered the fate that lies in store for Akiron. And I felt your mind recoil from these same visions, Captain. Even if you do not accept that these were moments from your *lihar*'s past incarnations—"

"Excuse me," Kirk interrupted. "My what?"

"Your *lihar*. What you call a soul, and the Vulcans call a *katra*." Kirk nodded his understanding and gestured for Gveter-ren to continue. "Whether or not you accept these lives as part of your own continuity of consciousness, can you accept that these were insights into real lives and real experiences?"

Kirk was not yet ready to commit himself to Gveter-ren's thought experiment. "I'm willing to concede it might be possible."

McCoy snapped, "Don't tell me you're buying into this malarkey?"

Spock replied in a cool baritone, "Actually, Doctor, there is ample evidence that a number of sentient species possess psionic skills that alter their perception of space-time and enable them to witness events across great distances. In some cases, these species even exhibit abilities that border on precognition."

The doctor harrumphed. "I'll believe that when I see it."

Scott added, "Keep an open mind, Doctor. I like hard data as much as the next bloke, but even science can't explain *everything*. Though this is a wee bit *out there*, if you take my meaning, Mister Spock."

"Be that as it may," Spock said, "such abilities do exist."

Gveter-ren nodded at Spock. "Thank you, Mister Spock."

"I did not say that I think *you* have demonstrated such abilities. I conceded only that there is scientific evidence for the existence of abilities that mimic or resemble them. The burden of proof is still yours to meet."

"Fair enough." The mystic turned his attention back to Kirk. "I will leave it to you to determine whether my gifts are genuine."

Kirk held up his palms in gentle protest. "I'm not qualified to—"

"Trust your feelings, Captain. Nothing more."

He lowered his defenses with reluctance. "Okay, I'll try."

"Close your eyes and breathe deeply. Cast your mind back to the first vision you experienced in the caves. Recall the sand grinding under your boot heels, the bite of sulfur in the air, the beams of your handheld lights slashing the darkness."

Imagining the expedition from just a couple of hours earlier, Kirk was impressed by the specificity of Gveter-ren's sensory details. He wondered if the old Kathikar had ever been to the dilithium mine, or if he simply was a gifted liar. "I'm remembering. I was walking—"

"—across the narrow stone bridge," Gveter-ren cut in. "Yes, I saw it. Your head felt light, you lost your balance."

"Yes." Kirk recalled his momentary blackout on the bridge.

"You saw yourself among reptilian bipeds. Your vision was heat based." The mystic paused for a few seconds. "Your second vision happened when you were near the craters. You saw yourself as one of a group of empathic scientists."

"That's right."

"Relax now, Captain."

Kirk exhaled a deeply held breath and met Gveter-ren's gaze. The Kathikar's forehead creased with effortful concentration. "My perception of your visions is that you saw the ends of two of your past incarnations. Regardless of whether you accept my interpretation of your visions, what is important is that you believe the lives you witnessed were real, and that the lessons imparted to you by the universe are valuable and relevant to the task that lies ahead of you and your crew."

Annoyed and confused, Kirk asked, "What lessons? All I saw was the same thing that just happened to me and my crew down in the mines. It gets dark and cold when the wights attack, and their touch wounds or kills. Hardly enlightening."

"You need to look more deeply than that, Captain. In my vision, you either absorb the lessons of the past and save my world from this onslaught of darkness—or you cast the lessons aside, and both our peoples suffer for it. You have failed in two past lives to stop these creatures, and two worlds have died. Unless you learn from your mistakes, my world will fall next—and you will be doomed to face these monsters again someday—either in this life, or the next."

Kirk looked at Spock, whose expression was a cipher. Then he cast a glance at McCoy and Scott. The engineer looked at the table; McCoy rolled his eyes and frowned. Kirk faced Gveter-ren. "I know I'll regret asking this, but what did you mean when you said I needed to look *more deeply*?"

"I am referring to regressive hypnosis, Captain. With your permission, I can help guide you into the past, to help you unlock your previous lives in greater detail so that you can take from them what you need to prevail in this life."

Kirk grimaced. "Great. I was afraid it'd be something weird."

Minutes later, while Gveter-ren was left to navel-gaze or admire the bulkheads in the briefing room, Leonard McCoy led the quartet of the *Enterprise*'s senior officers into sickbay. As soon as he was through the door, he barked at his staff of nurses, technicians, and junior physicians, "Everyone out! Now!"

The ship's medical personnel filed out in a swift and orderly fashion, leaving McCoy, Kirk, Spock, and Scott in privacy. The first officer cocked an eyebrow at McCoy. "Was that emotional outburst really necessary, Doctor?"

"Necessary? No. But neither is letting some witch doctor put our commanding officer into an altered state of consciousness."

"Calm down, Bones," Kirk said. "It's just an idea."

"And a damned foolish one. How much do you know about hypnotic regression, Jim?"

Kirk shrugged. "What am I supposed to know? Some guy waves a watch in front of my face, counts backward from ten, and I'm on the past-life nickel tour."

Spock looked askance at the captain. "Your gift for understatement remains as keen as ever, Captain."

"Thank you, Spock."

McCoy radiated concern. "Jim, listen to me. Hypnotic regression is a crock, pure and simple. It has no verifiable scientific basis whatsoever."

"Not in human science," Spock interjected. "However, studies conducted on Berengaria approximately seventeen years ago found that—"

"I don't care *what* they found, Spock! In case you've forgotten, our captain is *human*, not Berengarian." To Kirk the doctor added, "Hypnosis works on humans by inducing in the subject a state of altered brain activity similar to twilight sleep. It's a lot like lucid dreaming, except the hypnotherapist is able to direct the process because the subject becomes highly susceptible to suggestion. Once you're in that state, it'd be easy for Gveter-ren to shape your imagination and spin memories out of thin air, but to you they'd feel completely real."

"Hang on, now," Scott said. "My family always said my great-aunt Deirdre was psychic. They even have vids of her doing this regression-hypnosis thing when she was a little girl, and she started jabbering in Navajo—except she'd never learned how to speak Navajo. Seemed pretty real to me."

McCoy winced in vexation. "Yes, I know that some subjects of hypnotic regression have demonstrated short bursts of spontaneous xenoglossy, but that doesn't mean anything. Their hypnosis could've activated suppressed memory engrams of foreign languages that they heard earlier in life without comprehending what they meant. Most people who start speaking in tongues after hypnosis admit they have no idea what they've just said."

"That's all well and good, Bones," Kirk said, "but I started having these visions *before* I met Gveter-ren. How do you explain that?"

The doctor lifted his arms in mock surrender. "I don't know, Jim. Long-range telepathic suggestion? Maybe he controlled some piece of technology inside the mine that induces the visions? You'll have to forgive me—debunking psychic fraud isn't exactly my medical specialty."

"I don't know, Bones. Seems like kind of a reach to me."

"But being told you have to remember your *past lives* so you can live out some destiny to save one world and avenge two others sounds *reasonable*?"

Spock mirrored McCoy's grave manner. "I share Doctor McCoy's reservations, Captain. We do not know enough about the Kathikar's psionic abilities to make an informed judgment regarding Gveter-ren's credibility."

"Well, I think we can rule out psi-tech," Scott said. "The Kathikar haven't moved much past basic semiconductors, and their data networks don't have enough bandwidth to carry signals that could affect humanoid brainwaves. But if they *are* psychic, I'd love to know if they could contact my great-aunt. My grandfather always says Deirdre had a secret fortune buried somewhere in the Highlands, but she never—"

"Scotty," Kirk said, "we're not on a *treasure hunt* here."

Abashed, Scott dipped his chin. "Aye, sir."

"And even if we were," Spock added, "there is no evidence that the Kathikar possess any aptitude for necromancy—or for any other paranormal discipline."

McCoy's voice grew louder as his temper grew shorter. "Spock, you're missing the point here. Letting that kook put the captain under hypnosis for *any* reason is a recipe for disaster. He could plant triggered suggestions, alter the captain's memory, or manipulate him to who knows what end."

"Agreed." Spock faced the captain. "Doctor McCoy's concerns are valid. We lack sufficient knowledge of Kathikar politics or history to determine whether this Gveter-ren has ulterior motives. He might, in fact, be seeking to undermine our ability to stop the crisis."

Kirk sounded tired and irked. "And how do you propose we learn all that in the next five minutes, Spock? Because that's how long you all have before I go back to the briefing room and give him my permission to proceed."

"Then you have made up your mind to undergo the hypnotic regression?"

"Yes, Spock."

McCoy stepped in front of Kirk and held out his hands, stopping just short of physically restraining the captain. "Jim, think about what you're doing. If the Kathikar have psionic abilities, he might say one thing out loud while he puts you under hypnosis, but telepathically tell you something else once you're under."

Kirk looked at his first officer. "That's why I want Spock in the room for the entire procedure." He looked back at McCoy. "And you, too, Bones. Spock can use his abilities to keep tabs on Gveter-ren's mind games, and you'll monitor my brain-waves and bio readings every step of the way." He gestured at the nearest biobed. "We'll do the whole thing here in sickbay."

"Are you sure about this, Jim? Is there any way I can talk you out of it?"

"Yes, I am. And no, you can't."

"But it's completely insane!"

The captain shrugged. "Do you have a better idea?"

"No." McCoy shook his head in a final gesture of denial. "I'll have everything set up in five minutes. Scotty, go get the witch doctor, will you?"

"Sure thing." Scott hurried out of sickbay to fetch Gveter-ren.

Kirk trained a hopeful look upon Spock and then Bones. "Guys, I'm counting on you to make sure I don't get my id scrambled, okay? Because if I wake up and start clucking like a chicken, at least one of you is spending the rest of this mission in the brig."

14

Kirk lay on his back on the biobed, staring at a single point of intense, white light. The rest of sickbay was dark and silent except for the low thrumming of the *Enterprise*'s impulse engines and life-support systems. The comms had been turned off, along with almost every other system in sickbay. The display over Kirk's bed was also dark; its readouts were being routed directly to McCoy's medical tricorder, which had been set to silently alert the doctor if anything dangerous was detected in Kirk's vital signs.

Though he knew Spock and McCoy were standing only a meter or two away from him, he couldn't see them, nor could he see Gveter-ren, who stood at the foot of the bed and aimed the ophthalmological flashlight into Kirk's eyes.

"Concentrate on the light, Captain." The mystic's voice was slow and soothing. "Breathe deeply. Feel your body relax, starting with your extremities. The tips of your fingers and your toes are like smoke—weightless and free."

It was difficult for Kirk to move his thoughts in that direction. Letting go had never been his strong suit. He liked to control his circumstances before they controlled him; surrendering—whether to fate or to another person—made him uneasy. *No, it scares the hell out of me.* Hypnosis hinged on the subject's trust, and that was not something Kirk gave easily.

"Now your arms and legs are as vapor, dissipating into the air . . ." Slowly, the suggestions took root in Kirk's mind. He felt as if his body were becoming lighter, insubstantial, just a figment of his imagination. "Now your eyelids are growing heavy, Captain. Feel them drawing together. Let them close . . ." The point of light flared like a starburst as Kirk's eyes fluttered shut. He was overcome by the sensation of floating, of becoming a disembodied consciousness alone in the dark.

Gveter-ren's voice was soft and mellifluous. "You are poised upon the threshold now, Captain. As I count backward from five, you will cross over, leaving behind this life, this place and time, and you will journey back to another, one that you have lived before. When I reach 'one,' you will remember everything—what you see and hear, what you taste and smell and touch.

"Five . . . four . . ."

Kirk sank into the darkness.

"Three . . . two . . ."

A vortex of color and motion engulfed him.

"One."

• • •

Sveta holds her battle rifle level, its stock against her shoulder, her clawed forefinger relaxed but ready outside the trigger guard. She is near the rear of her platoon's formation as they follow a narrow path down the wall of the crater, navigating each switch-back with exaggerated caution. Dressed in body armor and heavy combat boots, Sveta and her comrades are less agile than any of them would like on the razor-thin walking trail. She, for one, is grateful not to have needed her backpack. That would have been one burden too many.

Above them, the night sky is hidden by a stormhead flash-ing with lightning. Thunder shakes the ground beneath Sveta's boots, and the humid air smells sweet. Rain is on the way. Not too soon, Sveta hopes. She's in no mood to fight beneath a downpour, and the thought of trying to make the hike back up the dirt path during a storm is even less appealing. One strong gale would be enough to send her and the rest of the platoon plunging to their deaths in the crater below.

She doesn't even know what her leaders expect them to find at the bottom of the crater. A monster? A gateway to another world? An alien spaceship? As usual, no one has told the soldiers anything except where to go and when to get there.

They reach the end of the trail and spread out across the level, rocky floor of the crater. The platoon commander barks orders. "Fan out by squads! Secure the pit's perimeter and give me a full recon! Move!"

No one questions orders, they just scramble to obey. Each trooper knows his or her job. The techs turn on their scanners and start *gathering data. Sveta and the other commandos set their weapons to maximum power and watch for trouble. On the far side of the planet, some big shots are watching it all on satellite video.*

Everyone is afraid to get too close to the pit in the middle of the crater. No one knows where it came from. It wasn't there yesterday. Now it gapes like an endless abyss, belching sulfuric fumes and inexplicably ice-cold vapors.

The temperature begins to drop, leaving the other members of Sveta's platoon shining like beacons in the sudden black chill. Frightened chatter crowds the comms. Desperate requests for orders are cut off by frantic calls for help.

Someone starts firing a weapon. Pulses of charged plasma are flying in every direction, melting sand into globs of glass, caroming off the crater's walls. Friendly fire strafes a commando standing only an arm's length from Sveta.

She has no orders, no targets. Just cold darkness and dying comrades.

The ground at her feet cracks open. She stumbles backward, loses her balance. Icy blackness spouts from the fissures in the crater floor. In seconds she is surrounded by a wall of cold shadow, and only then does she realize it's not some toxin, not some exotic phenomenon, but a malevolent intelligence. An enemy.

Sveta fires her weapon blindly, no longer caring who or what she hits, as long as she doesn't go down without a struggle, as long as she doesn't let the demons from the pit take her without a fight. She keeps firing until the creatures snare her in their frigid embrace. Her weapon's power cell goes dark.

A moment later, so does Sveta.

• • •

Kirk inhaled sharply and sat up in the biobed. Gentle paws pressed against his shoulders and eased him back onto the bed. Gveter-ren spoke in a reassuring tone of voice. "Relax, Captain. You are safe on the *Enterprise*."

"But the battle in the crater—"

"Was long ago and far away. Just a memory."

From the darkness, McCoy said, "Maybe that's enough."

The mystic kept his eyes on Kirk as he answered the doctor. "The captain experienced two distinct visions while he was in the cave. It would be best if we help him unlock both memories while we are here."

Spock said, "Captain, the decision is yours."

"I've come this far. Let's finish this."

"Very well." Gveter-ren stepped back to the end of the bed and turned on his borrowed medical flashlight. "Fix your eyes on the light, Captain."

Kirk remained skeptical of the notion of reincarnation, but he had been impressed by the clarity and richness of Sveta's recovered memory. *Could I really have been that person?* The notion intrigued him. After all, if reincarnation turned out to be more than a myth, who was to say that one could be reincarnated only as a member of one's own species? Even on Earth, some adherents of reincarnation believed a person might be reborn as an animal—so why not as an alien?

"Your body is becoming as a morning fog, Captain."

Step by step, Gveter-ren guided Kirk back through the stages of relaxation and surrender. Kirk's thoughts drifted, and soon he was lost in the twilight of his subconscious. An ebb tide of memory pulled him backward through his life, beyond the gray veil of oblivion from which his mind had awakened . . .

Jilur watches the data stream and is mystified. The numbers don't make any sense. He has spent years modeling the reaction, perfecting his formulas to predict every variable, fine-tuning every calibration to prevent a chaotic result such as this one.

Sensing Jilur's confusion and dismay, his wife, Mika, moves to his side and presses her hand to his back. "What's wrong, my love?"

"It looks like a feedback loop in the zero-point generator. I thought I'd accounted for that, but the negative charge is increasing rapidly."

Mika pokes at the control interface, tries to discern some error in Jilur's energy matrix, but he senses her frustration. "Everything is set properly. Where is all that negative charge coming from?"

"I don't know, but we either have to fix it in the next five minutes or else shut down the entire reactor."

They both know shutting down the reactor is not an option. It took more than a decade to plan and build this remote facility near the southern pole, and years more to ramp up its systems to the minimum charge needed for this experiment. If they turn it off now, the government will cancel their project and terminate their funding. Jilur and Mika will be ruined, professionally and financially. To come this close to proving his theory of dark energy only to fail would haunt Jilur to his grave. He cannot give up.

"Everyone!" he shouts to his fellow scientists. "Check your sensors! We need to know what's affecting the reaction. Report any deviation from the norm."

The others respond to his transmitted anxiety and work swiftly. Reports and data are fed to Jilur's master control screen, and Mika helps him organize the information in their search for the cause of the error. They rule out plasma imbalances in the distribution network, depolarized couplings in the aggregator, and a host of celestial phenomena ranging from gamma-ray bursts to sunspots.

Less than a minute remains to critical failure on the reactor. "Damn it," Jilur mutters. "We've eliminated every possible cause in the universe!"

Mika's eyes light up. "Only the ones in this universe!" She punches numbers into the system. "It's a dimensional fracture! The negative particles are slipping through a gap in the spacetime membrane." Pointing at a screen of sensor data, she adds, "See? Superheavy subatomic particles with abnormal spins!"

Only seconds remain. Jilur asks, "How do we compensate?"

"We punch through to the other dimension and create a positive node." Mika is already putting her plan into action. "We'll use it to shunt the excess negative charge back into a dimension where it won't affect the reactor!"

Jilur's heart swells with love and admiration for his wife as he watches her save their life's work with a moment of inspiration. She is genius incarnate.

The positively charged node is projected into the other dimension.

An explosion turns the lab white.

Then there is nothing but darkness and pain.

Jilur awakens to find his lab coat is on fire. He rolls side to side and extinguishes the flames. An acrid stench of burnt fabric assaults his nostrils as he scrambles off the floor and looks for Mika. She lies at his feet, stunned but alive.

The rest of his team has not been so fortunate. Many of them lie dead, scorched by flames or impaled by debris, twisted in grotesque poses. Slicks of blood spread across the once-immaculate laboratory floor.

But the greatest horror of all lies inside the reactor chamber. Beyond the transparent barrier, something black and vaporous takes shape. It is not just a chemical aftereffect of the accident. Jilur's empathic senses detect waves of fury radiating from the smoky entity inside the chamber. It is alive and sentient—and it is the most thoroughly malevolent being Jilur has ever encountered.

He shakes his half-conscious wife. "Mika! Wake up! We have to go!" She stirs but is too dazed to respond. Jilur looks at the creature coalescing inside the reactor and wonders how long that structure will contain it.

Then he has his answer.

The black shape passes through the transparent-steel wall of the reaction chamber as if it were not even there. The entity moves straight toward Jilur and Mika, its deadly intentions telegraphed by waves of icy-cold hatred.

Yewon forgive us. We opened the door to this thing. It's all our fault—we knew just enough to destroy ourselves.

He picks up Mika, hefts her fragile body over his aged shoulders, and tries to carry her out of the lab. Three staggering steps toward the door, he knows he will not make it. Then death's frozen hand grips his heart—and his wife's.

Tears rolled from Kirk's eyes as he gasped and returned to himself.

Gveter-ren stood at Kirk's side. "Two lives ended in tragedy, two worlds lost to horror and darkness." He placed a hand on Kirk's shoulder. "Now do you understand, Captain? Do you see why the arc of the universe has brought you to Akiron? Why you cannot allow this evil to prevail yet again?"

"Yes. I do." Kirk swallowed hard. "What now? How do I make use of these memories? What do I do?"

"Learn from your mistakes, before it is too late."

15

Hikaru Sulu stood and relinquished the command chair as Captain Kirk strode onto the bridge, with Spock just a few steps behind him. "No change in mission status, Captain," Sulu said, standing aside as Kirk swung himself into the center seat.

"Then it's time to try something new," Kirk said. "Mister Chekov?"

The teenaged navigator swiveled around to look at Kirk. "Yes, sir?"

"Plot a new orbital path, one that'll take us over the poles of Akiron rather than around its equator. I want to have a good look at the planet's polar latitudes." He turned toward Spock. "Reprogram the sensors to look for any signs of experiments involving dark matter or zero-point energy."

Spock responded with a doubting look. "What sort of signs, Captain?"

"I don't know." Kirk sounded frustrated. "Anything that might rupture the barrier between dimensions, or emit quark changelets."

A momentary pause. "Yes, sir." Spock faced his console and began reconfiguring the ship's sensors for their new assignment.

Sulu returned to his post at the helm as the relief flight-control officer moved to an aft science station. Checking the readouts to make certain all systems were nominal, Sulu saw that Chekov was already relaying new flight instructions for the adjustment to the *Enterprise*'s orbital profile. Sulu began executing the new course. The image of Akiron on the screen seemed to roll gradually sideways as the *Enterprise* arced away from the equator.

The doors to the bridge slid open with a whisper-hiss, and the dry, condescending voice of Ambassador Sarek filled the bridge. "Captain, I am compelled to ask you once again to cease your efforts to prolong this mission."

"I've already heard your case, Mister Ambassador. Unless you've got something new to add, my answer's not changing."

"Indeed, Captain, there is a new element factoring into my deliberations." The implicit challenge in Sarek's words snared the attention of the bridge crew, including Sulu. Sarek continued, "Have I heard correctly that you submitted to a session of hypnosis conducted by a Kathikar mystic?"

"What's your point?"

"Please answer my question, Captain. Is it true?"

Sarek's question provoked a dark glare from Kirk and a

keenly focused stare of interest from Spock. Kirk sighed. "My meeting with Gveter-ren inspired me to entertain some new ideas." Grudgingly, he added, "Technically speaking, I suppose one could say that hypnosis was involved."

Incredulous looks were volleyed between the members of the bridge crew—from Uhura to Sulu, from Sulu to Chekov, and so on—while Kirk simmered beneath the withering glare of the Vulcan diplomat standing beside him.

"Really, Kirk? Is this what your command has come to? Pseudoscience and psychological trickery masquerading as mysticism?" A slow, damning shake of his head. "Perhaps you were promoted too soon for your own good."

Kirk tensed and aimed all his attention at Sarek. "You're walking a thin line, Your Excellency. Step one inch over it, and you'll spend the return leg of your trip in the brig. Do I make myself clear?"

"Your hostility is unwarranted, Captain."

"That's a matter of opinion." Kirk looked at Sulu. "Report, Mister: Has the course correction been completed?"

Sulu spun back toward his console and checked the display. "Aye, sir. We're now in a polar-survey pattern."

"Well done. Spock? How soon can you have the sensors ready to start looking for active dark-energy experiments?"

Spock checked the data on his console. "According to Mister Scott, the sensors will be ready to initiate their new scanning protocols in one hour."

"Good. Keep me updated on your progress."

"Understood."

Sarek asked Kirk, "Do you believe that this new evidence which your crew seeks is related to the creatures attacking the Kathikar?"

"No," Kirk said, his voice rich with sarcasm. "I just thought it'd be fun."

The narrowing of Sarek's eyes was more than sufficient to express his displeasure with Kirk's snide retort. The ambassador faced his son. "Spock, do you endorse this foolishness, or will you speak in favor of reason?"

The first officer looked up from his console to reveal his cagey expression. Sulu could tell that Spock felt trapped in the battle of wills being waged between his father and his captain, and that he harbored serious inner conflicts about the matter. "The captain's proposal is, perhaps, not entirely without merit."

Kirk frowned at his XO. "Gee, thanks for the ringing endorsement, Spock."

Sarek stepped in front of Kirk's chair and met the young man's furious glare with his own cold gaze. "Starfleet might grant you many liberties, Kirk, but this charade cannot continue indefinitely—I trust you know that."

"What I know, Sarek, is that until someone at Starfleet Command says otherwise, I'm the captain of this ship. That means I expect my orders to be followed even if they sound wrong, stupid, or even completely crazy." Pushing himself back to his feet, Kirk continued, directing his comments to the bridge personnel around him. "Yes, I underwent some kind of unusual hypnotic therapy, and I experienced visions I can't explain. But I'm *not* crazy—I'm simply following the best leads and making decisions with the best information I have, and I need to know that I can count on every one of you to do your job and follow my orders."

The ensuing silence was gravid with the potential for disaster. Sulu searched his own conscience. He considered hypnosis and mysticism to be irrational ideas, but he was willing to give his captain the benefit of the doubt. For all his faults, Kirk was a reasonable man, a fair man. And Sulu had not forgotten that he owed James Kirk his life, for saving him from a fatal high-altitude plunge during the destruction of Vulcan. He would not let his captain stand alone now.

Speaking out with confidence, Sulu said, "You can count on me, sir."

Chekov nodded at Kirk. "And me, Keptin."

Uhura stood and faced Kirk. "I'm with you, too, sir."

Around the upper deck of the bridge, junior officers nodded their support to Captain Kirk, who permitted himself a humble smile and a small nod.

The last officer to reply was Spock. He looked at Sarek, and then at Kirk. "I await your orders, Captain."

"Continue scanning the polar regions, Mister Spock." To Sarek, Kirk added, "As soon as we have something to report, Mister Ambassador, I promise you'll receive a full briefing. Until then, I have to ask you to stay in your quarters, for your own safety." He shrugged. "Nothing personal."

"Of course not, Captain." Sarek bowed his head a fraction of a degree, the smallest increment of courtesy. "I will await your report." He turned and left the bridge.

Kirk settled back into his chair and looked anxiously at the image of Akiron's ice-encrusted northern pole. Sulu turned back to his work of making minor course adjustments to compensate for the planet's gravitational effects on the *Enterprise*'s orbit. A moment later he heard Kirk mutter under his breath.

"At least, I *hope* I'm not crazy . . ."

McCoy stared at the data tablet in his hand and forced himself to finish reviewing one more crewman's physical-fitness report. *Just one hundred thirty-eight more of these and I'll be done for another month,* he told himself in a failed attempt at self-motivation. Then he remembered that Kirk still hadn't taken his physical. He rubbed his eyes. *I should've become a bartender.*

Outside his office, the sickbay door opened. Spock walked in, saw McCoy in his office, and continued toward him. *Uh-oh. I know that look—it's the one that means bad news.*

Spock stopped in the doorway of McCoy's office. "Please pardon the interruption, Doctor, but I need to speak with you."

McCoy tossed his data tablet on top of his desk. "Fine, c'mon in." He gestured to a guest chair. "Have a seat."

The first officer stepped forward and stopped. "I would prefer to stand."

"Of course you would."

"Would you be so kind as to close your office door, Doctor? The matter I need to discuss is one of a sensitive nature."

"Certainly." McCoy pressed a button on his desktop that

shut the door, affording him and Spock a measure of privacy. "What's on your mind?"

Spock folded his hands behind his back. "I have developed serious reservations regarding the captain's state of mind."

This ought to be good. "What about it?"

"I am concerned that Captain Kirk's interactions with Gveter-ren might have compromised his fitness for command."

"Based on what evidence, Spock?"

"Less than an hour ago, when he returned to the bridge following his regression therapy with Gveter-ren, he began issuing orders based on what he had witnessed while under hypnosis. He altered our orbital profile and sensor protocols without any clear rationale."

McCoy elected to play devil's advocate. "Are starship captains normally expected to explain their orders, Mister Spock?"

"No. However, they also do not normally rely upon quasi-religious experiences to guide their decision-making."

McCoy shook his head. "I think you're blowing this out of proportion. I was there, remember? I observed the entire session, and I didn't hear Gveter-ren coach him or ask any leading questions. Whatever he helped Jim tap into, it was the same thing he saw when we were down on the planet a few hours ago."

Spock lifted one eyebrow. "How do we know that Gveter-ren did not shape *both* experiences, Doctor? If he possesses psionic talents, he might have planted the original visions telepathically as a prelude to inducing the captain's more detailed 'recollection' while under hypnosis."

"*If* he's a telepath? That's a mighty big 'if,' Spock." McCoy picked up a spare data tablet. "Let me show you something." He tapped into the ship's medical database, called up some files, and then handed the lightweight device to Spock. "Those are the captain's brainwave patterns and neurochemical levels before, during, and after the hypnosis session. Nothing abnormal, no unexplained spikes in neurotransmitters, no sign of irregular synaptic activity. If Gveter-ren had been telepathically invading the captain's psyche, there would have been traces."

"Not necessarily. Medical research into telepathy and other psionic disciplines is still in its infancy. Considering the Federation's limited contact with the Kathikar, it is possible, however unlikely, that they could be capable of as-yet undetectable psionic intrusions."

McCoy studied Spock. "Let's say your suspicion is borne out, and Gveter-ren has some never-before-discovered telepathic power. Why would he choose to manipulate the captain? What would he stand to gain?"

The question appeared to stymie Spock. "I admit it is difficult to imagine an ulterior motive that would be served by influencing the captain to intervene against the wights." After another moment he shed his mask of doubt. "Regardless, the captain's decision to let this unvetted foreign national place him in an altered mental state, and then to use it as a basis for command decisions, is highly suspect, wouldn't you agree?"

McCoy conceded his side of the debate with a sigh. "Yes, it's odd." He sat forward and leaned against his desktop. "But do me a favor, will you? Don't go making a big deal out of this with him—it's bad for morale. Let me talk to him, one on one, and see if I can knock some sense into that young head of his."

"By all means, Doctor. It was always my intention that you should be the one to broach this subject with the captain."

That revelation took McCoy by surprise. "Really? Well, I guess I should say thank you for the vote of confidence, then."

"Not at all. It is a simple matter of what is required by Starfleet regulations. If you, in your role as chief medical officer, determine that the captain has been compromised, psychologically or otherwise, by the influence of Gveter-ren, then it is your sole prerogative—and your sworn duty—to relieve Captain Kirk of command of the *Enterprise*."

16

"I have come to expect a certain degree of arrogance from the captains of Starfleet vessels," Sarek said to Admiral Deigaro, whose careworn features were rendered in unflattering detail on the screen in Sarek's quarters. "However, Captain Kirk's unrepentant intransigence regarding our mission on Akiron far exceeds anything I have ever before been asked to endure in the course of my diplomatic duties."

The admiral winced in a manner that Sarek took to mean Deigaro was experiencing profound physical discomfort. *"I know Kirk can be a bit of a maverick, Mister Ambassador, but that's sort of his privilege. Starfleet Command tries not to second-guess its starship commanders."*

"I understand your position, Admiral. I am not suggesting you adopt such interventions as a matter of normal operations. However, in this circumstance, I believe such action to be warranted."

"On what grounds?"

"Insubordination. He has failed to recognize my authority in political matters, and by taking action on the surface of Akiron without proper legal sanction, he has set the stage for a potentially disastrous interstellar incident."

Deigaro grimaced. *"Are you sure you're not exaggerating a bit, Your Excellency? Because I don't see anything wrong with a mercy mission."*

"The situation on Akiron is more complicated than it appears." Sarek reached out to his aide, L'Nel, who handed him a data tablet, from which he read aloud. "'Chief Minister Vellesh-ka was deposed in a coup approximately four hours ago, by a faction of religious extremists who are capitalizing on the current crisis for political gain.'"

"Yes, I read that in Kirk's report. I also know Vellesh-ka's been granted asylum on the Enterprise. *With all due respect, Mister Ambassador, what's your point?"*

"My point lies in the detail that I made clear to Captain Kirk, but which he omitted from his official report: Although the current planetary government of Akiron has been deposed, no clear successor has emerged. If there is no legal governing body, then there is no entity to grant permission to Federation civilians or Starfleet personnel to take action on the planet's surface. In its current anarchic state, Akiron is entitled to Prime Directive protection, and possibly aggressive interdiction. Any action taken by Captain Kirk or his crew on Akiron is illegal."

Deigaro sighed. *"I see. Your points are well taken, Mister Ambassador. I'll convene a meeting of the admiralty and ask for a consensus. If the majority agrees with you, we'll issue new orders to Kirk."*

"Thank you, Admiral." After a brief pause he added, "There is one more request I would like to make, if I may."

"Go ahead." Deigaro's weariness was evident. *"Ask."*

"Regardless of whether new orders are issued to Captain Kirk, it is time for the Federation Council to reassign me to a new task. As my services are no longer required on Akiron, the logical course of action would be for me to move on."

The admiral nodded. *"Got anyplace particular in mind?"*

Sarek called up a new file on his data tablet and relayed its contents over the encrypted channel to Deigaro. "I have sent you a list of assignments for which I think my skill set is suited."

A soft warble over the comm indicated that Sarek's data had been received. Deigaro took a moment to glance at it. *"Long list. I don't really have time to review all that. Can you pare it down to no more than five choices and resend it after you've made your selections?"*

"Of course, Admiral. Thank you for your assistance."

"You're welcome, Mister Ambassador. I'll be in touch. Deigaro out."

The admiral closed the channel, and Sarek's screen went dark. He swiveled his chair so that he faced L'Nel. "I wish to commend you. You did an excellent job of creating a secure subspace channel. Are you quite certain my conversation with the admiral will not be noticed by the *Enterprise*'s crew?"

"Yes, Mister Ambassador. I am absolutely certain."

"Good." Sarek stood and handed L'Nel his data tablet. "I would be most grateful if you could review this list again and recommend the five posts that you feel are most worthy of my attention."

L'Nel bowed her head. "I am honored to serve, Ambassador."

She took a few steps toward the door while Sarek walked to his bed and stretched his arms above his head. When he lowered his arms, he noticed that L'Nel was still inside his quarters, watching him out of the corner of her eye.

"Is there something else you wish to discuss, L'Nel?"

The young woman seemed reluctant to meet Sarek's gaze, choosing instead to avert her eyes toward the floor or bulkheads. "I have a question."

Sarek moved toward her in slow steps, as he might if he were approaching an easily spooked feral animal. "You may speak freely."

There was a hint of desperation in L'Nel's voice. "Did you ask Spock if he would consider taking me as his mate for his next *Pon farr*?"

Lying to her will serve no purpose. The truth might be difficult for her to hear, but in a matter of such importance, it is necessary.

"I asked Spock if he would consider taking a Vulcan mate."

"And what was his response?"

"He remains committed to his relationship with the human Nyota Uhura." Sensing his aide's grave disappointment, he added, "I apologize if I led you to believe my son's opinion on this matter could be swayed in your favor."

L'Nel's expression was coldly neutral. "It is of no consequence."

"Very well." They stood facing each other in silence for a moment, and then Sarek added, "It is time for me to retire."

"Understood. Good night, Ambassador." L'Nel turned and left Sarek's quarters. Her stride was swift and businesslike.

Sarek reflected that L'Nel seemed to have taken Spock's rebuff with perfect stoicism and calm, but he'd also sensed a quiet tension in her departure that led him to infer that his aide was far from untroubled by his son's rejection.

As he lay down on his bunk to try to sleep, he suspected that his next several hours on the *Enterprise* would prove to be anything but restful.

Kirk's fists moved in a rhythm, beating out a cadence on the blur of the speed bag. He had found that the classic boxing exercise helped him quiet his thoughts and relax. It brought him all the serenity of a meditation chant, coupled with all the satisfaction of getting to hit something.

Why do I feel like I'm getting beat up every time I turn around? I've got Sarek trying to pull rank, Spock looking for a reason to second-guess me, and a fur-faced holy man who wants me to believe in reincarnation. This sure doesn't sound like the job I trained for at the Academy.

He punched the speed bag faster until its impacts bled into a stutter.

From behind Kirk's shoulder, McCoy said, "Quite a beat you got goin'."

Kirk gave the speed bag one last hard swat, then caught it with both wrapped hands. He looked back at McCoy. "What can I do for you, Bones?"

"Take your physical, for one thing."

"Not right now, Bones. I'm a little busy."

"Yeah, I can see that. Training for a new career as a prize-fighter? You might want to spend more time on your foot-work." Reacting to Kirk's scathing glare, McCoy lifted his palms in a defensive posture. "Just trying to help."

Kirk resumed pummeling the speed bag. "I doubt that."

McCoy leaned against the bulkhead on the other side of the speed bag and worked at maintaining eye contact, even though Kirk was making a point of not doing so. "Would you mind telling me what's going on inside that head of yours?"

"Yes, I would." Kirk increased his tempo on the bag.

McCoy folded his arms. "Why do you think I'm here?"

"Because someone asked you to talk to me. Spock, or maybe Sarek." Kirk began alternating light taps with power hits. "Tell me I'm wrong."

The doctor rolled his eyes. "Wish I could." After a few seconds of watching Kirk beat the hell out of the speed bag, he added, "It was Spock."

"I figured. Sarek wouldn't go to you—he's probably too busy trying to find a way to go over my head."

"Okay, so you've guessed *why* I'm here. What do you think I came to talk to you *about*?"

Kirk grinned. "You think I've gone off the deep end. You think I'm giving orders based on mystical alien mumbo jumbo."

With a tilt of his head, McCoy said, "Now that you mention it . . ."

"Spare me the lecture, Bones. It's not like I'm asking someone to sacrifice a goat or do a rain dance." He slammed the bag with one mighty blow and then halted its motion with both hands. "All I did was order a course correction and ask Spock to run a sensor sweep for dark-energy generators."

McCoy nodded. "Yes—based on a vision you had under hypnosis."

Kirk walked away as he began removing the protective wrappings from his hands. "Okay, I'll admit the source of my intel was weird." He looked over his shoulder at McCoy, who was following him toward the locker room. "Look at me, Bones. Do I seem like a zealot to you? Do I seem irrational?"

"No more than usual."

"Touché."

Catching up to Kirk, McCoy said, "I'm not worried that you've gone all superstitious, Jim. What concerns Spock—and I have to say I think he has a point here—is that you might have been compromised by telepathic suggestion. We're afraid you're being manipulated."

The captain pulled off his hand wrappings as he entered the locker room. "Into doing what I already wanted to do? And by who? Gveter-ren?"

"Maybe."

Kirk shook his head. "I don't think so." He opened his

locker, tossed his hand wraps inside, and pulled off his sweat-soaked black T-shirt. "I'd know."

McCoy leaned against the row of lockers. "Would you, Jim? Are you sure? Are you willing to stake the safety of your ship and crew on it?"

"Yes. I am." He pulled off his sweatpants. "Have you considered that maybe my visions in the cave and under hypnosis weren't mystical at all? What if they were just products of my subconscious? A message from some deeper part of my brain about how to deal with this crisis?"

"Is that what you think they were?"

"I have no idea." Kirk removed his underwear and socks. "I just wanted to give you an answer I thought you'd accept." He closed his locker and walked toward the showers, once again with McCoy at his heels.

"Well, I'm at least relieved to know you don't put your faith in ghosts and Dark Ages quackery. But it sounds like you're not really buying the purely scientific explanation, either."

Kirk stepped into a three-sided shower stall and turned on a pleasantly hot, high-pressure spray of water. "I just call it like I see it, Bones."

McCoy stood back to avoid being doused by ricocheted streams from Kirk's shower. "So if you don't believe in the supernatural, and you don't believe in science, exactly what the hell *do* you believe in, Jim?"

Kirk considered that while he stood under a white deluge surrounded by gray vapor. "Honestly? I don't know *what* I believe, Bones."

As the captain rinsed the sweat from his hair, he heard Scotty's voice echoing over the ship's PA system. *"Scott to Captain Kirk."*

He shut off the water, and McCoy tossed him a clean, dry towel. Kirk dried his hands and face, and then he wrapped the towel around his waist as he walked to a companel on a nearby bulkhead. He thumbed open a response channel. "Kirk here. Go ahead, Scotty."

Scotty sounded excited. *"Sir, I think you need to come to the bridge on the double. Spock and I have something to show you."*

17

"I am not comfortable granting your request, L'Nel," said Tokor, an acolyte of the Temple of Mount Seleya and an eighth-year *Kolinahr* adept who had found refuge on Deneva following the destruction of Vulcan.

L'Nel looked back at Tokor from the comm screen in his home. There was a quality of anger in her manner that troubled Tokor. *"This is not a time to give free rein to your conscience. We face more pressing issues than the sanctity of the temple's secrets. We need to perpetuate our race and protect our culture."*

"I find no fault with your objective as stated. But I question the role you would have me play. I do not see how it serves the greater good."

The muscles in L'Nel's jaw tensed. *"Tokor, I do not have time to enumerate all the reasons why I need this information. I will be able to maintain this channel for only a few more minutes before I risk being detected by the* Enterprise's *crew."*

Tokor made a fist of his right hand and folded his left hand over it. "Your predicament is unfortunate but hardly sufficient to compel my cooperation."

She narrowed her eyes, lowered her chin, and leaned forward like a wild animal preparing to charge. *"Really? You seemed very eager to assist me when I approached you two weeks ago. Has your cowardice overcome your avarice?"*

"Having failed to persuade me with bribery or an appeal to my sense of pity, you resort to petty insults. A most illogical tactic. What arrows will you draw next from your conversational quiver? Threats of violence and blackmail, perhaps?"

L'Nel simmered for a moment, and then she collected herself. *"Why are you no longer inclined to assist me?"*

It was a reasonable inquiry. "The *fal-tor-pan* is not a ritual to be undertaken lightly. Its origins are ancient beyond record, and it is dangerous for both the patient and the priest. It has not been attempted in more than a century."

"I know all of that. You made it clear when last we spoke."

Tokor nodded. "Yes, but at the time I had only a passing familiarity with the ritual. I have since retrieved a copy of the ancient scrolls and studied its mysteries. The ritual was created to transfer a hosted *katra* from one living being to another—not to retrieve one from a *katric* ark."

"Perhaps. But theoretically it is possible, is it not?"

"I do not know. There are unsubstantiated accounts that Syrran freed the *katra* of Surak himself from an ark and bonded it to his own. However, no record exists of Syrran's method for this posthumous bonding."

"*I have already accounted for that. I will perform a reversal of the ritual that extracts a living* katra *from a patient and inters it in the ark, as a prelude to the* fal-tor-pan.*"

It was a labor for Tokor to conceal his horror at L'Nel's proposition. "That is not advisable. The ancient ways are not so easily malleable. Juxtaposing two such incantations might prove disastrous, L'Nel. I beg you to reconsider."

"*I will not. And your earlier supposition was correct: if you deny me the aid you pledged previously, I will make our arrangement public. For me, the penalty will be social opprobrium. For you, however, the consequences will be far more severe—beginning with your expulsion from the* Kolinahr.*"

Masking his dismay, Tokor asked, "Why are you doing this?"

"*Because our people's crisis demands it. We all have an obligation to one another to rebuild and repopulate. Spock, however, refuses to accept a Vulcan mate, choosing instead to pursue a sentimental relationship with a human woman. Since he will not listen to reason, corrective action is required.*"

"And you believe that you possess the authority to mete out such justice?"

She was unfazed by his accusatory question. "*I think that we all bear a responsibility to act in the best interests of our people, and to do our best to make certain that our fellow Vulcans do the same—even when they do not wish to. As we have been taught, 'The needs of the many outweigh the needs of the few—'*"

"Or the one." Tokor frowned. He resigned himself to playing his inescapable role in L'Nel's despicable scheme. "If I honor my pledge to help you, will you honor your promise to deliver me the ark?"

She nodded. *"I will. You have my word, the* katric *ark will be yours."*

He sighed, and then he accessed his virtual library to find the documentation of the *fal-tor-pan* ritual. "I am transmitting the information you desire now. Please promise me that you will use it with the utmost caution."

"I will." A ping from her console drew her attention for a moment. *"The data has arrived. Thank you."* She lifted her hand in the Vulcan salute. *"Live long and prosper, Tokor."*

He returned the gesture. "Peace and long life, L'Nel."

She terminated the connection. Tokor stared at the darkened screen. Despite all the years he had spent working to master his emotions, he was wracked with guilt. Because of his one moment of weakness, an innocent man was going to die.

18

Kirk's hair was still damp from his post-workout shower as he stepped onto the bridge. To his right, Scott and Spock huddled over the sensor display at Spock's post. Kirk moved to join the chief engineer and first officer. "Spock, Scotty: fill me in, quickly."

"Right." Scott punched up some data on the screen in front of him. "We recalibrated the main sensor array to look for those quarks you mentioned. Our first couple of passes over the planet's northern pole came up empty—but then we started our southern survey." The image that appeared on the screen was a detailed map of Akiron's southern polar region.

Spock nodded at the screen. "The region has no major landmass. It consists primarily of pack ice and glaciers anchored to a handful of small islands." He tapped a key on his console, and a tiny grid on the map enlarged to fill the screen. "On one of those islands we detected an artificial structure that houses a generator whose particle emissions are consistent with those of systems designed to harness zero-point energy." Spock pressed another key, changing the image to one of subterranean topography. "The island is the remnant of a dormant volcano. It appears to be linked to the same vein of gray dilithium we found in the mine."

"Okay," Kirk said, "we found the generator. What's it powering?"

Spock glanced at Scotty, who put on a sheepish look. "No idea, sir. We've got a pretty good picture of its subatomic emissions, but no clue what they're being used for. Look at this, though!" He called up another screen of waveforms and raw data. "Subspatial phase distortions like I've never seen!"

Kirk grimaced at Spock. "Help me out, here."

"Evidence that the island's zero-point generator has caused a breach in spacetime that could have granted the wights access to this dimension."

At last, information I know how to use. "If we shut down the generator, will that stop the wight attacks?"

"Whether that alone will be sufficient is unknown, Captain," Spock said. "However, it is very likely a prerequisite to any permanent solution."

That was enough to spur Kirk to action. "Spock, put together a landing party. If we can't get the Kathikar to shut that thing off, we'll do it ourselves." He turned toward Uhura. "Lieutenant, hail the facility on the island."

"Aye, sir." Uhura worked at her console while Kirk and the others resumed their discussion.

"Sir," Scott said, "you might not want to beam down there

in person this time. For all we know, that base—or lab, or whatever it is—might be swarming with wights. It could be a trap for anybody dumb enough to walk in."

Spock replied, "Unlikely, Mister Scott. Based on the data we've collected, it would appear that the same subspace disruptions responsible for opening a passage to a neighboring dimension would also act as a potent repellent for entities from that reality now residing in ours." To Kirk he added, "In fact, the interior of that island facility might very well be the only safe place on the surface of Akiron."

Uhura looked over her shoulder at Kirk, Spock, and Scott. "Captain, I'm getting a response from the base on the island. It's a warning from the Kathikar military to cease and desist all efforts at contact."

"A military base," Kirk muttered with disdain. "I should've known."

Spock dropped his voice to a confidential hush intended only for Kirk and Scott. "Captain, if we beam an armed landing party into a Kathikar military base, it could be construed as an act of war."

"With who? The planet has no government, Spock."

"At a minimum, we will risk inciting a violent confrontation with whatever armed forces are stationed there."

"Can't we just hit the island with low-intensity blasts from our phaser banks?" Kirk asked. "Do it right, we could stun everyone on the island."

"Aye," Scott said, "and risk ripping a hole in the universe." He punched up another screen packed with symbols, graphs, and formulas. "That's a blast-hardened structure. Any shot that can knock out the personnel inside it will be strong enough to cause a catastrophic reaction in the zero-point generator. If that happens, kiss Akiron good-bye, and maybe half this sector with it."

Kirk shot an incredulous look at Spock. "It wouldn't be *that* bad, would it?"

"Actually, I think Mister Scott might have underestimated the potential zone of destruction."

"Okay, scratch that plan." Kirk weighed his options. "They don't have any shields. Use the transporters to beam up the base's personnel, put 'em in the brig, and then we'll beam down and take the generator offline."

"Normally," Spock said, "that plan would be commendable as much for its ingenuity as for its nonviolent nature. Unfortunately, the same subspatial disruptions that brought the base to our attention also interfere with our transporters. We cannot use the transporter safely within fifty meters of the base's perimeter as long as the generator remains active."

Kirk shrugged at Spock and Scott. "I'm out. You two got any ideas?"

Spock said, "If the base is under military control, perhaps its personnel will respect an order from an authority they recognize—even if that authority technically no longer wields power."

"The chief minister." Kirk nodded. "Who just happens to be resting comfortably in exile here on the *Enterprise*. Good thinking, Spock. Let's go have a word with Vellesh-ka. Mister Sulu, you have the conn."

As Kirk led Spock and Scott toward the exit, Uhura said, "Captain! We've just received a recorded message from Admiral Deigaro at Starfleet Command."

Kirk paused, shot a surprised look at Spock and then at Uhura, and then turned back toward the main viewer. "Put it on-screen, Lieutenant."

"Aye, sir." Uhura routed the incoming message to the forward screen, where Admiral Deigaro's face appeared.

"Captain Kirk," said Deigaro, *"you are hereby ordered to leave Akiron and return Ambassador Sarek to Starbase 21 as soon as possible. This is a priority-one command directive. Deigaro out."*

The screen blinked back to the image of Akiron's southern pole.

Kirk scowled at Spock. "Well, it didn't take your father long to find a way to do an end run. Give him my compliments the next time you see him." To Uhura, he added, "Lieutenant, find out how Sarek got a message to Starfleet Command." He started toward the door. "Back to work, gents."

Spock said in a stern voice, "Captain. What are you doing?"

"What does it look like I'm doing, Spock? I'm on my way to ask Vellesh-ka to tell his island commandos to stand down and turn off the generator."

"Captain, that would be a direct contravention of Admiral Deigaro's order to leave Akiron and, by extension, terminate our mission."

Kirk stepped to within a few centimeters of Spock, to make it clear that he wasn't backing down, either literally or figuratively. "I understand what's *implied* by Admiral Deigaro's orders. However, I am choosing to *interpret* his orders based on his *precise* choice of words."

Spock stood his ground despite Kirk's intrusion into his personal space. "I do not understand."

"Admiral Deigaro said we were to leave Akiron and bring your dad to Starbase 21 *as soon as possible*. Well, at the moment, I have work to do—turning off that generator and saving the Kathikar—and I can't leave until that's done. So, at the moment, it's *not possible* for me to leave Akiron. But as soon as it is, Spock, I assure you, we'll leave with all due speed."

It was difficult for Kirk to read all of Spock's subtle microexpressions, but he was fairly certain that somewhere beneath that icy façade, his first officer was at least slightly amused.

With the slightest twitch of one eyebrow, Spock said, "That is a very *creative* interpretation of the admiral's orders, Captain."

Kirk slapped Spock's shoulder. "Thanks, Spock. I'll take that as a compliment. Now, let's go ask Vellesh-ka what his army is making down there."

"It's a death ray," said Vellesh-ka.

Getting the deposed chief minister to talk about his military's secret polar base had proved easier than the Starfleet officers had expected, though Spock found the glibness of Vellesh-ka's answer less than satisfying. Noting Kirk's and Scott's stunned reactions, Spock asked their Kathikar refugee as diplomatically as he was able, "Could you be more specific, Chief Minister?"

Vellesh-ka got up from his chair and began pacing in front of the three officers. "A few months after the mining company opened a passage to the Underdark, they discovered a peculiar variant of dilithium. It was useless for starship engines, so the miners treated it as garbage. My military's research division, however, uncovered a potential use for this new substance."

"As a weapon," Kirk said with obvious disapproval.

"Yes. We financed the project with the profits from the dilithium mine. It helped solve a number of theoretical problems related to accessing zero-point energy, but its secondary effects were even more impressive: it could generate bursts of energy across vast distances—our first tests produced effects along the outer reaches of our solar system."

Scott interrupted, "Let me guess—you were trying to make a weapon with interstellar range."

"More than that. A weapon of mass destruction that could strike any world in known space without warning. A weapon that would make Akiron a major player in interstellar politics rather than a mere commodity to be fought over and used up and thrown away." The minister bowed his head, ashamed. "When the experiment on Redivel Island began to go awry, I wanted to shut it down, but the project's military liaison assured me his people could bring it under control. I was under pressure from key members of Parliament to keep the project active. They warned me that if I shut it down, they'd take my seat with a no-confidence vote. So I capitulated—and now my people are paying the price for my failure."

Kirk affected a consoling demeanor. "Chief Minister, my

crew and I think we can help your people if we can get your military to turn off that dark-energy generator. We've tried asking them, but they refuse to speak to us. We're hoping you'll be willing to order them to stand down."

"I can try. When the wights began attacking in numbers, I placed the military on high alert, which liberates most of our combat units to take independent action. Many of them are operating in radio silence."

That news prompted a concerned look from Kirk. "Seeing as their weapons likely won't have any effect on the wights, your troops might be doing more harm than good. I think it's time to pull them back."

Vellesh-ka sighed. "You may be right, Captain. Let me speak to the men at Redivel Base. Perhaps I can make them see reason before it's too late."

"That's what I was hoping you'd say." Kirk activated the comm unit on Vellesh-ka's desk and opened a channel. "Kirk to Lieutenant Uhura."

"Uhura here. Go ahead, sir."

"The polar-island base is called Redivel. Hail them again and tell them it's Chief Minister Vellesh-ka calling." He looked at the minister. "Is there a recognition code or some other way to get them to answer the hail?"

"Tell them it's a Code *Orexem* alert."

Facing the comm, Kirk asked, "Did you get that, Uhura?"

"Aye, sir. Hailing the base now."

"As soon as you get them on the line, patch us in."

Vellesh-ka rubbed his paws together while he waited.

"I want to make clear, Captain, that I cannot guarantee the troops at Redivel will obey my commands."

"I understand, but I have an obligation to exhaust all diplomatic options before I resort to the use of force. If we can resolve this by talking instead of by shooting, it'll be better for everyone."

Uhura said over the comm, *"Patching you through to the base now, sir."*

Kirk nodded at Vellesh-ka. "You're up."

Vellesh-ka sat down in front of the comm terminal, on which appeared the white-furred visage of another Kathikar, who wore a dark gray military uniform.

"This is Chief Minister Vellesh-ka. To whom am I speaking?"

"Chief Minister, this is General Adrig."

"General, are you aware of the global crisis currently transpiring?"

"Affirmative. We've fortified our position against the wights."

"The time for such measures is past. Your base's zero-point generator is part of what enabled the dimensional breach being used by the wights. I am ordering you to shut down the generator and stand down your forces."

After a long pause, Adrig replied, *"I'm sorry, sir. I can't do that."*

The minister's voice pitched upward with indignation. "I beg your pardon, General? I gave you a direct order!"

"I'm aware of that, Chief Minister. Just as I'm also aware you've lost control of the government. And now my communications officer informs me that you're speaking to me from a Federation starship in orbit—which means you've abandoned not only your office but also our planet."

"I have done no such—"

"*You're not in command anymore. That means I'm no longer obliged to follow your orders.*"

Vellesh-ka was flustered but struggled to remain calm. "General, if you will not hear me as your head of state, then hear me as a fellow citizen, as one Kathikar to another: Our people's only hope of survival lies in defeating the wights, and we cannot do that as long as your base's ZP generator remains online. For the good of all Akiron, I beg you, please—turn it off and let the Starfleet crew help."

"*I do not hear the words of cowards. I need to protect my men and guard this technology—I won't let it fall into enemy hands. Warn your Federation friends not to interfere in my mission or set foot on my island.*" A manic gleam widened the general's eyes. "*It will take my men ten minutes to charge the dark-energy weapon. I'm giving the* Enterprise *exactly that long to break orbit. After that, if the Starfleet ship is still there, I'll blast it out of existence.*" Adrig terminated the transmission, and the screen went dark.

"Well," said Scott, "that's a fine how-do-you-do."

"Could've gone worse," Kirk said.

Spock asked, "What shall we do with our ten minutes of grace, Captain?"

"Assemble a strike team. Because in five minutes, we're gonna go down there and flip the switch that turns that thing off."

19

The landing party materialized knee-deep in snow behind an icy hill on Redivel Island. Kirk, Spock, Scott, and their nine-person security team were swaddled in identical suits of white-and-gray camouflaged arctic gear that concealed their faces and protected them from the scouring blasts of ice driven by off-key howls of freezing-cold wind. The security personnel carried phaser rifles; Kirk, Spock, and Scott were armed with phaser pistols, and Scott had his portable toolkit.

Kirk activated his faceplate's night-vision filter, which cast his surroundings in a synthetic frost-blue twilight, and then he turned on its holographic status display. As he looked at his men, their surnames and ranks appeared above their heads, enabling him to tell who was who. Other data on his faceplate helped him get his bearings and gauge the distance to the target: they were sixty-one meters from the perimeter of the base that housed the zero-point generator.

Along the bottom edge of his field of vision was a countdown to the fulfillment of Adrig's threat to open fire on the *Enterprise*.

"We've got four minutes and forty seconds," Kirk said. "Phasers on heavy stun. Move out!"

Spock, Scott, and Kirk split up as they charged over the hill, and each led three members of the security team on a frontal assault under cover of darkness.

Sprinting in the snow was clumsy and exhausting, and Kirk felt winded by the time he had crossed half the open ground to the base's electrified fence, which, according to his faceplate's display, had been set for lethal effect.

Then came the cracks of rifle shots. Atop the roofs of the base's solidly constructed buildings, muzzle flashes lit up the night. One of the officers running beside Kirk was slammed backward, all her forward momentum arrested.

Searchlights snapped on and swept in blinding slashes across the wide, empty stretch of snow that bordered the base's fence.

Kirk fired, and then so did the rest of the landing party. Brilliant pulses of phaser energy converged on the searchlights and shot them apart in flurries of sparks and shattered glass. As the base's exterior was plunged back into darkness, several of its guards were dropped by stunning blasts from the *Enterprise* team.

A handful of sentries continued to pepper the landing party with harassing fire. As he neared the perimeter fence,

Kirk changed his phaser's power setting to full and disintegrated a ten-meter-wide section of the electrified barrier ahead of him with two shots. He led his people through the gap and ducked into a recessed area along one building's wall, gaining himself at least a bit of cover.

The landing party regrouped single file against the wall behind him. Resetting his phaser to stun, he looked over his shoulder at his team. "Suppressing fire on the snipers while I lead Spock and Scotty inside. Got it?" His men nodded. "On three. One. Two. Three!" He broke cover at a full run, heading straight for the base's secured access door. Pops of semiautomatic rifle fire were drowned out by the shrieks of phaser pulses that lit up the night with crimson flashes.

Kirk ducked into the doorway, spun around, and joined in the effort to keep the snipers at bay or at least blinded. Spock pushed into the doorway behind him, firing at snipers in the other direction, while Scott used his tricorder to hack the electronic and biometric locks on the door.

The readout on Kirk's faceplate indicated that they had less than three minutes before the Kathikar troops fired their weapon at the *Enterprise*. He flinched as a stray bullet ricocheted off the concrete wall above his head. "Time's a factor, Scotty!" he shouted above the din of combat.

"Almost there!" Scott's tricorder chirped and he exclaimed, "Open sesame!" The door behind Spock and Kirk let out a pneumatic gasp as it swung inward. Scott slung his tricorder at his side, drew his phaser, and did his part to keep the snipers occupied. "Go! I'll be right behind you!"

Spock and Kirk hurried inside the base's headquarters. Scott unleashed a steady barrage as he backed in after them.

Kirk keyed his suit's communications transceiver. "We're in. Move up and have at least one man hold the entrance."

"Acknowledged," said Lieutenant Damrow, the ranking security officer.

Hunched low and moving fast, Kirk prowled through the corridors of the base's headquarters, trusting his instincts to lead him to the command center. He rounded a corner to discover the flicker of massive display screens—and then he caught a blur of movement just in time to duck back behind cover before a hail of bullets ripped divots from the corner in front of him.

"I think we found the command center," he said to Spock and Scott.

"Apparently," Spock said. "We have one minute and fifty-two seconds until the weapon is ready to fire."

Kirk leaned forward and asked Scott, "You thinking what I'm thinking?"

"Aye, sir." Scott held up a small cylinder. "Photon grenade." He armed it with a push of his thumb, stepped forward, pivoted, and hurled it blindly around the corner and down the corridor into the command center.

All three men covered their faces a fraction of a second before the ultrapowerful flash grenade detonated with a muted *whoosh* and a blinding effect for anyone unlucky enough to be within sight of it. Cries of pain and chaotic stutters of weapons fire followed, and then there were only the groans of its stunned victims.

"Move up," Kirk said. "Secure the command center. Scotty, find the weapon's controls and shut it down."

They rounded the corner and jogged forward into the command center, whose personnel were lying on the deck beside the dazed General Adrig. Spock and Kirk disarmed the fallen soldiers, and then they used lightweight but ultrastrong polymer ties to bind the enemy troops' hands behind their backs and their legs together at the ankles.

By the time they finished, the rest of the landing party had arrived. Lieutenant Damrow said, "All enemy personnel subdued, sir. No fatalities."

"How's Harrington?" Kirk asked, referring to the security officer who had been hit during the initial charge to the fence.

"She's fine. Her body armor absorbed most of it."

From the other side of the room, Scotty let out a worried, "Um . . ."

Kirk turned toward the chief engineer. "What's wrong?"

"I can't shut down the weapon. The Kathikar's wild shots ripped up their own consoles. It's all goin' haywire!"

Spock joined Scott at the weapon's control panel. "Mister Scott is correct. The Kathikar's weapon is already locked onto the *Enterprise*, and it is set to fire in eleven seconds." He tried manipulating several of the console's buttons. "Its interface is not responding." He turned toward Kirk, his eyes betraying his alarm. "We cannot disengage its targeting mechanism or abort its firing sequence."

Kirk pulled his communicator out from under his cold-weather jacket and flipped it open. "Kirk to *Enterprise*! Raise shields and brace for impact!"

The first salvo rocked the *Enterprise* hard enough to throw Sulu halfway out of the command chair. Clinging to one of its arms, he called out, "Damage report!"

Chekov replied over the wailing red-alert klaxon, "Shields holding, but not for long!" Another blast quaked the ship. The lights on the bridge began flickering. "We're losing main power!" The young Russian looked back at Sulu, his face contorted with fear. "Warp drive offline, shields will fail in two minutes!"

"Helm, increase to full impulse, put us above the northern pole. Use the planet for cover." Sulu pressed a comm switch on his chair's armrest. "Bridge to engineering. Route all weapons power to shields!"

A loud drone accompanied the power increase to the impulse engines. As Akiron's southern pole slid out of sight on the main viewscreen, Chekov said, "If we move to the northern pole, we won't be able to beam up the landing party."

"If we *don't* do it, we'll be a cloud of debris," Sulu said.

Uhura looked up from her station. "Captain Kirk is hailing us."

Sulu replied, "On audio."

Kirk's voice crackled from the overhead speakers. *"Sulu, report!"*

"Shields damaged, warp drive offline. We're taking evasive action, which means we'll be out of transport range."

"Do what you have to do, but protect my ship!"

"Acknowledged. Is the landing party safe?"

"We're fine, and looking for a way to shut this gizmo off."

A warning signal shrilled from Chekov's console. "Subspatial distortions!" He analyzed the incoming data on the fly. "Moving with us—*tracking* us!"

The *Enterprise* trembled and lurched to port. A momentary failure of its inertial dampers and artificial gravity hurled the bridge crew out of their chairs and against the overhead. Then the artificial gravity came back online and slammed the crew back onto the deck as the main bank of lights went out.

Struggling to get his bearings in the meager half-light cast by the bridge's consoles, Sulu struggled back into the command chair. "Report! What happened?"

"Power failures on all decks," Chekov said.

At the science station, Ensign sh'Vetha recoiled in horror from the sensor display. "The subspace disruption is generating pockets of negative energy," said the Andorian. "They're passing through our shields and penetrating the hull."

Sulu opened an internal comm channel. "All decks, intruder alert! Security, repel boarders!" He closed the channel and said, "Helm, increase speed! We have to get clear of the weapon's emitter!"

Ensign Katuscha replied, "But we *are* clear of it, sir!"

"Then what—?"

"Another emitter," Chekov said. "It's part of a global array."

He looked at Sulu, more afraid than he was before. "Shifting our orbit won't help us."

Damn. What was I thinking? Why would they build a weapon with interstellar range if they couldn't fire it in any direction they pleased? Of course *there's a global network of emitters.* Sulu asked Ensign sh'Vetha, "Can we destroy the emitters with phaser shots?"

"Not without causing massive civilian casualties. And our phasers are currently offline to help power the shields."

I won't slaughter millions to save hundreds. Unless the captain knocks out the weapon's generator, we're done for.

Sulu's morbid reflection was interrupted by a report from Chekov: "Internal sensors are tracking the invaders! They are converging on sickbay!"

"Evacuate sickbay!"

"It's too late," Chekov said. "All escape routes are cut off." He looked crestfallen. "They have no place to run."

One minute McCoy was tending to a handful of patients with minor injuries; the next, people were stampeding into sickbay, screaming in terror.

Pushing his way through the crush of running *Enterprise* crewmen, he shouted, "What the hell's going on here?"

An enlisted engineer—McCoy guessed the man couldn't be much older than twenty—shrieked, "They're coming! They're everywhere! Run!"

Not content to get his facts from crazy people, McCoy shoved through the flood of people logjammed at the main entrance of sickbay and bladed through the crowd in the dark corridor. If there was one thing he had learned about panicked crowds, it was that they tended to run roughshod over the slow or the weak, which meant there were probably wounded people left in its wake who needed his help.

Dodging through the thinning stream of frightened people retreating past him, he struggled to see clearly in the feeble light thrown off by stuttering companels along the bulkheads. Up ahead he heard someone groan, and he started running. As he rounded a curve, he saw an injured enlisted woman lying on the deck at his feet—and then a wash of numbing-cold air and a blood-curdling shriek drew his attention farther down the passage.

Wights were emerging like smoky phantoms through bulkheads and swarming on a fallen young Tellarite ensign, who let out a cry of agony and terror. Part squeal, part scream, it sent a chill of fear through McCoy.

Then the swarm began moving toward him.

In fluid motions, McCoy spun, kneeled, picked up the fallen woman at his feet, hefted her over his shoulder in a fireman's carry, and made a run for it.

Pure adrenaline drove him. His heart slammed inside his chest, his breaths were fast and shallow. There was no time to think, no time to plan. All he could do was run. All that mattered was to get away.

As he ran, he heard more screams from the corridor ahead.

He ducked inside sickbay, which was packed wall to wall with people. He locked the door behind himself, then looked around in dismay.

Good God. We're cattle in a pen. Herded to the slaughter.

He braced himself to meet a grisly, painful end.

Someone shouldered past McCoy, heading toward danger.

It was Gveter-ren. He chanted under his breath, his demeanor firm but serene, and he held his jewel-tipped walking stick in front of him like a spear.

A trio of wights slipped through the locked door as if it weren't even there. The wizened Kathikar mystic growled and lunged forward, thrusting his walking stick at the vaporous entities. As the translucent jewel at the end of his staff made contact with the misty apparitions, there was a flash of emerald light— and then it was the wights' turn to fill the air with cries of pain.

One by one, the wights dispersed or recoiled from the touch of Gveter-ren's walking stick. For a moment, McCoy felt a glimmer of hope.

Then dozens of people inside sickbay screamed.

McCoy turned and went numb with shock. Wights were coming up through the deck, down through the overhead, from every side through the bulkheads. Demons of smoke and shadow were turning sickbay into a circle of hell.

Gveter-ren held his staff over his head and in a voice hoarse with age and effort, shouted a string of alien words that even the universal translator couldn't understand. And he summoned a miracle.

A brilliant viridian flash from his staff's gemstone became

a steady bath of green light that flooded every corner of sick-bay. The wights shrank and fled, leaving some of their victims shaken but not yet paralyzed.

The elderly mystic kept on chanting, maintaining the glow from the gemstone, but his legs trembled, and McCoy was certain the old Kathikar was on the verge of collapse. McCoy put his hands under Gveter-ren's shoulders and held the man up, then ordered the crewman beside him, "Help me! Keep him standing!"

McCoy and the crewman supported the fragile holy man, who continued to chant as if he were talking in his sleep. There was no way of knowing how long Gveter-ren could keep his incantation going. All McCoy knew was that if the mystic's spell ended before the attack did, they were all doomed.

"I need a solution, gentlemen." Kirk stood behind Spock and Scott, who were huddled over the control panel for the Kathikar dark-energy weapon. "*Enterprise* can't take this for much longer."

Spock looked up from his tricorder readout. "Fortunately, the same damage that prevents us from turning the weapon off has also impaired its function, preventing it from firing at full power—which would have destroyed the *Enterprise* in a single shot, regardless of whether its shields were raised."

"That doesn't exactly qualify as good news, Spock. Wights are inside my ship." Kirk slapped Scott's shoulder. "Give me a plan, Scotty. Something. *Anything.*"

The engineer was despondent. "The control systems are goosed. Best we can do is pop the cork on this bugger."

"In English, Mister Scott?"

"We'll have to blow it up."

"Great." Kirk didn't like where this was going. "Spock, didn't you say we'd wipe out half the planet if we destroyed the generator?"

Spock thought for a moment. "Only if we cause an uncontrolled detonation using the ship's weapons." The look in his eyes told Kirk that his first officer was concocting a new plan. "We can induce a less energetic but equally effective reaction by creating a feedback loop between its primary and secondary phase coils."

"But we can't do that from here," Scott said. "We'd have to go down into the generator and cross-circuit the buggers manually."

Encouraged, Kirk asked, "How long will it take?"

Scott said, "Four minutes."

At the same time, Spock said, "Sixty seconds."

"Scotty, I'll pretend not to notice you've been inflating your repair estimates. Once it's done, how long 'til it blows?"

Spock answered, "Ninety seconds."

Kirk grimaced. "Blast radius?"

"Approximately sixteen kilometers."

"So much for reaching safe distance," Kirk said. "I don't know about you, but I can't run sixteen klicks in ninety seconds, and *Enterprise* can't beam us up with its shields raised."

Scott raised his eyebrows. "Well, in theory, the weapon

ought to shut down about eight seconds before the whole thing goes boom. That'll stop the subspace disruptions and give us a window for transport."

"Eight seconds? To beam up all twelve of us, plus the base's personnel?" Kirk shook his head. "And I thought we were cutting it close. Okay, go—get to work. I'll brief *Enterprise*." He watched Spock and Scott sprint away to the base's lower levels, then he flipped open his communicator. "Kirk to *Enterprise*. Sulu . . . you're not gonna believe this."

Sulu was perched on the edge of the command chair, fists curled atop the armrests, brow creased in concentration. Sickbay was locked in a desperate standoff, and the landing party had triggered a reaction that would disable the Kathikar weapon—and disintegrate them and more than two dozen stunned Kathikar unless Chekov, who had gone belowdecks, worked his transporter magic like never before.

He opened a comm channel. "Sulu to Chekov. Are you ready?"

"Affirmative! All transporter pads energized."

"Good work. Wait for the captain's signal." To the bridge crew, Sulu added, "Look sharp, people. We only get one shot at this."

Everyone had their orders. Katuscha had maneuvered the ship back into transporter range, and Chekov had linked all of the *Enterprise*'s transporter platforms to a jury-rigged master console. As soon as the Kathikar weapon ceased its barrage, Ensign sh'Vetha would pinpoint all life signs on Redivel Island and feed their coordinates directly to the transporter system, where Chekov would lock them in and beam them up—in less than eight seconds, or else not at all.

"The weapon's generator is failing," sh'Vetha said. "Get ready!" Seconds later, she began tapping rapidly at her console. "Relaying coordinates!"

Over the comm, Chekov announced, *"Locking on! Energizing!"*

A bright flash bloomed in the darkness of Akiron's antarctic region.

"That's not good," Sulu mumbled. Raising his voice, he said, "Chekov, tell me you got them." No answer. "Chekov, report!"

"The landing party's aboard! And the Kathikar troops are on their way to the brig."

Sulu switched comm channels. "Bridge to sickbay. Report!"

"Secure," said Doctor McCoy. *"Lots of wounded, and more than a few paralyzed. I need casualty reports from all decks, ASAP."*

Sulu hid his concern behind a mask of professional calm. "Understood, Doctor. Bridge out." He sat back, forced himself to draw and release one deep breath, then opened a ship-wide channel. "All decks, secure from general quarters. Make damage and casualty reports to the bridge, on the double." He closed the channel and felt as if he had been hollowed out.

I hate being in charge. I hope I never get promoted to command.

20

Kirk sat at the head of the table in the briefing room, annoyed to be back in the middle of another group discussion when he would have preferred to be in his command chair *doing* something to solve the crisis instead of *talking* about it.

Spock stood in front of the display screen on the bulkhead, narrating his latest findings to Kirk, Scott, McCoy, Ambassador Sarek, and Chief Minister Vellesh-ka, whom Sarek had insisted be invited to this discussion.

"Although the controlled demolition of the Redivel Island generator was successful in halting the attack on the *Enterprise*," Spock said, "the explosion has had at least one unintended consequence. It has triggered a massive local rupture in the membrane between this dimension and that of the wights." He called up a computer-generated cutaway image of the planet's core. "The effect has been focused by Akiron's vast deposits of gray dilithium, and it is spreading rapidly."

Vellesh-ka asked, "What will happen when it reaches the surface?"

"It will have the same effect as the touch of the wights," Spock said. "The planet will become a lens that focuses an inexhaustible 'death ray' from another dimension into our own. When it does, every living thing on Akiron will die."

A heavy silence settled upon the room.

McCoy asked, "How long do the Kathikar have left, Spock?"

Spock switched the display to a screen of complicated data. "According to my calculations, the effect will become irreversible in eight hours."

Kirk asked, "Is there anything we can do to stop it?"

"Not at this time. We lack sufficient data to predict how the phenomenon might react to external forces."

Scott shook his head. "What a waste. We're about to lose more dilithium in a day than we've found in two centuries."

"My God," McCoy said with equal parts anger and shock. "Billions of people are about to die, and all you can think about is the *dilithium*?"

The doctor's ire elicited a confused shrug from Scott. "I'm an engineer."

"Guys," Kirk snapped, "enough." Chastised, McCoy and Scott turned their stares toward the viewscreen.

Vellesh-ka looked back and forth between Kirk and Sarek. "Can't you rescue my people? Evacuate them from the surface?"

Kirk lifted his brow in surprise. "In eight hours? I'm afraid not, Chief Minister. It would take at least twelve hours for another starship to reach us, but even that wouldn't make much of a difference. The *Enterprise* could carry, at most, maybe a few thousand refugees—"

"If we pack them in like sardines," McCoy cut in.

"—but in eight hours we could beam up only half that many," Kirk continued. "If your people had at least basic interplanetary travel capability, we could arrange a convoy out of the danger zone, but since you don't—"

"I understand," Vellesh-ka said, nodding sadly.

Spock said, "There is another fact to consider." He gestured at a new screen of graphs and data superimposed over a star map of local space. "Because of the unusually high concentrations of gray dilithium in Akiron's core, the effects of this rupture in the dimensional membrane will not be limited to this world, or even to this star system. Because of the peculiar physical properties of gray dilithium, the deadly emanations from Akiron will pose a threat to dozens of neighboring star systems. Any inhabited world within twenty light-years will be at risk of suffering near-instantaneous extinction-level events, and this region of space might become impassable to unshielded vessels."

Scott looked aghast. "Are you sure about those calculations, Mister Spock?"

"I am quite certain, Mister Scott."

Sarek, who until that moment had seemed content merely to audit the briefing, looked at Vellesh-ka. "What compelled your people to build such a weapon, Chief Minister? Why even conceive of such an abomination?"

The Starfleet officers were shocked silent by Sarek's pointed inquiry. Vellesh-ka closed his eyes, and his already shamed expression took on a grim cast. "We were afraid. Afraid that despite the income we gained from letting off-worlders exploit our world's dilithium reserves, we would be marginalized, taken for granted, taken advantage of."

Spock replied, "There are a number of ways your people could have ensured a larger role in Federation politics. The advances your scientists have made in the field of zero-point energy, had they been applied to peaceful technologies, would almost certainly have led to partnerships with many of our member worlds."

"Yes, yes. And I proposed as much to my parliament. But that kind of research and development can take years or even decades, and the military had a use for the technology now—and the technological prowess to bring it to fruition." He shook his head. "Our military and our defense industries have secretly held control of our government for centuries. If Akiron survives this disaster, perhaps it will finally be possible to change that."

McCoy said, "Let's just hope that, come tomorrow, you have a *reason* to worry about politics."

"No matter what happens, Doctor, come tomorrow, politics will no longer be my concern. If Akiron is saved, I will have to resign my office and confess my part in this debacle." Vellesh-ka looked at Sarek. "However, if my world dies and others are put in peril because of my failure as a leader, I will have to insist you direct Captain Kirk to take me into custody and deliver me to your civil authorities, so that I may stand trial for my negligence and incompetence, and answer for the lives that have been lost because of my timorous judgment."

Kirk replied, "That's very noble of you, Chief Minister. I won't second-guess how you answer to *your* people, but I plan to make sure you never need to answer to *mine*—because we're going to find a way to stop this before it gets that far." He looked around the table, rapidly doling out orders. "Scotty, find out everything you can about gray dilithium; see if it has some as yet unknown property we can use to negate the energy buildup in the planet's core.

"Spock, look for a way to close the gap in the dimensional membrane.

"Bones, keep running tests on the victims of the last wight attack. Analyzing the damage the wights do to living tissue might give us some clues to blocking their effects." He planted his hands on the tabletop and stood. "We'll reconvene in one hour. Dismissed."

Uhura found it difficult to keep her mind focused on her work. Beyond the emotional distress of having a front-row seat to the impending doom of a planet, she was still bothered by her recent arguments with Spock.

It shouldn't have surprised me. He's never been one to take a sentimental view of things. I'd thought the death of his mother and the end of Vulcan would change that, but I guess some people just are who they are.

What surprised her even more than her disagreements with Spock was how often she found herself in concurrence with James Kirk. Though she was too disciplined an officer to undermine morale by speaking ill of her commanding officer, she still harbored doubts about the *Enterprise's* very young and still relatively untested captain. Despite those misgivings, however, she had of late found her opinions in harmony with Kirk's—especially when he was at odds with Spock. *The captain talks like a maverick, but he acts like an idealist. Maybe that's why I'm beginning to like him so much.*

Sarek's return to the *Enterprise* certainly hadn't helped matters. As chilly as Spock's logic often seemed to Uhura, the ambassador's reason was as cold as absolute zero. Even more perplexing to Uhura, even though Sarek had married a human woman and with her had conceived Spock, the Vulcan ambassador seemed to disapprove of his son's romantic relationship with Uhura.

She was at a loss to understand why. *Is it because we're shipmates? Or because I was his student? Or does he want me out of the way so Spock can do his part to help repopulate the Vulcan species?* No matter which explanation she considered, the hypocrisy of Sarek's position rankled her. Who was he to make such decisions for his son? Or even to presume he had the right?

Her resentment of Sarek's interference in her and Spock's personal business had made her welcome the captain's order to investigate the ambassador's clandestine communications with Starfleet Command. The first question she had needed to ask herself was how Sarek had gained access to the *Enterprise's* subspace communications array. She had suspected that a member of the crew might have left a comm terminal unsecured, but a quick review of the ship's comm system logs had refuted that notion. All terminals' access logs and usage details had been verified; if Sarek had used one of them to send a signal back to Earth, he had hidden his tracks so well that even Uhura couldn't uncover them—and while she had great respect for the ambassador's intellect and experience, she didn't believe for a minute that he possessed the skills for that kind of subterfuge.

But maybe his aide does.

Regardless of who deserved the credit—or the blame— the question remained unanswered: How had it been done? *It would have to have been something that I wouldn't flag. Something routine.* An idea occurred to her: There were numerous automated functions in the *Enterprise*'s comm system. Among them was a burst-transmission module that sent regular updates of logs and sensor data back to Starfleet Command as long as the ship was in communications range. Though it had been designed as a means of securing mission data in the event of a starship's unexpected loss or destruction, the module might provide someone on the ship a covert means of communication with someone who wasn't.

Uhura called up all logs of burst-transmitter data traffic from the previous twenty-four hours. Most of them seemed perfectly ordinary—but two did not.

The majority of the *Enterprise*'s signals back to Starfleet Command were small and quick—just rapid uploads of compressed, encrypted data. The two logs that had drawn Uhura's attention were orders of magnitude larger than the others.

Just what I'd expect from a full-bandwidth comm signal, Uhura reasoned. She isolated the two files and locked them against tampering or deletion, in case the person who had created them belatedly thought to expunge them from the *Enterprise*'s signal buffers. Confident the data had been secured, Uhura began her analysis, starting with scans for any identifying metadata embedded in the files.

It took a few minutes to extract even rudimentary information from the first file. In addition to Starfleet's standard encryption protocols, the file was protected by high-level diplomatic ciphers. A smile tugged at Uhura's mouth. Sarek and his aide might as well have left their names on their handiwork; the cipher's presence was the digital equivalent of leaving one's fingerprints at a crime scene.

Breaking it would not be easy. Starfleet was not privy to the encryption schemes used by the Federation civil authorities except on a need-to-know basis. Uhura was certain, however, that it could be done. It was only a matter of time. Already she had identified the origin point of the transmission as Sarek's quarters, at a time when the ship's internal sensors had verified his presence there. The communication had, apparently, been a two-way real-time conversation lasting four minutes. Reconstructing the actual conversation would entail retrieving scattered bits of cached data from scores of subspace booster relays between Earth and the *Enterprise*, but Uhura knew a few methods for doing so that were sneakier and more reliable than those taught at Starfleet Academy.

The second piggybacked transmission intrigued Uhura

even more than the first one had; its origin point had been the quarters of Sarek's aide, L'Nel, and its recipient was not on Earth but on Deneva. Its duration was also very brief—less than five minutes—but it had entailed a transfer of data from Deneva to the *Enterprise*. Tellingly, the second comm hijacking had been secured with the same cipher that had been used for the first one. Apparently, L'Nel had unfettered access to Sarek's diplomatic codes and was not afraid to use them.

Setting her decryption program to run in the background, Uhura started writing a security patch for the *Enterprise*'s burst-transmission module. She made a special note to send it to Starfleet Command when it was finished, with instructions to distribute it throughout the fleet as soon as possible.

You're a clever one, L'Nel, but you've just pulled this trick for the last time.

21

Kirk was on the move between his quarters and the bridge, and he was in no mood to be waylaid—not by Doctor McCoy's umpteenth demand that he show up for his physical, or for anything else. Naturally, Ambassador Sarek chose that moment to emerge from an intersection and fall into step beside Kirk.

"I need a moment of your attention, Captain."

Kirk quickened his step. "Not a good time, Ambassador."

"There rarely is one." Sarek and Kirk parted to pass a pair of slow-moving junior officers in the middle of the corridor. As they converged on the other side without missing a step, Sarek continued. "It is vital that we discuss—"

"No. We're not talking about it, Sarek. I've explained my reasons for continuing the mission. I'm done debating you."

Sarek nodded. "Rightly so. When I counseled you to withdraw from Akiron, we were unaware of the full scope of the danger. Now that the circumstances and consequences have changed, so must my response to the matter."

"Wait." Kirk stopped and turned to face Sarek, who halted beside him. "You're changing your position?" The ambassador nodded. Kirk was flabbergasted. "So now you agree that we have to get involved in the Akiron crisis?"

"Yes. It is imperative that we find a solution."

Kirk resumed walking, and Sarek matched him stride for stride. "I'm sure the Kathikar will be glad to hear you've come around."

Confusion creased Sarek's brow. Kirk detected a note of suspicion in the Vulcan diplomat's voice. "Why should my reversal of opinion be of any consequence to the Kathikar?"

"Well, an hour ago, you wanted me to break orbit and leave them all to die. But now that you're on board with the rescue plan—"

"I never said I supported your efforts to save the Kathikar."

Once again Kirk came to a halt and looked at Sarek. "Say what?"

Sarek spread his arms in an "isn't it obvious?" gesture. "I have been persuaded of the necessity of Starfleet's immediate involvement in the Akiron crisis—not of the necessity of saving the Kathikar. Spock stated the threat most clearly, Captain: left unchecked, the dark-energy phenomenon that is killing all life on Akiron will become a threat to life in several neighboring star systems and a hazard to interstellar navigation. That is the more pressing emergency, and the only one that directly concerns Federation interests."

"Wow." Kirk walked away to help contain his disgust. "For a second there, I was afraid you'd grown a heart. Glad you dodged that bullet."

Apparently unwilling to let Kirk leave in peace, Sarek followed him. "I am not without compassion, Captain, but I do not let emotion define my priorities."

"I'm sure that'll be a great comfort to the Kathikar." Kirk rounded a corner and headed toward the bridge, in the core of the *Enterprise*'s primary hull. Then he turned and stepped into Sarek's path, adopting an aggressively confrontational stance. "Tell me, Ambassador: If I were to let logic alone dictate my decision-making, how would I tell my crew to deal with the Akiron crisis?"

Sarek arched one eyebrow. "Because the planet itself is acting as a lens for the dark-energy effect, the logical solution would be to shatter that lens."

Kirk couldn't believe what he was hearing. "Hang on—are you suggesting we *destroy the planet*?" He spent a few seconds at a loss for words, his jaw agape. "You've got to be kidding me! After the nightmare you lived through, after what happened to Vulcan, how can you stand there and recommend *that*? How can you condemn an entire world and billions of people to die?"

"As I have already told you, Kirk, I do not allow my emotions to guide my decisions. I am aware that destroying Akiron would cost billions of lives, but it also would save tens of billions of other lives. For every species consigned to oblivion on Akiron, dozens more would be saved on other worlds throughout local space. The needs of the many outweigh the needs of the few, Captain—even when our definition of 'few' is, in a case such as this one, purely relative." He shrugged. "In any event, the question will be moot in less than eight hours. Once the dark-energy phenomenon has laid Akiron waste, destroying the planet by means of a concentrated bombardment will be an act of self-preservation on our part—and it will be of no concern to its former inhabitants, who by then will be extinct."

"Not if I can help it." Kirk turned and continued toward the bridge.

Sarek trailed him by a few paces. "Why do you persist in this hopeless effort, Kirk? Why do you insist on putting your crew in mortal danger?"

"Because it's the right thing to do, Sarek. I had to *watch* your homeworld die. I *saw* it happen, and there was *nothing* I could do to stop it. I've never felt that helpless in my entire life." He suddenly felt ashamed and wondered why he was baring his soul this way to a man he hardly knew, but the truth was burning inside him like a white-hot coal, and it needed to come out. "I won't just sit by and watch that happen to another world. Not today, not *ever,* no matter what it takes— I'll lie, beg, kill, or die to stop it. If that means defying you, or disobeying a direct order from Starfleet Command, so be it. But I won't be passive, Sarek. I won't accept defeat. And I won't turn my back when people need my help."

They arrived at the entrance to the bridge, stopped, and faced each other. Sarek bowed his head slightly. "I respect your passionate embrace of altruism, Captain, but certainly you must see that your judgment is clouded by guilt and driven by a need to overcompensate for your perceived powerlessness."

"What I see is a lot of people making excuses for taking the easy way out. I don't plan on being one of them."

"Be that as it may, Captain, your intransigence in the face of such overwhelming odds is highly illogical."

Kirk cracked a bitter half smile as he walked onto the bridge. "Not to the Kathikar."

"Scotty, get your trained monkey off my ceiling."

Montgomery Scott looked over his shoulder to find Doctor McCoy scowling up at Keenser—a short, vaguely reptilian-looking alien engineer who had transferred to the *Enterprise* from the Delta Vega outpost so that he could continue to serve with Scott. Keenser had a natural affinity for scaling walls and clinging to even the tiniest protrusions; because his species had evolved on a world with numerous deadly terrestrial predators, he was driven by instinct to seek out the highest possible vantage point, wherever he happened to be.

At the moment, that entailed dangling upside-down from the hub of a swiveling medical scanner that was mounted to sickbay's overhead.

"Oi!" Scott shouted at his diminutive assistant engineer. "You heard the doctor, you green bastard! Get down! He's got enough problems wi'out you nabbin' a hudgie on his gizmos like some bloody numptie!"

Keenser let go of the swing-arm's hub, twisted nimbly as he fell, and landed on his feet between two rows of biobeds. Then he cringed and scurried off.

"Sorry 'bout that, Doc," Scott said. "Can't take him any-where, y'know?"

McCoy frowned at Scott, then returned to making his rounds of the patients still recovering in sickbay from the re-cent wight attack. "I thought you were supposed to be unravel-ing the secrets of gray dilithium." He ran a tricorder scan of an unconscious crewman. "What're you doing up here?"

"Multitasking. I've got a platoon of particle analyzers work-ing on the crystal samples we brought back from the planet. Not much I can do to speed them up, so I'm working another angle while I wait."

McCoy moved on to his next patient. "Dare I ask?"

Scott activated his own tricorder, which filled sickbay with its high-frequency oscillating tones. "Looking for subatomic residues in the bulkheads and the deck. Witnesses said the wights came through the floors and walls. Figured maybe they left footprints of one kind or another. Didn't really have a baseline to check the data Spock brought back from your first trip to the planet, but I've got specs for every molecule in this ship." He looked around expectantly. "If something's gone wonky, I'll find it."

"Don't get your hopes up. Those things move like ghosts."

An alert chirped from Scott's tricorder. "Got something!" Scott took perverse satisfaction in McCoy's look of glum surprise. He coaxed the flood of raw data into shape. "As I thought—residual negative charges! Ion trails."

"Stunning. That tells you what, exactly?"

"Don't be such a killjoy, Doctor! Each fact is useful. It adds to the big picture. The more we know, the better questions we can ask."

McCoy harrumphed. "I know the question you should be asking."

Scott lowered his tricorder. "And that would be . . . ?"

"Why the hell did those things converge on sickbay?"

Scott shrugged. "It's where everybody ran to. The creatures were probably just following the crew as they retreated."

"I don't think so, Scotty. I was in the corridor, and I saw what those things did. They didn't *follow* our people to sickbay—they were *herding* them toward it. Or, to be more precise, I think they were heading for sickbay all along, and the crew just happened to be in the way."

Looking around the compartment, Scott wondered aloud, "What would draw them here?" He eyed various pieces of equipment. "None of this seems all that appetizing to a negative-energy creature."

"I doubt it was my equipment drawing them in." McCoy sidled over to Scott and lowered his voice. "I think the wights came to sickbay because of our Kathikar visitor over there." He pointed to the biobed farthest from the entrance. On it lay Gveter-ren, the elderly mystic, asleep and curled around his gnarled black wooden staff. "He's the reason any of us survived the attack."

Scott stared in surprise at McCoy. "What do you mean *he's* the reason you survived? What happened down here, Doctor?"

McCoy's face reddened with embarrassment. "When the wights came in," he said, his voice barely more than a whisper, "we were defenseless. They were everywhere." He stole a fearful look at Gveter-ren. "Then he started wielding that stick of his like a weapon—and it *worked*, Scotty. Every wight he jabbed with that thing went *poof*—gone in a flash of green light. Then he held it up, spouted some gibberish, and blasted all the wights at once. It was amazing."

Scott grabbed McCoy by his tunic and struggled not to raise his voice. "And you didn't think this was *worth mentioning* in the bloody briefing? Are you out of your mind?"

"Actually, *that's* what I'm afraid of." McCoy twisted free of Scott's grip. "What was I supposed to say? That I witnessed a miracle? That I saw an alien priest exorcise demons with magic? How could I be sure I wasn't hallucinating?"

Scott walked past McCoy and headed directly toward the slumbering Gveter-ren. "Always start with the assumption that you're not crazy, Doctor. Then assume there's a perfectly reasonable scientific explanation for everything you saw." Edging up to the mystic's bed, Scotty leaned over to take a closer look at the stone that topped the Kathikar's walking stick. "I'll bet you a pint that's pure gray dilithium." He activated his tricorder and scanned the crystal.

Within seconds, his hunch was confirmed. "Aye. Called it." He turned off his tricorder and faced McCoy. "You said he was chanting something when he fought the wights?"

"Yes, but I didn't catch a word of it."

"Right, here's my theory. This furry old bugger has some

kind of psi talent, right? And maybe gray dilithium helps him to focus it the way regular dilithium focuses energy inside our warp core. Wasn't magic that saved you, Doctor, just science you didn't know yet."

McCoy nodded. "Interesting idea. How do you propose we test it?"

Scott folded his arms. "Good question." After a moment's thought, he resigned himself to the inevitable. "I think we need to ask Spock for help."

The doctor sighed. "I was afraid you'd say that."

22

Vellesh-ka had expected the *Enterprise*'s sickbay to be like the hospitals on Akiron—dim and quiet, a sedate haven of tender ministrations and dignified recovery. Stepping through its open door, he found instead a painfully bright flurry of activity—technicians carrying in tools and machine components, nurses and medical technicians hovering impatiently over the comatose and, in the middle of it all, some kind of jury-rigged contraption under construction.

Skulking through the frantic tableau, the chief minister made his way to the bedside of the only other Kathikar on the ship. Looking down at the elderly monk, Vellesh-ka wondered what he would say to him if he awoke. Then the mystic opened his eyes, as if he had heard Vellesh-ka's silent musings.

"Greetings, Chief Minister," said Gveter-ren, his manner serene.

"Hello, Elder. I'm told you're the hero of the hour."

Gveter-ren mustered a weak smile and looked at the slap-dash machine being assembled by the ship's chief engineer and first officer, with assistance from a dozen specialists in red and blue tunics. "I feel more like a test subject than a hero. They've put me through three rounds of experiments already."

"To what end?" asked Vellesh-ka, out of concern for the elder's health.

"They're trying to figure out how I stopped the wights."

"Why don't you just tell them?"

"I did—I told them I beat the fiends with faith."

Vellesh-ka rolled his eyes. "I'll bet they *loved* that."

"They found my explanation less than satisfactory." He winced as he lifted his head a few centimeters off the pillow to watch the Starfleet officers work. "They seem particularly interested in my walking stick—or, I should say, the crystal that serves as its headpiece. They've scanned it over and over, and they injected me with something to help them study my brainwave patterns. Then they made me hold the staff and repeat the prayers I used to drive off the wights."

Vellesh-ka cast a skeptical glance at the twisted black stick inside the hulking mass of metalwork and wires. "And what did they find?"

"Nothing yet. But, as you can see, their work continues."

The chief minister nodded. "They are nothing if not persistent."

The monk began coughing—intermittently at first, and then with greater ferocity, until it became obvious that he was fighting for breath. Vellesh-ka turned to summon aid, only to see a nurse hurrying to Gveter-ren. The human woman pressed the nozzle of a small cylinder against Gveter-ren's throat. There was a soft hiss as she injected him with medicine. The old mystic stopped coughing; a few moments later his breathing became slow and regular. He looked up at Vellesh-ka with reddened eyes and smiled. "Getting old is not for the faint of heart."

"True," said Vellesh-ka. "Living in an aging body is like being a passenger on a ship that's gradually sinking."

Gveter-ren narrowed his eyes at his visitor. "I mean no offense, Chief Minister, but what are you doing here? I might be an honored elder to the adepts at the monastery, but I hardly merit a courtesy call from a head of state."

Vellesh-ka looked away and sighed. "The government has fallen. It was overthrown by Tergan-besh and his rabid mob of religious extremists." He was unable to suppress a grimace as he looked back at Gveter-ren. "A turn of events that no doubt meets with your esteemed approval, I'm sure."

"Why would you assume that? Do you think that all persons of faith are cut from the same cloth? I have no more affinity for Tergan-besh and his throng of hateful zealots than you do, Chief Minister—I can assure you of that."

As Vellesh-ka's eyes widened, Gveter-ren continued. "Don't look so surprised. If you had ever taken the time to learn about the Order of Oernachta, you'd understand. We're not evangelical; we teach new adepts to seek the truth within themselves and find their own relationship with the eternal. What we believe cannot be preached; each of us finds his own path. No one can be forced or coaxed to follow our ways; only those who come to us of their own free will are ready to learn." He frowned. "Tergan-besh and his ilk, however—they'd stamp out orders such as mine for being heretics. I have no desire to see him or his faithful place their hands on the levers of power in the military or the civil government."

"Unfortunately," Vellesh-ka said, "that is exactly what has happened. Even if Captain Kirk and his crew are able to save our world from the wights, we will still need to save it from our countrymen." A deep thrumming sound from the scanner in the middle of sickbay turned Vellesh-ka's head. He looked at Gveter-ren's staff inside the machine and furrowed his brow. "Do you think that they can stop the wights in time to save our people?"

Gveter-ren took a moment to think. "Perhaps. It will depend."

"On what?" He pointed at the scanning device. "On that thing?"

"No, Chief Minister. It will come down to a question of faith."

That was the least heartening news Vellesh-ka could have imagined hearing at that moment. "These are a secular people, Elder. If our survival hinges on their embrace of our religion—" He was silenced by the monk's raised hand.

"I'm talking about a different kind of faith. The belief in oneself, in the delicate balance between fate and free will. And not for all these people but for one in particular: the captain, the one known as James Kirk."

Dumbfounded at the revelation, Vellesh-ka asked, "Why him?"

"Because I have been given a glimpse of what is to come. He, like many of his people, places his faith in this ship, in its tools and its weapons, in technology. But if he is to save our world—and break his past lives' cycle of failure—he must learn to rely not on any of these things . . . but to trust in *himself*."

Kirk entered sickbay as Vellesh-ka was walking out of it. For a moment, Kirk considered asking the chief minister what had brought him there, but there was more pressing business in need of Kirk's attention.

Gathered in the middle of the medical compartment were McCoy, Scott, and Spock, all huddled around the control panel for an unwieldy assemblage of high-tech components, about whose function Kirk could only speculate. It, or perhaps the object lying inside it, was the reason his three senior officers had asked him to come down to sickbay, but it was not the reason he had made the trip in such haste.

"Bones," Kirk said in a voice that filled sickbay, "you'd better start talking, and the excuse you're about to give me had better be really damned good."

McCoy turned and raised his hands in a defensive posture. "Hang on, Jim. I didn't mean to hold out on you. It's just that the whole experience with Gveter-ren and the wights was so surreal that I didn't know how to—"

"Bullshit. I went through the same Academy training you did. I know we see some really weird stuff out here, and that we can't always explain it when it happens. But dammit, Bones, I need to know *everything* that happens on this ship when it's relevant to the mission. And if you saw that guy"—he pointed at Gveter-ren—"whup the crap out of the wights with nothing but a stick, *I need to know about that.*"

"I understand," McCoy said, "and I'm sorry. But before you string me up from the warp core, would you at least give us a minute to show you what we've found?" He gestured at the Frankenstein's monster of a device that dominated the middle of sickbay. "It's really something else, Jim. Please."

Kirk frowned at McCoy and looked at Spock. "You first."

"Working from Doctor McCoy's detailed account of Gveter-ren's intervention against the wights, Mister Scott ascertained that the means used to ward off the attack likely involved some interaction between Gveter-ren's staff and some innate psionic talent of the Kathikar."

Scott pointed at the walking stick inside the scanning device. "It's all about that crystal! Something about the matrix in the gray dilithium captures wavelengths of projected brainwave activity and—"

"Long story short," McCoy cut in, "it's a lens for psionic energy."

"Precisely," Spock said. "It focused and amplified Gveter-ren's natural psionic talents, enabling him to project positive mental energy that dispelled the wights from this dimension and forced them back into their own."

McCoy struck a cautious tone as he added, "There's a catch, though."

"There always is," Kirk said. "Spell it out for me."

Scott answered, "The same piece of rock that helps that ol' bugger send the beasties away also draws them in, like honey for flies."

"Wonderful." Kirk looked to Spock. "If the crystal amplifies psionic energy, can you use it the way Gveter-ren did?"

"Unfortunately, no. The psionic talents of Kathikar operate at very different wavelengths than do those of Vulcans. The crystal would be of no use to me. And before you ask, we spoke to Chief Minister Vellesh-ka while he was visiting with the monk. He does not appear to possess the requisite psionic talent to make use of the crystal in Gveter-ren's staff."

Kirk ran his hand through his hair while he pondered his options. "Okay, let's reason this out. Even if there are other Kathikar who have talents like Gveter-ren's, we have no way to test for them, and since the whole planet's been turned into one big traveling riot, we can forget about setting up an organized search for candidates to wield his staff."

McCoy replied, "Hell, for all we know, what he did might have been the product of a unique set of factors—his natural ability, his mental discipline, the prayer he invoked. We have no way of knowing."

Kirk held one hand against his aching forehead. "Spock, if we know the Kathikar's psionic talents don't work on a Vulcan frequency—"

"I have already searched the memory banks for any close

matches among known species. There are three—the Dopterians, the M'Lik, and the Szenhai—but no members of those species are among the *Enterprise*'s crew."

"Great." Kirk pounded the side of his fist against the scanning device. He looked down at the chunk of gray dilithium attached to the head of the walking stick, and an idea came to him. "Hang on. Spock, did you say that the energy field Gveter-ren created dispelled the wights—sent them back to their own dimension?"

"Yes, sir. Internal sensor logs confirmed it."

"Scotty!" Kirk grew more animated as a fledgling notion took shape in his thoughts. "If we can replicate that effect on a larger scale, could we get rid of *all* the wights and close the gap between our two dimensions?"

"Aye, but that would take a lot more brainpower than we've got to work with." To Spock he added, "No disrespect intended, of course."

Clapping his hands once to draw attention back to himself, Kirk said, "I've got it. We're going about this all wrong, guys. Forget about finding another Kathikar and trying to replicate this effect naturally. We need to think bigger than that—a lot bigger." He pointed at the chief engineer. "Scotty, if we can measure the kind of energy that feeds this crystal, then there must be some way we can replicate it, generate it, mimic it. I don't care what you call it or how you do it, but get it done. We need to create an energy pulse that matches Gveter-ren's psionic wavelength and then boost it by a few orders of magnitude."

McCoy snapped, "And do what with it? Make a bomb?"

"Exactly! You said yourself the energy field he produced caused no harm to living tissue, but it blasted the wights back where they came from. Scotty, I need something that can do that on a planetary scale, and I need it while there's still time to save the Kathikar."

Scott seemed energized by Kirk's fiery resolve. "Right! I'm on it, skipper!"

"Spock," Kirk continued, "help him find a way to incorporate this technology into small arms, the ship's shields, anything and everything. If this is our only defense, I want it online as soon as possible."

"Understood, Captain. I will have recommendations for a landing party to deploy the weapon ready within—"

Gveter-ren declared in a loud rasp, "Kirk must go alone!" Scott, McCoy, Kirk, and Spock turned to regard the feeble old Kathikar lying on a biobed behind them, one shaking paw held up and outstretched toward the captain. "Only Kirk can succeed. Anyone else who tries will die."

Kirk was struck by the monk's words; they resonated with truth. He felt it in his bones, in the core of his being. Gveter-ren was right—whatever the endgame of this mission proved to be, it was Kirk's to see done.

Spock drew breath, no doubt as a prelude to dismissing Gveter-ren's declaration. Then the deck lurched as if the *Enterprise* had slammed into something solid, and the next sound Kirk heard was the red-alert siren.

23

Bone-jarring concussions rocked the *Enterprise* and made Sulu wonder why these things always happened when he was sitting in the command chair.

"Raise shields!" he shouted over the thunderous din. "Damage reports!"

The bridge crew scrambled to recover their bearings and check their consoles. Chekov was the first to respond. "Shields are up but losing power fast!"

"Sh'Vetha," Sulu yelled over the continuing barrage, "what's hitting us?"

The deck lurched, and the Andorian science officer struggled to stay on her feet while she peered into the hooded sensor display. "I don't know, sir. No other ships on sensors." A punishing blow blacked out the overhead lights for several seconds and rained sparks across the deck between her and Sulu. "I'm reading massive pulses of negative energy beneath our secondary hull!"

Sulu tensed. "Negative energy? Like from the death ray?"

"Exactly! But there are no emissions from the planet's surface." She slammed her palm on her console. "I can't figure out where it's coming from!"

Uhura looked up from her station to tell Sulu, "I'm getting reports of wight attacks in the engineering section! Three crewmen down!"

Chekov added, "Temperatures falling rapidly on all decks below main engineering and aft of frame fifty-two. Life-support unable to compensate."

"Evacuate those sections!" Sulu thumbed a switch on the chair's armrest. "Bridge to security! Intruder alert, engineering section!" Switching to the ship's all-call internal channel, he added, "Captain Kirk to the bridge!"

Kirk had only begun peeling himself off the deck in sickbay when another impact tremor knocked him back down. A few feet away, Spock, Scott, and McCoy were faring little better, all of them tumbling as the onslaught continued.

Sulu's voice echoed from the overhead comms, *"Captain Kirk to the bridge!"* Resisting the ship's chaotic rocking motion, Kirk crawled to the nearest companel, used a biobed to pull himself to his feet, and opened a reply channel. "Kirk here! Report, Sulu!"

"It's the wights, sir! They're attacking in main engineering!"

"How? Was there another weapon on the planet?"

"Unknown, sir. We—" Another quake made the decks reso-
nate with a sound like thunder and pinned Kirk against the bulkhead. Sulu continued, *"We can't pinpoint the source, and—"* Static
spat from the comm speaker, and then the channel went dead.
Kirk jabbed at the controls in a futile effort to restore contact.

Gveter-ren said in a brittle voice, "The wights know you're
here, Captain. They no longer need my people's weapon to attack your ship."

Turning toward the elderly monk, Kirk said, "What do
they want?" He stalked across the violently pitching deck and
plucked Gveter-ren's staff from the scanner. "Is it this they're
after? Is this why they're attacking my ship?"

"No, Captain. It draws their attention, but it's not what
they want."

Kirk stumbled through the flickering half-light to the mystic's bedside, and grabbed him by his shirt. "Then tell me what
they *do* want!"

"They've come for *you.*"

Kirk let go of the monk and looked at his officers. "Bones,
prep for wounded. Scotty, get to engineering, bring main
power back online, and find some way to close this new rift.
Spock, you're with me: we need to get to the bridge."

In what Uhura could think of only as a perverse affirmation
of the law of supply and demand, the number of damage and

casualty reports flooding into her communications console increased in direct proportion to the number of system errors and power failures choking off the ship's available comm channels.

"Wights coming through the bulkheads on deck thirty-one!" declared one panicked report, overlapped by another reporting, *"Two down in auxiliary fire control!"* One emergency channel was jammed by an open transmission from a compartment filled with screaming. Several channels were cluttered with security-division chatter as deck officers tried to coordinate rescues and counterattacks.

Sulu looked at her. "Have you raised the captain yet?"

"Not yet. Internal comms are overloaded."

"Keep trying. Helm, widen our orbit. Let's see if getting some distance from the planet makes any difference."

Ensign Katuscha replied, "Aye, sir." A moment later she added, "Error in flight controls, sir. Helm's not responding." As Uhura turned to see what was going on, the ensign said, "I'm getting a weird power spike—"

The helm console erupted with violet lightning. Forks of dark energy enveloped Katuscha, who convulsed and tumbled from her chair. Crackling tendrils of electricity migrated across the deck, onto other consoles.

Sulu leaped from the command chair. "Engage overrides!" He lunged to the helm and threw himself into the maelstrom of lightning as he reached for the console. Uhura looked away for a split second to engage her station's override protocol, which isolated its command functions, tapped a reserve battery for energy, and disconnected it from the ship's main power grid.

When she looked back, Sulu was hurtling through the air. He landed hard on the deck, knocked unconscious. Uhura sprang from her chair and dashed to Sulu's side. She touched his throat and found a weak pulse. "He's alive, but only barely." To sh'Vetha she said, "Get the medics."

Chekov kneeled beside the fallen Ensign Katuscha. He lifted his fingers from the woman's throat and said to Uhura, "She's alive, but fading fast."

Around the bridge, junior officers glanced at one another, all wearing expressions that telegraphed the same desperate question: *Who's in command?*

Uhura whispered to Chekov, "Do something!"

Recoiling, he whispered back, "Me? You outrank me!"

The ship rumbled again. Uhura stood, smoothed the front of her uniform, and sat down in the command chair. "Mister Chekov, transfer helm and weapons control to your console. Ensign sh'Vetha, I need an update on the rift below engineering." Banishing all fear from her face and voice, she held up her chin with pride. "Look sharp, people. I need intel and options, and I need them *now*."

Spock and Kirk blundered like drunks down the corridor, which seemed unable to make up its mind which way it wanted to roll. In between wild lurches, *Enterprise* personnel were running—though whether they were moving away from something or toward something, Kirk had no idea.

Kirk reached the next intersection a few steps ahead of Spock, then stumbled to a halt as he heard a faint echo of panicked shouting. He looked back at Spock, who stopped as Kirk asked, "Do you hear that?"

"Yes." Spock looked around. Backtracked a few paces to the intersection and listened again. Pointed farther down the corridor. "It is coming from this direction." He hurried toward it, and Kirk followed him.

They arrived at a pair of turbolift doors, which did not open. Kirk pressed the call button, but nothing happened. "Looks like they're offline."

"A standard safety precaution aboard starships," Spock said. "Turbolifts lock down during main-power failures."

More frightened cries resounded behind the closed doors, ratcheting up Kirk's desire to take action. "We have to help them, Spock." He pointed a few meters past the turbolift doors. "There's an emergency access ladder over here."

"Captain, they are in no imminent danger. The prudent course of action would be to continue on our way to—"

"Spock, if the wights come up that turbolift shaft, those people'll be sitting ducks. They won't even get a chance to *run*. I won't let that happen to them."

Kirk released the locks on the access panel, pulled it free of the bulkhead, and tossed it aside. Beyond it yawned a shadowy chasm of metal. Crawling through the opening onto a narrow walkway that traversed the maintenance nook running parallel to the turbolift shaft, he said to Spock, "C'mon!"

"One moment, Captain." Spock stepped away, and Kirk

heard another bulkhead panel being opened. Spock returned a moment later with a pair of emergency tool kits and two compact flashlights. He handed one kit to Kirk and slung the other's strap across his torso. After Kirk had donned the satchel-like kit, Spock handed him a flashlight.

Kirk turned on the light, whose beam slashed through the darkness in the turbolift shaft. He looked back at Spock. "Ready?"

"Yes."

Kirk shuffled a few steps sideways to make room for Spock, who climbed through the open panel onto the walkway. Standing beside Kirk, he aimed his flashlight beam down to the trapped turbolift, from which a woman's faint cries of *"Help us!"* and *"Can anyone hear us?"* now were audible.

"We're on our way!" Kirk shouted. "Just stay calm. Are you hurt?"

"I'm okay, but the other passenger's not."

Spock shouted, "There are two of you, then?"

"Yes. We were heading to our posts when the lift stopped. Some kind of blue electricity shot out of the panel and stunned him."

Kirk opened his kit and took out a carbon-nanofiber safety line with a self-powered retracting winch. He secured the line to his uniform belt and the winch to a welded beam on the walkway. Spock did the same as Kirk put away his flashlight and began descending a ladder built into the turbolift's wall.

"Don't move," Kirk called down the shaft, feeling his way in the darkness from one icy cold rung to the next. "We'll be there in a few seconds."

As soon as Kirk's feet were within half a meter of the top of the turbolift, he leaped from the ladder and landed in a crouch. He retrieved his flashlight, turned it on, and sought the lift car's emergency access panel. A few seconds later he found it and released its magnetic locks. Spock stepped off the ladder, kneeled beside him, and helped him lift the heavy hatch open.

Kirk pointed his flashlight slightly away from the face of the young woman squinting up at him from inside the lift. He recognized her as Ensign Dehler from the sciences division. "C'mon, let's get you out of there." He aimed the light at her unconscious lift mate, an enlisted security guard named Katumbe. "Him first."

Kirk moved to climb down into the turbolift, but Spock stopped him with a gentle touch on the shoulder. "I should go, Captain. It will be easier for me to lift the crewman up to you than it would be for you to lift him to me."

Taking his first officer's advice as a matter of simple fact, Kirk gestured for Spock to proceed. "Okay, go."

Spock put away his flashlight, detached his safety line, and lowered himself with speed and agility through the narrow portal in the top of the lift. The Vulcan quickly hefted the unconscious Katumbe over his shoulder.

Then, to Kirk's surprise, his slightly built first officer squatted and leaped straight up. With his free hand, Spock grasped the edge of the hatchway and—despite bearing the burden of another person's deadweight—did a one-armed pull-up that brought the stunned security guard within Kirk's reach.

Kirk grabbed Katumbe under his armpits, pulled him

out of the turbolift, and laid him down on top of it. Then he helped Dehler, who had received a helpful boost from Spock. As Kirk had expected, Spock needed no help to climb out of the stalled conveyance. Reunited atop the lift, they faced each other. "Good work, Spock. Let's get these people to safety."

Spock reattached his safety line and once again took Katumbe in a fireman's carry. Kirk reached for the ladder. Dehler stood between him and Spock, who carried Katumbe with little apparent effort.

Then came a gust of unnaturally cold air that Kirk knew was bad news.

He looked down over the turbolift's edge and saw a wall of pure blackness coursing up the shaft, extinguishing the self-powered safety lights. Spock glanced down, then looked back at Kirk. "Haste would seem to be in order, Captain."

Kirk hugged Dehler to him as he triggered the winch for his safety line. "Express elevator, going up!" Spock switched on his winch, as well.

They and their passengers began a frustratingly languid ascent. Beneath them, the deadly tide of dark energy seemed to accelerate.

"I'd kind of hoped these would be speedier," Kirk said.

"Indeed," Spock replied, staring down at the rising threat.

A few meters shy of the walkway, Katumbe stirred back to consciousness and mumbled, "What's happening?"

"We're rescuing you," Kirk said. "Get ready to run."

"Um . . . yes, sir."

Spock reached the walkway first, detached the safety line

from his belt, and abandoned it as he pushed Katumbe toward the opening in the bulkhead to the corridor. The man jumped through, followed by Spock.

Kirk saw his breath condensing into vapor as he and Dehler reached the walkway. As soon as she had her footing, he said, "Go!"

She didn't argue. By the time Kirk had freed himself from his safety line, Dehler was somersaulting through the open panel. Frost formed on the inside of the turbolift shaft as Kirk dived back into the corridor and rolled to his feet. "Run!" he shouted to anyone who would listen.

Then he grabbed Spock and followed his own order.

Scott's first clue that something was wrong should have been that while he was running in one direction, everyone else was running the other way. Dodging and shoving his way through the oncoming tide of bodies, he could barely see where he was going. The lights flickered erratically, rendering the frantic movements of the fleeing crewmen in jerky stop-motion.

All at once the corridor ahead of Scott was empty, and he sprinted through the next intersection. The passage on his left was blocked by searing flames and toxic smoke spouting from a ruptured bulkhead. The passage on his right led to a maintenance compartment that he knew had no other exits—in other words, a dead end. His destination was the turbolift just a few more meters ahead.

He reached the lift as a gust of frigid air washed over him.

Lights went out like snuffed tapers in the corridor ahead of Scott as a wall of impenetrable darkness made its inexorable advance.

That cannae be good. He anxiously pressed the lift's call button. Seconds passed as the darkness closed in, and Scott realized the lift was offline. *Definitely not good.* He made a hasty retreat.

Crossing the intersection, he was met by a terrible sight: a second barrier of unnatural darkness had cut off his escape route and was creeping toward him.

Bugger. Monsters in two directions, fire in the third, and a dead end in the last. Determined to delay the inevitable for as long as possible, Scott made a run for the maintenance compartment. Without main power, the door did not open at his approach. Fortunately, it was not locked, and Scott forced it ajar—pulling it first, then getting his shoulder into the gap and pushing with his back and his legs until it was open wide enough for him to slip past.

Looking back through the barely open door, he saw the wights flow like a black wave into the dead-end passage. Empowered by fear and adrenaline, he slammed the door shut behind him, despite knowing the wights would likely pass through it with ease. *I cannae stay here. Those things'll eat me alive.*

Scott took a quick inventory of the room's contents. *Not much help here.* He spied a plasma-welding station, some duotronic cables, a bin of scrap metal, some antigrav load-lifters tagged with repair tickets, and not much else.

He felt the air getting colder by the second. *Think! What do these things want? What're they hungry for?* The answer hit him: *They eat energy! Let's give the wee beasties a snack, then.*

Moving with speed and purpose, Scott opened the toolkit slung at his hip as he stepped over to the plasma torch. With a few deft zaps, tweaks, and twists, he detached the unit's power supply, which was linked to a dedicated generator inside the maintenance bay. Using some of the duotronic cables and bits of scrap metal, he fused the power line to the compartment's bulkhead. Then he glanced over his shoulder and saw the first hints of frost on the door.

He looked down to make sure he was standing on the insulated panel in front of the welding station, and then he flipped the switch that activated the generator.

Bright arcs of raw electricity danced and crackled across the deck, the bulkheads, and the overhead. In seconds the chilly air inside the compartment grew hot and stifling, and the tang of ozone became oppressive. The generator registered its protest in the form of a rising drone and wisps of acrid smoke—its release of energy was typically much more controlled than this. Electrifying the entire compartment would likely burn out the capacitors on the unit in a matter of seconds—assuming the wights' appetites didn't drain it first.

Either way, they're not coming through the walls yet—which means I just bought myself a few more seconds to think.

Squinting against the blazing pyrotechnics he had unleashed inside the maintenance bay, Scott searched for a backup generator or another expendable energy source that he could sacrifice to keep the wights at bay, but he found none. *What I really need is another way out of here.* An image took shape in his mind, and he smiled. *If an exit's what I need, I'll make* one.

He opened his satchel and pulled out a phaser. The compact sidearm had become a standard piece of equipment in his toolkit ever since he had narrowly survived being attacked by a colossal predator called a *hengrauggi* while repairing an outdoor communications antenna during his prolonged tour of duty on the frozen hell known as Delta Vega. He adjusted the weapon's power and beam settings to an optimal combination for cutting through duranium, took aim at the bulkhead, and opened fire. *No extra points for neatness*, he reminded himself while he cut an uneven portal through the wall. He closed the circle, and the slab inside it fell away into the open space behind the bulkhead. Great clangs of impact echoed inside the *Enterprise*'s vast superstructure.

The generator sputtered and then groaned as its fuel and battery cells ran out. Just as quickly as the room had been turned sultry by the electrical fury Scott had unleashed, the chill of the wights' touch returned.

He put away his phaser, took two running steps, and dived through the hole in the wall, being careful not to touch its still glowing-hot edges.

Scott arrested his fall by grabbing a vertical structural support and hugging it for dear life. He looked down into a deep but narrow chasm of crisscrossed beams and wiring. *That'll do nicely.* He drew his phaser. Aimed at a non-load-bearing cross-beam several meters directly beneath himself and fired a short burst that vaporized it, giving him a clear drop to his destination. Then he pulled a thick bundle of cables loose from the support he was holding, giving himself some slack under his feet.

Through the hole in the bulkhead he saw the wights enter the maintenance compartment. *Time to go.* He pushed off from the beam and slid down the cables. As he dropped, he kept his foot wedged between the cables and the beam, prying them loose with his weight and momentum as deck after deck blurred past.

Judging his position inside the ship strictly by instinct, he dislodged his foot from the cables and pressed it against the support, slowing his descent by friction. Noting the subsystems around him and the markings on the bulkhead in front of him, he deduced that he had reached the uppermost deck of main engineering.

Above him, the wights surged into the *Enterprise*'s superstructure.

He drew his phaser and set it to a lower power level than he had used to cut through the bulkhead above. He hoped his mental calculations were accurate, because if he had set the phaser too low, he wouldn't be able to cut through the bulkhead in time to escape his monstrous pursuers. If he'd set it too high, he might wound or kill unsuspecting *Enterprise* personnel on the other side—or, worse, rupture part of the ship's warp drive, risking a potentially catastrophic explosion.

He quickly scored a sloppy oval in the panel with his phaser beam, then he pushed off from the bulkhead beside it to build momentum. Swinging back toward the panel, he stretched his legs and shut his eyes a moment before impact.

The panel broke loose as he made contact, and he heard it peal like a church bell as it slammed onto the deck in engineering. He landed feetfirst on top of it and tumbled forward, still clutching his phaser. When he rolled to a stop and looked up, a dozen enlisted engineers were gathered around, staring at him.

"Don't just stand there!" Scott snapped as he scrambled to his feet. "Yerka, Tejwadi, get some portable gen-packs and set up force fields around engineering—give the ghosts somethin' to chew on while we work. Everybody else, with me: we've got to get the mains back online!"

"We're losing altitude fast," Chekov announced over the banshee wails of the *Enterprise*'s overtaxed, unshielded hull.

All that Uhura could see on the main viewscreen was the golden nimbus of superheated gas that had enveloped the ship as it began its shallow plunge into the atmosphere of Akiron. "Engage navigational thrusters, full reverse!"

"All thrusters are at maximum," Chekov replied. "No effect!"

Uhura looked at sh'Vetha. "What about our tractor beams? We could reverse the polarity, make them into repulsor beams, and push off the planet."

"Without main power, we have no tractor beam," sh'Vetha said. "And even if we did, it wouldn't be able to compensate for the mass of the planet and our relative velocity." She glanced at her console with a pained expression. "Hull temperature is at seventeen hundred Kelvin and rising fast. If it goes above forty-one hundred, we'll have to abandon ship."

Looking over his shoulder at Uhura, Chekov said, "Don't worry, dat will never happen." Turning forward, he added under his breath, "We'll crash *long* before the hull temperature reaches two thousand."

Lost in worried thought, Uhura didn't notice that sh'Vetha had left her post until the Andorian woman was standing beside the command chair. She whispered to Uhura, "Our descent is unrecoverable. We should abandon ship *now*."

"No. We don't know that."

"If we wait much longer, there won't be enough time to launch the shuttles and get people to escape pods before the ship hits the surface. At most, we have another ninety seconds to give the order."

Uhura turned her fiercest glare at sh'Vetha. "Then we'll wait ninety more seconds. I won't abandon ship, not until I hear the order from the captain."

Disbelief contorted sh'Vetha's blue face. "For all we know," she said, antennae twitching, "the captain and Mister Spock are already dead."

Swallowing her anger left Uhura clenching her jaw. "We don't know any such thing, and you should know better than to say that out loud on the bridge—or anywhere else. Understood?"

Sh'Vetha mimicked Uhura's taut manner. "Yes, sir." After

a tense pause, she asked, "Permission to prep the emergency log buoy?"

"Do it *quietly*." Uhura shooed the ensign back to her post with a curt nod. As sh'Vetha stepped away, Uhura focused alternately upon the increasingly grim spectacle on the main viewscreen, and upon the clock ticking away the crew's precious remaining seconds.

Uhura's rational side—the part of her that had been trained and honed by Starfleet Academy into a top-notch line officer—knew that sh'Vetha had probably made the correct recommendation for the circumstances. With power and comms down, the helm unresponsive, and hostile life-forms loose inside the ship, evacuating the *Enterprise* was prudent and justified.

But her emotional side would never let her give up on Spock, not when there was a chance, however slim, that he might still be alive.

Get control. Do your job. Remember your oath as an officer. Regardless of whether she ordered the crew to abandon ship, Uhura knew that she would be aboard until the bitter end, as would the rest of the bridge crew. With sixty seconds left until the point of no escape, she steeled herself for the worst. "Mister Chekov, compute our most likely crash trajectory."

"Already done. Current projections indicate we will hit the surface just outside a major city."

Uhura looked at sh'Vetha. "Casualty projection?"

"If our antimatter pods rupture, twenty-two million Kathikar will die."

That was not an answer Uhura could accept.

"Mister Chekov, I know we can't slow our descent, but can we accelerate and control it enough to put the ship down in the planet's ocean?"

The towheaded young Russian thought for a moment. "Maybe." He turned and began working at his console. "If I adjust our angle of approach, and fire navigational thrusters at maximum burn—" He nodded. "Yes. I can do that."

"Make it happen, Ensign. Just because we have to go down in flames, that doesn't mean we need to take innocent people with us."

Sarek hunkered down inside his quarters, surrounded by his three advisers and his aide, L'Nel, as the *Enterprise* shuddered and groaned like a wounded beast.

Sangare, the human scientist, remarked, "I'm no expert in starships, Mister Ambassador, but I think that's a *very* bad sound we're hearing."

"Maybe we should head for an escape pod," said Lesh, the Tellarite economist. "If we wait for an evacuation order, we might not reach one in time!"

"No one leaves unless ordered by the ship's crew," Sarek said. "We are safer if we remain together and follow established safety protocols."

The Andorian lawyer, th'Noor, asked, "What if one of those life-devouring creatures comes in here, Ambassador? Should we stay entrenched then, as well?"

"Common sense would prevail in such a circumstance." Sarek buried his irritation at th'Noor's openly antagonistic query. "If fleeing becomes the most prudent course of action, we shall, of course, do so."

The low groan of the ship's strained hull was pierced by a high-pitched shriek of buckling metal. Lesh cringed and looked fearfully toward the ceiling. "Are you *hearing* that? How can fleeing not be the prudent course, Ambassador?"

L'Nel asked th'Noor, "Did you say the invading creatures 'devour life'?"

"Just Kathikar life. Others they merely paralyze."

The aide turned toward Sangare, who nodded in confirmation. "The data the ship's crew shared with me suggests an energy-disrupting entity."

Eyes wide with alarm, L'Nel stood from the huddle. As she turned away, Sarek took hold of the young woman's sleeve. "What are you doing?"

"I must retrieve the ark from my quarters." L'Nel's tone was as unyielding as it was desperate. "Let me go, Mister Ambassador."

"Sit down, L'Nel!" Sarek met her manic stare with his own cool gaze. "If you leave here, you might get in the crew's way during an emergency."

She twisted free of his grasp and backed away. "I consider that to be an acceptable risk. In this case, the needs of the one outweigh the needs of the many." Turning her back on Sarek, she quickened her pace toward the exit.

Sarek called after her: "L'Nel! Stop! You must remain here!"

"No." She paused in the open doorway just long enough to add, "I must protect the ark!" Then she was gone without any heed for the danger ahead of her.

As the door slid shut, Lesh grumbled to no one in particular, "I'll bet she's really heading for the escape pods." To Sarek he added, "If she gets to go—"

"Stay still and be silent. This is no time for a debate."

The Andorian wore a dubious look. "Really? It seems to have been an opportune time for your aide."

"My aide might soon find herself in need of new employment. Do you three wish to join her in that predicament?" None of Sarek's advisers replied in the affirmative. He arched an eyebrow in reproach. "As I suspected."

Kirk charged onto the bridge to see that Akiron's surface on the main viewscreen was much closer than he would have liked. Taking his place in the command chair as Spock reclaimed the science console, Kirk said to Uhura, "Sum it up for me."

Uhura remained calm and businesslike. "We're diving toward the planet, we have thirty seconds before we're too far gone to use escape pods, and instead of wiping out a major city I chose to scuttle the ship in an ocean."

Her response drew a look of quiet approval from Spock, and Kirk nodded once in agreement. "Well done. Damage report?"

"Main power, comms, and shields are down."

Chekov added over his shoulder, "Helm unresponsive, Keptin."

"Emergency log buoy is prepped," Uhura said.

"Peachy," Kirk said. "Unless anyone has any final flashes of brilliance—"

"Actually," Spock interrupted, "I *do* have a plan, but without internal comms I am unable to convey the details to engineering."

Chekov swiveled his chair so that he faced the first officer. "Can't you just make a direct signal from your communicator to Mister Scott's?"

Leaning forward with anticipation, Kirk ordered Chekov, "Explain."

The young ensign shrugged. "The ship routes all our comm signals automatically, but only because it knows the ID codes on our devices. If you look them up in the memory banks, you can enter them manually."

Spock blinked. "Quite correct, Mister Chekov." He pulled out his communicator and flipped it open.

Scrambling from his chair to Spock's side, Kirk said to Chekov as he passed him, "Good work, Pavel! You just earned two days' extra shore leave." He kept to himself the added condition, *If we live through the next two minutes, that is.*

Keenly aware of seconds passing while Spock accessed the code and programmed his communicator to hail Mister Scott's device, Kirk asked his first officer, "You are aware that if we decide to try your plan, we won't have time to abandon ship if it fails, right, Spock?"

Spock tapped in the final digits. "It is your decision to make." He opened the channel. "Do you wish to evacuate the ship?"

It was going to be an all-or-nothing gamble. If Kirk took the safe path, he might preserve his crew's lives for a few hours, at least until the wights caught up to them on the planet's surface. If he took a chance on saving the ship, he might end up killing them all in the next four minutes. For Kirk, it was not so difficult a choice after all. "I don't like to lose. Try your plan, Spock."

"Spock to engineering."

The chief engineer's voice squawked over the speaker of Spock's communicator: *"Scott here!"*

"Mister Scott, I have devised a possible means of repelling the wight incursion aboard the *Enterprise*. It will involve generating—"

"—a subspace field pulse at an inverse cycle to the wights' native frequency," Scott said, finishing Spock's thought. *"Already on it, Mister Spock, but with the main computer down, I'm missing—"*

"—the precise frequency modulation," Spock said, picking up the chief engineer's thought, "which I am sending to you now via this communicator signal. Do you have a tricorder at hand?"

"Aye, sir. Interplexing now." Kirk heard the oscillating whine of a tricorder over the open channel, and then Scott said, *"Ready, Mister Spock."*

Spock punched up some files on his console and adroitly

relayed them through his communicator to Scott. "Data transfer commencing." As the operation continued, Spock asked, "How do you propose to generate a pulse of sufficient power and area to purge the ship of wights?"

"I figured I'd run the whole shebang through the dilithium crystal chamber and generate the pulse using the coils in the warp nacelles."

Something about that gave Kirk a twist of fear in his gut. "Whoa. Firing up a warp pulse in an atmosphere? Isn't that kind of dangerous, Scotty?"

"No more dangerous than striking the surface at a thousand kilometers per hour."

"Point taken. Good luck."

"Aye, sir. Scott out." The channel clicked off and went silent.

Kirk looked up expectantly at Spock. "Is this gonna work?"

"Mister Scott's notion of using the warp nacelles themselves to create the subspace pulse is the most efficient method, and possibly the only one with the potential to seal the dimensional rift through which the wights are attacking us."

Kirk sensed his first officer was evading the subject. "That's not what I asked you, Spock. I asked you if this is going to work. Specifically, is there even a snowball's chance in hell that we're getting out of this alive?"

Spock arched an eyebrow and shrugged. "It is . . . possible."

It was less than the ringing endorsement Kirk had hoped for. "All hands, brace for impact," he said, moving to his command chair.

Chekov looked back from his station, his face a portrait

of dismay incarnate. "Can I have my two days of shore leave *now,* Keptin?"

Kirk watched a dark and forbidding expanse of open ocean fill the frame of the main viewer as the *Enterprise* continued its barely controlled descent.

"Ask me again in three minutes, Mister Chekov."

Injured personnel came in two and three at a time, almost nonstop, packing into the *Enterprise*'s sickbay faster than the nurses and junior physicians could triage them for McCoy, who had his hands full performing a series of emergency surgeries.

He snapped at a nurse, "Clamp that artery, dammit!" Although he tried hard not to contaminate his gloved hands, the patient on the table in front of him had an open chest wound that spouted tiny geysers of blood every which way as McCoy struggled to repair the damage caused by shrapnel and a nasty chunk of sharp-edged metallic debris lodged against the man's pericardium.

His junior physicians had their hands full, as well, moving without pause from triage to their own fast-response surgeries, treating everything from severe burns to broken bones to toxic-fume inhalation.

The worst part was the row of patients McCoy couldn't bring himself to look at, because they had been assessed during triage as unrecoverable. At last count there were more than a dozen paralyzed victims of the wights. Each of them was pale and cold to the touch. Knowing there was nothing he could do now to revive them, McCoy had ordered them placed into stasis for their own protection.

He looked up from his latest completed surgery. *That's good enough for now.* The shrapnel and debris had been cleared, the patient's pericardium was intact, and the bleeding was under control. "Nurse, close for me, please," he said, turning about-face to cope with the next life-or-death crisis.

A different nurse stepped up and helped him change his soiled surgical gown and gloves for fresh ones. Prepped for action, he looked down at the woman on the biobed in front of him. Her arm was all but severed just above the elbow. "My God," McCoy groused, "she looks like she got put through a grinder." He held out his open hand. "Osteofuser." If he was going to save the woman's arm, he would have to rebuild it from the inside out: bones first, then cartilage, tendons, blood vessels, muscles, and skin. It would not be quick or easy.

He was half finished fusing her bifurcated humerus back together when sickbay filled with shrieks of terror. McCoy knew what he'd see even before he looked up: wights were everywhere, emerging through the deck and bulkheads.

Another sound drowned out the screaming: the angry shrieks of phasers. Security personnel who had come in as patients were now reacting as combatants. Their blue beams slashed ineffectually through the wights and scorched the walls and floor. Halting his surgery, McCoy waved his arms and shouted, "Hold your fire, dammit! Phasers won't do anything but get us all killed!"

A small, stumbling figure pushed through the knot of bodies in the middle of sickbay. It was Gveter-ren, recovering his walking stick from the scanning device. Clutching the gnarled black staff, he turned toward the wights and began his chanting. In an instant the wights ceased their predation on the other patients and converged instead upon Gveter-ren, who collapsed beneath the assault.

McCoy wanted to run to the monk's side, to save him somehow, but all he could do was stand aside and watch the gray-furred old Kathikar sacrifice himself. Paralyzed by his obligation to stay with his patient, McCoy prayed for a miracle.

To his surprise, he got one.

Scott led a team of engineers in a mad dash down the length of the engine room, their movements stuttered by the strobing of the overhead lights. They each carried a bulky coil of power cables over one shoulder and wore tools slung at their hips. Their running steps were lost in the banshee wail of the ship's hull as the *Enterprise* continued its plunge toward the surface of Akiron.

Arriving at the junction points for the struts that joined the ship's secondary hull to its warp nacelles, Scotty pointed at the access hatches. "Walsh, Sovani, get these open! Lofvok, climb up to the starboard nacelle and run a bypass on the main warp coils—I need to tap whatever residual charges they have left. Go!" Then he looked at Keenser. "You're bypassing the port nacelle!"

Keenser cringed and shook his head in a vigorous but mute refusal.

Scott was in no mood for his assistant's neuroses. "Are you bloody kidding me? Every other minute of the day I can't keep your feet on the deck 'cause you've found something you need to climb. Now I'm asking you to go for the best freestyle climb of your life and you *don't want to go*?" His outburst prompted only more nervous headshaking from his assistant. "Why not, you gutless green monkey?" The squat alien responded with a flurry of clicks and gestures that Scott had learned to understand during their shared tenure on Delta Vega. Boiling over with rage, Scott said, "You *won't* get melted." He thought for a moment. "*Probably* won't get melted." He put some steel in his tone. "But if you don't do this in the next sixty seconds, we'll all go up in flames when this ship slams into the ocean. So *go!*"

Duly chastised, Keenser grumbled as he clambered through the access hatch and disappeared up the nacelle's maintenance passage, dragging the end of an unspooling length of power cable with him, up into the ship's warp drive.

Turning to face the rest of his team, Scott resumed issuing orders. "Patch the mains into this relay! Bypass the safeties! We need to squeeze every drop o' juice out of those nacelles in one hot burst—because that's all we're gonna get before this starship gets turned into a submarine!"

Everyone scrambled into motion—passing tools and cables, replacing circuits, and forging new connections in their shared race against calamity.

Scott checked his chrono several times each minute,

hyperconscious of time's passage, of seconds slipping away, of opportunities being lost.

Then Lofvok, a small and slender humanoid alien, emerged from the access passage for the starboard nacelle, looked at the chief engineer, and reported, "Ready, sir!" Seconds later, Keenser shot out of the port nacelle, tumbled across the deck, and landed at Scott's feet with his fists clenched in a gesture that was his species' equivalent of a thumbs-up.

"Right! Here we go, people!" Scott powered up the interface for the bypassed nacelles, checked the phase-variance settings, and triggered the pulse.

A majestic hum resonated through the deck and bulkheads, rising in pitch and volume, and then it thrummed like a musical chord of pure power as the engine room flooded with a blinding, golden radiance.

Either I've just saved us, Scott mused, *or I've just blown us up.*

Kirk felt the subspace pulse—it was like a tingle on his skin, a ripple of gooseflesh, a shiver of anticipation. Then he heard it—it was rich and deep beyond measure, like the sound of being submerged in an ocean. Finally, he saw it, an amber glow that came from nowhere even as it seemed to be everywhere.

Either Scotty's just saved us, or he's just blown us up.

The radiance faded, the sound diminished, and the galvanic sensation that had snared his attention petered out, leaving behind a lingering warmth. Hoping for the best, Kirk said, "I want reports: damage, casualties, ship's status."

"Impulse engines are back online, Keptin," Chekov said, never taking his eyes from his console as he worked. "Helm sluggish but responding."

"Take us back to standard orbit, Mister Chekov." Looking at Spock, Kirk asked expectantly, "Are the wights still on board?"

Spock peered at his sensor readouts. "Negative. The ship has been purged, and the dimensional rift we detected has been closed."

"Chalk that up as a win for our side. Secure from red alert, maintain yellow alert, all decks." Kirk asked Uhura, "Do we have comms yet?"

"Yes, Captain. All internal channels are available."

He thumbed a switch on his chair's armrest and opened a comm to main engineering. "Kirk to engine room. Scotty, you still with me?"

"Aye! But one more bout like that, and this fine gray lady of ours'll be a smear on the planet's surface. I need time to get the mains back online before you go pulling any more dodgy stunts." He added belatedly, *"Sir."*

"Understood, Mister Scott, but repairs'll have to wait. What I really need you to do is figure out what we just did right, then find a way to make the same thing happen for Akiron. Put everybody you can spare on that until further notice."

"Acknowledged. Scott out."

As Kirk terminated the channel, Spock stepped up beside the command chair. "Despite the fact that we only narrowly survived this most recent altercation with the wights, I presume you do not intend to break orbit and refrain from further conflict."

"You presume correctly, Spock. I'm just gettin' warmed up." Looking over his shoulder, Kirk added, "Uhura, get me a status update on our diplomatic passengers."

"Aye, sir."

McCoy's halting, shaken voice squawked from the overhead speaker.

"Sickbay to Captain Kirk."

"Kirk here. Go ahead, Bones."

"Jim, you'd better get down here. He's asking for you."

The message perplexed Kirk. "Who is?"

"Gveter-ren. He's dying."

Kirk rushed into sickbay, followed by Spock. McCoy intercepted them almost as soon as they were through the door. "He's back here." The doctor led them past numerous wounded crewmen. Blood of many colors blotted out the rank insignia of the casualties, making it impossible for Kirk to tell enlisted personnel from officers; it pooled in dark swirls on the deck under his boots and stained the surgical smocks of the medical staff.

"What happened, Bones? I thought he was recovering."

McCoy sighed. "He decided to be a hero." Casting a dour look over his shoulder at Kirk, he added, "Like a starship captain I happen to know."

Kirk took the rebuke as a compliment. "I'm sure he just did what he thought was right." He ignored McCoy's frown and Spock's arched brow—both of which seemed cut from the same dubious cloth. The trio edged through a knot of medical staff who were on their way to treat other patients, and then the three officers arrived at the bedside of the mortally wounded Gveter-ren.

The elderly Kathikar had looked careworn and fragile when he had first come aboard; now he looked like a husk of himself. His gray fur had become brittle and was falling out in clumps. Burst capillaries had turned the whites of his sunken eyes red. His skin looked as brittle as parchment left in the desert, and his voice was as dry as sand. "Kirk," he rasped.

Leaning in close, Kirk grasped Gveter-ren's trembling paw in one hand. He was careful not to squeeze it for fear of crushing it. "I'm here."

Gveter-ren's head lolled toward Kirk. He wheezed softly while laboring for breath. "You stand now . . . at the threshold."

Kirk shook his head in confusion. "The threshold? Of what?"

"Of your . . . future." The dying monk's eyelids were slowly closing. He seemed to be resisting it, as if he knew that once they shut, they would never reopen. "Only you . . . can save . . . my world. My . . . people." He coughed for several seconds;

it was an ugly, wet sound. After he recovered a portion of his composure, he added, "Do not . . . let others . . . choose your path."

"Never have. Don't plan to start now."

That drew a wan smile from Gveter-ren. "Good." His paw closed around the captain's wrist with more strength than Kirk had thought the old mystic still possessed. "I see . . . greatness . . . in you, Captain." The timbre of his voice deepened as he continued. "You were not born . . . to live an ordinary life."

Kirk recoiled upon hearing such a clear echo of the words that Christopher Pike had spoken to him years earlier, in a bar back on Earth—words that had spurred Kirk to enroll at Starfleet Academy. Words that had changed his life.

Gveter-ren pulled Kirk toward him and gasped out his final words.

"You, James Kirk . . . are a man . . . of destiny."

A pained, shallow breath passed over the monk's lips. The strength left his hand, which went slack and released Kirk's wrist. The Kathikar's eyelids fluttered most of the way shut. With a gentle pass of his hand, Kirk eased them closed.

He stood over the body of an alien who, hours earlier, had been a stranger to him, but whose death now felt like a grievous loss. "I barely knew him." Kirk hoped that voicing his thoughts would coax them into order. He looked at McCoy. "Should we ask the chief minister about his people's funeral customs?"

"Hardly seems like our top priority right now, Jim. Hell, for all we know, the Kathikar might be like us and have dozens or even hundreds of different customs. Vellesh-ka might not even know Gveter-ren's funeral rites."

Spock said, "If it will help, Doctor, I can forward you all files in our memory banks regarding the Kathikar's practices concerning their dead." Apparently reacting to the mild looks of surprise his comment elicited from Kirk and McCoy, Spock added, "Starfleet protocol recommends we show the same respect for the customs of other cultures as we do for our own."

McCoy put on a chastened frown. "Yes, of course. Thank you, Spock." To Kirk he added, "What about you, Jim? Are you okay?"

"I don't know, Bones. He really expected me to save his world and his people. Me and no one else."

"No one could ever hold you to something like that. You're just one man—you can't bear that kind of responsibility alone."

Kirk shook his head. "It's not the responsibility that's eating at me. It's that he *believed* in me, Bones. The only other person who's ever come close to showing *that* kind of faith in me is Captain Pike."

"You cannot control what others believe about you," Spock said. "And one might argue that it is better to *know* oneself than to *believe* in oneself."

Too tired for riddles, Kirk asked, "What's your point, Spock?"

"Simply this: whatever you believe—about Gveter-ren, your destiny, or anything else—is ultimately irrelevant. Whether one holds beliefs as a matter of conviction or as a means of consolation, all that matters is what one *chooses* to do." He let that sink in, and then he asked, "What are your orders, Captain?"

"Let's get back to the bridge. As soon as Scotty comes up with some way to stop the wights and save Akiron, we're going back down to the planet's surface." Heading for the door with Spock at his heels, Kirk added with adamant resolve, "It's time for a rematch."

24

It was an impossible task, and Montgomery Scott knew it. *If I had a month to work out the numbers, maybe I could unravel this Gordian knot. But in two hours? That's insane. What does the captain think I am? A miracle worker?*

He stood in the middle of the shambles that until a short while ago had been the *Enterprise*'s main engineering compartment. All around him, every spare hand on the ship was clearing debris, pulling out damaged components, installing new cables, and running complex diagnostic programs to recalibrate the ship's finely tuned warp-drive system, which had been rendered inoperative by the wight attack.

As much as Scott wanted to be in the thick of the repair efforts—not just directing the work but actively getting his hands dirty, both figuratively and literally—Kirk had made it explicitly clear that he wanted Scott's full attention on the task of weaponizing the subspace pulse that had driven the wights off the ship.

Unfortunately, the pulse had drained all the residual energy from the ship's warp nacelles, and the *Enterprise* had no means of recharging them until the warp drive was restored. Most baffling of all, none of the systems appeared to have been physically damaged, so Scott and his crew were at a loss to explain why the system remained stubbornly offline. Not that bringing it back up would matter, he knew. Even at full capacity, the *Enterprise*'s warp drive couldn't generate a pulse big enough to disperse all the wights plaguing the surface of Akiron, and the technology didn't exist to generate subspace pulses with devices small enough to use as small arms. Scott frowned. *The captain might as well ask me to change the laws of physics.*

A commotion behind Scott, at the warp core, offered him a much-needed distraction. Several engineers were gathered around the dilithium-crystal articulation chamber and swearing like the sailors of old. Keenser was perched on top of the articulation frame, eyeing the problem from above. He beckoned Scott closer, and the chief engineer shouldered through the cluster of his subordinates to see what was going on. "Break it up, lads. Let me have a look."

As he slipped past the last man in his way, Scott saw the cause of the other engineers' consternation: several high-grade dilithium crystals—which normally were transparent—mounted inside the articulation frame had been turned gray and cloudy. "Bloody hell." Scott leaned in for a closer peek.

"That looks familiar." He tried to imagine some way that the subspace pulse he'd generated could have done that to the crystals, but nothing about that scenario made sense. Then a more worrisome possibility occurred to him. *Those dark-energy buggers were inside the crystal housing. They did this.*

It made sense, Scott thought. The wights had seemed to congregate inside the dilithium mine on Akiron, and whatever Gveter-ren had done to drive them off had involved focusing his energy through his staff's gray-dilithium headpiece.

He held that thought for a long moment. *The gray dilithium,* he repeated silently to himself. *It amplified whatever energy his mind was producing . . .*

All at once the plan began to take shape. "Keenser," he said, backing away from the articulation chamber, "retrieve those gray crystals and bring them to my workbench. Hartung, go up to sickbay and get the dead monk's staff—I need that crystal too. On the double, Ensign! Go!" Breaking free of the gaggle of engineers, Scott moved quickly through the engine room, snapping at people as he moved from one console to another, pushing people out of his way. "Stop what you're doing! I need your workstations, all of them, right now! Everybody step back!" At each station, he initiated another part of an absurdly complex simulation, one for which he would need every bit of the ship's computing power that he could hijack.

Passing an enlisted mechanic, he grabbed her sleeve and pulled her with him as he moved on to commandeer the next console along his path. He pulled out his communicator, flipped up its cover, and opened an intraship channel. "Scott to sickbay!" Then he handed the communicator to the startled young mechanic and told her, "Keep this open and near me at all times."

The chief medical officer replied over the portable comm, *"McCoy here."*

"Doctor, I'm patching in to your medical database, and I need you to release to me all of Gveter-ren's brain scans."

"Scotty, that's privileged medical information. I can't—"

"I need it to save his planet, Doctor. Also, I sent up one of my people to get his walking stick. I need that, too."

After a short delay during which Scott imagined he could hear the proverbial wheels turning inside McCoy's head, the doctor replied, *"I'm removing the confidential seals on his brainwave data—and only his brainwave data—now. And your engineer just left with the walking stick."*

"Thank you, Doctor." Scott grew more excited by the second.

Slaving all the engineering workstations into a single distributed computing apparatus, Scott ran comparative analyses of every bit of data he had about gray dilithium, Gveter-ren's brainwaves, the phase variance of the wights' dimensional rifts, and the subspace pulse that had repelled their attack. He prowled back the way he had come, checking the incremental but steadily growing progress being made on his daisy-chained network of consoles.

By the time he returned to his master status console, he was able to watch the final steps in his massive number-crunching operation. The resultant flood of data, graphs, and formulas was staggering at first, but Scott quickly saw the common factors and felt a swell of pride as he realized his crazy idea might just work after all. The captain would have his weapon, and, if Scott worked quickly enough, the Kathikar might survive this nightmarish siege from another dimension.

He smiled, cracked his knuckles, and said to Keenser, "Bring me my tools."

"I'm still workin' out the kinks, mind you," Scott cautioned over the comm, *"but I'm pretty sure this'll work. Better than sharp sticks and harsh words, at any rate."*

Kirk stood beside Spock at the science console and asked, "Exactly what kind of weapons are we talking about, Mister Scott?"

"A rifle, to start, and I've got my people crunching numbers and making parts for something a wee bit bigger—a gizmo that'll really give those spooky buggers a wallop if I'm right."

"Good work," Kirk said. "How soon can you have a prototype?"

The chief engineer sounded cagey. *"I'll need at least an hour to hammer something into shape, but it shouldn't take much longer than that."*

"See that it doesn't. The lives of four billion Kathikar depend on your punctuality." Kirk added as an afterthought, "No pressure. Bridge out." He closed the channel and looked at Spock, who seemed lost in grim contemplation. "Out with it, Spock. What's stuck in your craw now?"

Spock replied in a low voice, "I am concerned by the degree of zeal you have expressed for this mission, Captain. Even if you are able to repel the wight incursion at this late stage, your efforts will not restore the countless thousands of lives already lost on the planet's surface, or those of our paralyzed shipmates."

"I'm aware of that, Spock. I'm not expecting to raise the dead. All I'm hoping to do is prevent a tragedy from becoming an apocalypse." Looking around his bridge, his gaze landed on Sulu's empty chair. "As for those in sickbay . . . they all knew the risks of wearing the uniform. And I won't dishonor them by letting their suffering be in vain." He walked back to his command chair, leaving Spock alone to consider what he'd said.

As Kirk settled into his seat, Uhura announced, "Captain, I'm receiving a priority-one subspace transmission from Admiral Deigaro at Starfleet Command."

Wonderful. Kirk heaved a deep sigh. He'd had very few dealings with the admiralty so far in his brief tenure as a starship captain, but he had worked enough lousy jobs to know that a call from the boss was usually not a good thing.

"Put him on the main viewscreen, Lieutenant."

"Aye, sir." Uhura routed the message with the press of a button.

The on-screen image of Akiron was replaced by the weathered visage of Admiral Deigaro, who wasted no time launching into a tirade. *"Kirk, what the hell are you still doing at Akiron? I gave you a direct order to leave hours ago."*

Kirk did his best to conceal his ire at being berated in front of his crew. "Actually, sir, you gave me a conditional order, and I've interpreted it based on my objectives and my understanding of the situation on the planet's surface."

Fury and befuddlement put deep creases in Deigaro's already wrinkled forehead. *"Excuse me? What do you mean, I gave you a 'conditional' order?"*

Shrugging nonchalantly, Kirk said, "You directed me to leave Akiron and transport Ambassador Sarek to Starbase 21 *as soon as possible*. However, since my mission here is unfinished, it's not yet possible for me—"

"Spare me your semantic games, Kirk. You knew damned well what my orders meant, which means you're currently one smart-ass remark away from being court-martialed for insubordination." Leaning forward so that his stern face filled the viewscreen's frame, he continued, *"This is a direct order, Kirk: your mission to Akiron is officially terminated. Break orbit and depart immediately for Starbase 21 at your best possible warp speed."*

"As it happens," Kirk said, "we don't currently *have* warp speed, Admiral."

"I'm warning you, Kirk: don't test my patience."

Spock stepped down from his post to stand beside Kirk's chair. "Captain Kirk has reported truthfully, Admiral. The *Enterprise* is currently without warp drive."

Hooking a thumb in Spock's direction, Kirk said to Deigaro, "See? If you won't believe me, you can at least believe him, right?"

"You don't need warp drive to break orbit. My order to termi-

nate your mission to Akiron stands. Withdraw from their system at your best possible speed and prioritize the repair of your warp drive."

Kirk couldn't stop his hands from curling into fists. "With all respect, Admiral, the Kathikar have only a few hours left to live unless we *do something*. These people asked for our help, and I don't think it's right to turn our backs on them because of some political red tape."

Deigaro glared at Kirk. *"First of all,* Captain, *if you want to treat me with 'all respect,' you can start by not debating my direct orders. Second, who do you think you are? You've barely been in that chair long enough to make an ass-print on the seat. Goddammit, I have* scars *older than you, boy. If you want to stay in Starfleet long enough to actually call it a career, you'd better learn to respect the chain of command, starting right now."* He shook his head. *"I know you've got guts, Kirk, and I can see you've got heart. But a starship captain also needs to have discipline—and that's one virtue you have in short supply."* Hardening his stare, he added, *"Give the order to your crew, Kirk. I want to hear you say it."*

As hard as he tried, Kirk couldn't issue the order. He knew he'd be in a world of hurt if he openly defied an admiral on an open channel, but he couldn't bring himself to give up, not when he was so close to his mission's end.

Static clouded the picture on the viewscreen, and chaotic noise garbled and drowned out Deigaro's next shouted words. The signal terminated, and the image on the main viewer reverted to the majestic curve of Akiron's northern hemisphere.

"Sorry, Captain," Uhura said. "We seem to be experiencing a temporary failure in our long-range subspace comm system." Reacting to Kirk's amused half smile, she added with cool calm, "I'll ask Mister Scott to add it to his repair list."

"See that you do, Lieutenant," Kirk said, his smile widening. "I'm eager to resume my conversation with the admiral at the earliest *possible* moment."

"Understood, sir," Uhura replied, turning back toward her console.

Kirk's smile faded as he looked up at his first officer. "Spock, it seems only fair to warn you that I have absolutely no intention of obeying Admiral Deigaro's order to abandon an entire planet of innocent beings to horrible deaths. Since this makes me unequivocally guilty of insubordination, I'll understand if you need to relieve me of command and put me in the brig."

Spock arched an eyebrow. "And who will put me in the brig with you?"

With his smile restored, Kirk said, "Glad we're finally on the same page, Spock." He got up and gestured for Spock to follow him to the science console. "Let's get to work—we have a lot to do in the next sixty minutes."

25

Drifting slowly back from silent oblivion to pained conscious-ness, Hikaru Sulu was certain he heard the ocean—until he realized that the crashing waves drawing him up toward the light were merely the tides of his own breathing.

The last thing he remembered was standing on the bridge and engaging the override switch on the helm. Next had come a flash of light, and then . . . nothing. Darkness and sound-less confusion, a stream of thoughts both disembodied and disjointed, a fluid progression of free-association images, fol-lowed by an endless sensation of falling through a featureless void.

He broke through to awareness not with a start or a gasp, but with a gradual upward creep of his eyelids. Light flooded in, washing away details and leaving him just as blind as he'd been with his eyes shut. Sounds remained muffled, as if his ears were stuffed with cotton. He sussed out a few distinct voices in the wall of sound—one male, two female—but was unable to tell what they were saying.

His body felt impossibly heavy. There was a faint, tingling sensation in his fingertips, but he couldn't move them. Closing his eyes, he drew a deep breath, concentrated, and succeeded in wiggling the digits of his right hand. *It's a start.* He focused on repeating the effort with his left hand. Soon he was able to move both hands and flex his fingers. *Not bad.*

Marshaling his strength, he rolled to his right and pushed himself up from the bed. Propped on his right elbow, he opened his eyes and saw that he was in sickbay. The medical staff had their hands full; every bed had a patient, and more people were lying on the deck or sitting with their backs to the bulkheads. The metallic scents of blood were mingled with the pungent odor of disinfectant. He was surrounded by maimed and paralyzed shipmates.

Sulu dragged his legs over the bed's edge and let them dangle above the deck as he sat up. The effort made his head spin. Nausea churned inside him like some grotesque beast trapped in his stomach, and warm, sour bile snaked up his esophagus. He choked down on the surge of acidic reflux and winced at the burning sensation and vile taste it left in the back of his throat. Suppressing a sudden urge to vomit, he swallowed instead.

When his vertigo passed, his headache began. At first

it was a dull ache deep inside his skull. It quickly bloomed into a brutal, crushing pain that left him seeing free-floating puce-and-lavender spots everywhere he looked. Rubbing his forehead, he discovered his skin felt feverishly warm and was coated in sweat. He palmed the perspiration from his hand across one leg of his trousers.

From behind him came Doctor McCoy's accusatory query, "And just where do you think *you're* going?" As the helmsman blinked and struggled to focus his eyes, McCoy stepped around the biobed to stand in front of him.

"I need to get back to my post." Sulu leaned forward to slide himself off the biobed and stand up. He didn't get very far.

McCoy put a hand to Sulu's chest and stopped him. "No, Lieutenant. What you need to do is lie down and let me do my job."

Protesting with a feeble shake of his head, Sulu lied, "I'm fine, Doctor."

"The hell you are. You're lucky your brain didn't get hard-boiled by that jolt you took. You've got neurological damage throughout your body, and your brain chemistry's completely out of whack."

Sulu tried again to get out of bed. "I've suffered worse."

McCoy restrained Sulu with apparent ease. "Really? When?"

Damn. Called my bluff. "I won't lie to you, Doc. I feel like I got run over. But I can tell just by looking around that I'm not the worst-hurt person here. Matter of fact, I'd bet I don't even make the top fifty."

"Why don't you let me be the judge of that?"

Sulu pushed himself up and off the bed more quickly than he had before. On his feet in front of McCoy, he said, "Go ahead, Doc. Test me."

McCoy lifted a medical tricorder and scanned Sulu. "Your vitals are saying the same thing I am: you're barely out of shock and ought to stay in bed."

"I don't care." Sulu tried to step around McCoy despite being unsteady on his feet. "There are other people in here who need you more."

He halted Sulu with one hand. "Just because they need me more doesn't mean you don't need me at all. Get back in that bed."

"I'll be fine. I have advanced combat training."

"Yeah, I heard about that. Fencing doesn't train you to cope with the kind of punishment your body's just taken. Lie down."

"No. The ship's in danger, and my place is on the bridge." Sulu held up one hand to ward off McCoy's rebuttal. "As soon as the captain says the crisis is over, I'll come back and let you run all the tests you want. I promise."

McCoy frowned. "If I order you to bed, you'll just sneak out, won't you?"

"Probably, yes."

His answer prompted a disgruntled sigh from the doctor. "Everyone wants to be a hero 'til he drops dead at his post. . . . Go."

"Thanks, Doc." Sulu shuffled past McCoy and left sickbay before the doctor changed his mind. Loping down the corridor, he fought to suppress the pain engulfing his body. *All I have to do now is reach the bridge without passing out.*

Spock entered his father's guest quarters to find them in disarray. Sarek stood surrounded by his three advisers, who milled about in quiet confusion, muttering softly among themselves as they picked up the ambassador's personal effects from the floor or righted overturned pieces of furniture. Though they looked disheveled and mildly bruised, none appeared to be seriously hurt.

Protocol, however, still compelled Spock to ask after their conditions. "Father, I trust that you and your staff are unharmed."

"We have been fortunate in that regard. Though I cannot speak for my aide, L'Nel, who left us during the attack and has not yet returned."

"Shall I dispatch a security team to confirm her status?"

"Unnecessary," replied L'Nel as she stepped through the open doorway behind Spock. "I am unhurt." To Sarek she added, "I apologize for leaving without permission, Ambassador, and I hope you will not judge my actions too harshly."

Sarek regarded L'Nel with a look of quiet disapproval; it was one that Spock knew well, having seen it many times during his youth. "There is a difference between leaving without permission and defying an explicit instruction not to go."

"Forgive me, but you know why I thought it necessary."

"We shall speak later, L'Nel, in private." The aide bowed her head in contrite acknowledgment. Resuming his typical façade of cool logic, Sarek looked at Spock. "Have you come to bring me a message from Captain Kirk?"

"I have. He wishes to inform you that while the immediate threat to the *Enterprise* has been contained, there remains a risk of further attacks."

Sarek folded his hands together at his waist. "I see. Would I be correct to infer from your statement that Captain Kirk intends to continue his efforts to rescue the Kathikar from the entities laying siege to their world?"

"Yes. That remains the mission of Captain Kirk, and, by extension, the crew of the *Enterprise*. However"—he looked around the room at th'Noor, Lesh, Sangare, and L'Nel—"the captain does not feel it prudent to endanger you or your staff any longer. In order to ensure your safety, he has decided that the five of you will be placed on a shuttle with Vellesh-ka. You will be assigned a pilot and a security officer, and you will depart the *Enterprise* as soon as possible. The shuttle will withdraw to a safe distance at the edge of this star system until either the *Enterprise* or another Federation starship can bring you safely back aboard."

Looking pointedly unenthused by that scenario, Sarek asked, "And what does Starfleet Command have to say about Captain Kirk's proposed action?"

"To the best of my knowledge, Starfleet is unaware of the particulars of the captain's plan. However, his decision to continue our mission on behalf of the Kathikar runs contrary to Admiral Deigaro's direct order for us to withdraw."

Th'Noor was aghast. "In other words, Kirk's gone rogue!"

Spock fixed the agitated Andorian with a challenging glare. "I do not think hyperbole is a useful response, Mister th'Noor."

"I don't think I'm exaggerating, Mister Spock. Defying orders, committing a capital ship and its crew to an unsanctioned military campaign—how else are we to characterize your captain's actions in this matter?"

He bristled at th'Noor's aggressive style of argument. "It is my opinion that the captain is acting in accordance with his conscience, and in keeping with the finest traditions of Starfleet—whose officers, if history is any guide, tend not to consider blind obedience to superiors to be a virtue."

Lesh, the Tellarite, asked Sarek, "Are you just going to stand by and let this happen, Ambassador? Does the rule of law mean so little to Vulcans?"

Caught between his staff and his son, Sarek stood silent for a moment, his mien pensive. "This is not a simple matter. We are outside the jurisdiction of the Federation. Although some aspects of interstellar law appear relevant to the situation, it is ultimately the prerogative of starship captains to interpret and apply it as they see fit in each unique circumstance."

A derisive snort telegraphed Lesh's contempt. "In other words, we're just going to let Kirk do whatever he wants." He folded his arms and looked at th'Noor. "I hate having to agree with an Andorian, but you're right—he's gone rogue."

Sangare, the human science adviser, faced Spock. "Does

your crew have a viable strategy for combating the aliens at-tacking Akiron?"

"Yes. Based on data we have gathered during the past sev-eral hours, we have developed a working hypothesis that our chief engineer is applying to the fabrication of weapons and active countermeasures."

Sangare replied, "Such as . . . ? I'd appreciate some details, Mister Spock."

"The details are considered classified until such time as our logs are released by Starfleet Command. Let it suffice to say I do not think the captain would have given the order to proceed with the mission if he did not believe there was a rea-sonable likelihood of our success. He is headstrong—but not suicidal." He looked at his father and added, "Time is of the essence, Ambassador. I must ask you and your staff to gather your personal effects and proceed to shuttlebay one."

L'Nel stepped between Spock and Sarek. "Do not listen to him, sir. Captain Kirk is trying to remove us from the ship so that he can better stifle dissent, at exactly the time when such an opposing view is most needed."

Sarek's tone was sharp as he asked L'Nel, "Do you have proof of these accusations?" He scowled. "I will not predicate my decisions on hearsay and speculation." Calming himself, he looked at Spock. "My son, tell me truthfully: Do you con-sider this course of action to be the one that is most logical?"

"No—but it is the right thing to do." He wondered if Sarek would understand his answer. In the end, it was not important. What mattered was that Spock understood his own motives and the conflict between logic and emotion that had produced them, and he considered his conclusion ethical. If his father could not or would not accept his reasoning, that was a matter for another time and place. He lifted his hand in the Vulcan salute. "Live long and prosper, Father."

Returning the gesture, Sarek said, "Peace and long life, my son."

Spock lowered his hand. "Good-bye, Father."

26

Spock followed Kirk into the engine room, whose deck was cluttered with debris, discarded components, dropped tools, and loose cables. Standing in the midst of that muddled tableau was Commander Scott, his hands and attention steady on a spot-welding task behind a glare shield. He was flanked by several engineers.

"Scotty," Kirk called, his voice echoing inside the cavernous space, "time's up, we gotta go. Please tell me you've got something."

Scott switched off his plasma welder. "Aye, some real beauties!" He raised the glare shield to reveal a heavily modified Starfleet phaser rifle. "Took a wee bit of jury-rigging and a few new lines of code, but I swapped out the emitter crystal with a custom-cut piece of that gray dilithium."

Kirk's eyes widened. "Whoa! You put a dilithium crystal in a phaser rifle?"

"You bet your boots I did!" Scott flashed a broad smile. "And I changed its power frequency and prefire capacitance modulation to match the brainwaves of your late great pal Gveter-ren. Pull the trigger on this bad boy and the wights'll feel like they got a jolt of his mental mojo times twenty!" His smile vanished as he paused and then added, "Well . . . in theory."

"In theory," Kirk deadpanned.

"Mister Scott," Spock said, "have you tested this prototype weapon?"

"Not exactly, but it works great in the simulation."

"No doubt." Spock picked up the rifle and studied it. "Will these modifications affect the weapon's rate of power consumption?"

Folding his arms, Scott nodded. "Aye, no way around that. Pushing a beam through a dilithium crystal takes a lot more juice than shooting it through a regular superconducting lattice. At best you might get a few dozen shots per power cell."

"What else have you got, Scotty?" Kirk made rapid circling gestures with his hand. "How do we deal with the big picture?"

"Ah, for that we come to my masterpiece." Scott led Kirk and Spock to another workbench, on which a small blocky shape lay beneath a drop cloth. Scott rested his hand on the cloth. "I wracked my brains trying to think up some way to gin up a phase pulse big enough to affect the planet. No matter how I came at it, I didnae see any way to wring that much punch out of our warp drive. *After all*, I thought, *you can only push so much through our dilithium crystal matrix*. Then my pal Keenser showed me that a few of our crystals had gone gray—and it hit me: the planet's core is loaded with the stuff, aye? So we use the *planet itself* as the phase amplifier." He pulled away the sheet with a triumphant flourish to reveal a nondescript gray box with a carrying handle, a few buttons, and a small LED display screen. "She may not look like much, but set her off in the right place and you'll be in for a show!"

Kirk picked up the box, ostensibly to test its weight.

Spock considered the implications of the chief engineer's proposal. "Where, exactly, would be the correct place to trigger this device for maximum effect, Mister Scott?"

Scott shrugged. "Only place that really works is the very bottom of the dilithium mine you lads went pokin' round in before. Probably dead smack in the middle of that cave full of wights. Your tricorder readings from that cave show a pit in there that leads to a rich vein of mixed dilithium a few kilometers down."

"Invading that cavern is an extremely hazardous proposition," Spock said.

"Nice understatement, Spock," Kirk said. "It's more like a suicide mission." He looked at Scott. "You're sure this thing'll work?"

"As sure as I can be, sir. If our sensor readings of the planet's dilithium layer are accurate, setting off this pulse generator in the heart of it should create a temporary phase disruption that'll affect the whole planet at once."

Spock furrowed his brow. "Would the effects of such a pulse be powerful enough to affect the *Enterprise* in orbit?"

"Aye. Once the device is triggered, we'd have less than a minute to bugger off to safe distance. Otherwise we'll be a brick in space."

Kirk looked concerned. "And how far is safe distance?"

"About half a million kilometers. At full impulse we can make that with a few thousand meters to spare."

"Half a million kilometers," Kirk repeated. "Outside transporter range."

Scott nodded. "Afraid so." Clearly eager to change the subject, he continued in a more chipper vein. "I can have six of these rifles ready in three hours, so—"

"We don't have three hours," Kirk said, "we have less than one. And one rifle's enough, Scotty, because I'm going in alone."

Spock struck a confrontational stance in front of Kirk. "Captain, I cannot permit you to endanger yourself in this manner. I should be the one to go."

"Nonsense, Spock. You heard Gveter-ren, just as I did. This is my task."

"It is illogical for you to base your command decisions on the near-death ramblings of a religious figure. As this ship's commanding officer, your place during a crisis is on the bridge."

"So is yours, Spock. The only reason we're in this situation is because I bucked orders and stayed on to help the Kathikar. Dozens of my crew have been paralyzed, and I'm probably facing a court-martial if I survive. I'm not risking the safety of my ship or any more of my crew for this mission. I got us into this; it's up to me to get us out.

"I'm going in alone," Kirk continued. "I'll travel light—just the pulse bomb and this rifle. Scotty, can you rig a delay on the bomb's trigger?"

"Aye. Take me five minutes."

"Do it. Spock, are the comm boosters still in the caves?"

"Yes. They do not appear to have drawn the wights' notice."

"Good. Once I drop the bomb, I'll give you a heads-up and try to get back to the beam-out point that Scotty cut with the ship's phasers. If I don't make it by the time you need to break orbit, leave me behind. That's an order."

Sarek heard the whoop of a yellow alert resound through the *Enterprise*'s corridors as he approached the door to L'Nel's quarters. The portal slid open ahead of him, and he entered to find all of his aide's personal effects in the same places he had seen them during his previous visit, hours earlier.

L'Nel knelt before the *katric* ark's low altar, on which a cone of incense smoldered, filling the air with a sharp fragrance of citrus. Her back was to Sarek, who stepped toward her. "L'Nel, it is time for us to depart. The shuttle is ready. The rest of us have been waiting. Why are you not packed?"

"I am not going with you, Sarek. Depart without me."

Her answer was unexpected. "Unacceptable." Sarek moved closer to her. "Captain Kirk's orders were clear: we are to leave the *Enterprise*. Why remain behind when you know that Kirk intends to place his vessel and crew in peril?"

"Now you choose to respect Kirk's orders?" L'Nel turned to face Sarek, who saw that the young woman was wearing a ceremonial sash like those once favored by the priests and adepts at Mount Seleya. He glanced past her to see the *katric* ark uncovered on the altar. L'Nel continued, "How fickle you are, Sarek."

He wrinkled his brow at L'Nel's insult. "A curious remark."

"But not undeserved. You were quick to oppose Kirk's agenda when you had the upper hand. Where is your resolve now, Ambassador?"

"It would be irrational to subject ourselves to unnecessary risk." Sarek gestured toward the door. "Bring your artifact. We must go."

L'Nel stepped toward Sarek and lowered her chin. "No, *you* must go."

"Enough of this." Sarek grabbed her wrist.

She pulled him forward, off balance, and hit him with her free hand. He fell, momentarily airborne, and landed hard on his back. Striking the deck knocked the air from his lungs and left him gasping in vain like a landed fish. He touched his throbbing nose and felt warm blood trickle from his nostrils.

Short of breath, he asked, "Why, L'Nel?"

She answered him with a swift kick to his rib cage. "Because you coddle your son." Her voice was toxic with contempt. "You always have."

He rolled over and tried to crawl away from L'Nel, but she grabbed the folds of his robe, lifted him from the deck, and flung him across the room. He slammed against a bulkhead and landed on an end table that collapsed beneath him.

"All his life," L'Nel said, "given the choice between the Vulcan way and the human way, he has chosen the human way. Even when he professed to share our values, he scorned them. Refusing admission to the Vulcan Science Academy? Taking a human lover? Where did he learn such defiance, Sarek? A son's first template is always his father."

He looked up and lifted his hand, hoping to beg for mercy and stave off her next assault. Her foot smashed into his chest and spun him around before the ship's artificial gravity pulled him back to the deck. Then L'Nel clutched a handful of Sarek's gray hair and roughly yanked his head up so he could see her squatting in front of him. "Had it been up to you, he might never have been betrothed to a Vulcan girl at all. You would have denied me even the *promise* of a fiancé."

Fiancé? The word struck a faint chord in Sarek's memory: Spock had been pledged at the age of seven to a daughter from a respectable family. *But certainly she must have died when . . .* Horrified realization set in as he looked into the eyes of his assistant. Behind the manic gleam there was something familiar; there always had been, but he had not seen this woman in more than two decades—how could he possibly have recognized her? But now he saw who she really was, and he forced himself to say her name through bloodied lips: "T'Pring."

"Very good, Ambassador. I am honored you remember me, though I regret that your death will follow as a consequence."

Sarek pushed himself backward in retreat with his feet and

palms. "You do not need to do this, T'Pring. Spock will honor your betrothal."

"Will he? Are you quite certain? Because he seems rather smitten with his human lover at the moment. Not that it matters—Spock is not the one I want."

For a moment, Sarek wondered what T'Pring meant by that—and then his gaze landed upon the *katric* ark several meters away, on the low, makeshift altar. "What are you planning?"

"I am fulfilling my duty as a Vulcan. Even if Spock had not spurned me, this would still have been necessary. I will not spend my life waiting for a fiancé who betrays me for a human, or for a husband who spends years at a time in deep space. I deserve better than that." She pointed at the *katric* ark. "I deserve a mate who will value me. Who will stay with me. I deserve the man who was to be my own." She let go of Sarek and walked to the altar. "Circumstance took Stonn from me. The ancient rite of *fal-tor-pan* will bring him back—and ensure that when the *Pon farr* burns in Spock's blood, the right man's *katra* thrives inside his mind and seeks me out."

Dragging himself across the floor, Sarek said through a mouth brimming with bright green blood, "This is madness, T'Pring. You cannot use the *fal-tor-pan* to resurrect a dead man's *katra* inside another man's body!"

She replied with the clinical detachment of a surgeon describing a medical procedure. "You can if the living man's *katra* has first been expunged."

"No!" Sarek spat up blood onto the deck. "You would kill Spock."

"His body will live, and it will do so in service to a *katra* more worthy of a place in the new Vulcan society." She turned her back and faced the altar. "You raised your son to be weak, Sarek. I will make him strong."

I am too weak to best her in hand-to-hand combat. And she will stop me before I can use the communications panel on the wall. I must flee and summon the ship's security personnel.

As silently as he was able, Sarek stood and lurched toward the door.

T'Pring turned, sprang, and intercepted him in a blur. She landed a knifing blow with her hand against his throat and kicked him in his solar plexus. As he doubled over, her hand clamped down with a viselike grip on his shoulder. There was a momentary jolt of excruciating pain, and then Sarek felt himself slip away, trapped in the hands of the woman who had come to murder his son.

27

T'Pring drew a deep breath and cleared her mind. She would need all her focus and strength to prepare her mind-meld skills for the *fal-tor-pan* ritual. It was a perilous and difficult undertaking even under the best of circumstances; attempting it under severe time pressure, when the ship was in crisis, would not have been her choice, but she accepted the challenge that circumstance had foisted upon her.

Purged from her thoughts was the mental image of Sarek, bludgeoned and unconscious, lying only partially concealed in the next room. He knew too much now, and if the refusion ceremony went as planned, it would be imperative that she terminate the ambassador—preferably in a manner that disintegrated his corpse, as it would be almost impossible for T'Pring to mask the blunt-force trauma she had already inflicted upon Sarek. If the ship's chief medical officer were to conduct even a cursory autopsy, the true cause of Sarek's death would be readily apparent, and T'Pring's efforts all would be for naught.

Be calm. At peace. Empty yourself.

It was a struggle to quiet her mental tempest. She had planned and schemed for months to create this opportunity. In the upheaval that had followed the destruction of Vulcan, she had stolen a dead woman's name and abandoned her own, at least temporarily, in the service of her true mission: to resurrect Stonn.

She lit a row of incense cones with reverent care. Each cone released a different fragrance intended to stimulate a different portion of T'Pring's mind, as directed by the ancient texts. An essence of floral *kisek* quelled her anger. The cool freshness of *n'tai* imparted vigor and alertness. A mix of fruit fragrances, including *j'pem* and *yela*, enhanced her calm.

Still her memories haunted her, too vivid to be suppressed or contained . . .

T'Pring and Stonn stand together inside a small, spartan sanctuary near the Halls of Ancient Thought, deep within the massive temple at Mount Seleya, exchanging their pledges of fidelity while Sural, a priest, serves as their sole witness.

"I forsake my previous pledges," T'Pring says to Stonn, "and commit to be your faithful mate and spouse. I undertake these vows with clear—"

Thunder crashes, drowning out every other sound in the

world, and then a sharp crack fills the sanctuary as its ancient stone walls are split by fissures. Dust rains down from the ceiling, which sags precariously. Sural ushers Stonn and T'Pring toward the door. "Quickly! Before it collapses!"

They run for the exit. T'Pring is the first one out. Stonn is only a stride or two behind her when the ceiling caves in. Sural is buried instantly, and a huge slab pins Stonn to the floor. Turning back, T'Pring calls her lover's name and coughs as she waves away the thick cloud of ruddy dust. When she finds Stonn, the top half of his body is outside the door, and the lower half is trapped beneath tons of rock, no doubt pulverized.

She clasps Stonn's weakly twitching hand. "I will summon help."

"There is no time." Stonn coughs up a mouthful of dark green blood and frothy spittle. "My death is near. Fetch me a katric ark from the Hall." Perhaps sensing her reluctance, her denial of the unfolding tragedy, he adds with greater insistence, "Do not argue, T'Pring! Go, now. Hurry."

She sprints away from Stonn, into the Halls of Ancient Thought, and begins a desperate, fumbling search for an empty katric ark. As she scours the alcoves and antechambers, adepts and priests and visitors flee the temple, all of them running toward the remote platform used for shuttle landings.

Eyeing the ancient urns arrayed on the shelves around her, she despairs of finding one that has not been claimed—and then she sees it: a free vessel. She seizes it and hugs it to her bosom as she escapes mere steps ahead of another collapse. On her way back, a priest sees her break away from the crowd, and he grabs her. "Where are you going? We must evacuate!"

She twists free of his grasp, pushes him away, and resumes her panicked dash back to Stonn. When she reaches him, her beloved is clinging desperately to life. T'Pring gently presses the katric *ark into his trembling hands. He closes his eyes and mouths words in an ancient dialect of Vulcan, words that all Vulcan children are taught as soon as they are old enough to understand the concept of death. In just over a minute he finishes, and his hold on the ark slackens.*

"It is done," he whispers through teeth stained green with blood. As T'Pring retrieves the ark, Stonn adds, "Take it and flee . . . my love."

Logic tells her to run without hesitation. Instead, she stays for two more minutes, unable to bring herself to leave until Stonn exhales his terminal breath.

The temple is collapsing around her. Great pillars topple, and the floors heave and warp, forming peaks and canyons. T'Pring shields Stonn's katric *ark with her arms as she charges headlong through a final wall of amber haze and out of the temple. Overhead, the sky is black with clouds and flashing with lightning. Fierce, hot winds whip up rust-colored sandstorms that blot out the landscape. T'Pring makes her final mad dash for the shuttle pad, at the far end of a narrow rock bridge that is fracturing violently. Huge chunks of it tumble away into an abyss, leaving only unstable slivers of the path.*

One shuttle remains on the pad, and a lone figure stands outside its open hatch, waving frantically for T'Pring to hurry. Over the rumble of the temple's final implosion and the rolling thunder that seems to be consuming her world, she hears the shriek of the shuttle's engines—its pilot is clearly eager to lift off.

She reaches the pad as the last of the bridge falls away into the chasm, and she ducks inside the shuttle, which is packed with other refugees from the temple. The man who ushered her inside pushes in against her as he seals the door, and then the shuttle ascends— straight up at first, and then rocketing forward, away from the planet and into orbit. Looking past the man beside her, T'Pring watches through the door's viewport as Vulcan, her homeworld, crumbles and devours itself. There is a final conflagration—and then it is gone as if it had never existed. All that remains is empty space. Stars and cold darkness.

She clutches Stonn's katric *ark to her breast and swallows her tears, knowing they will have no place in her new life of forced exile.*

T'Pring held the *katric* ark in both hands. Her thoughts were silent. She was ready, committed. When the ritual was complete, Stonn would live again.

Which meant it was time for Spock to die.

28

The flood of signal traffic crossing Uhura's console told her that the *Enterprise*'s crew was growing anxious as the captain prepared for his solo mission to the dilithium mines on Akiron. The deck officers and crew chiefs were scrambling to secure the ship against another wight attack, or another power failure, or against any of a number of new potential disasters. Tensions were high.

Uhura shared some of that concern. The thought of letting Kirk go alone into danger went against all her Starfleet training, and she imagined it must also bother Spock, who was usually even more of a stickler for protocol than she was. She gave the young captain credit for bravery, but she worried that sooner or later they would all end up suffering because of his recklessness.

She glanced over her shoulder at Sulu, who sat in the

command chair. *Speaking of recklessness.* The helmsman had returned to duty looking like a walking corpse. He had half limped, half staggered onto the bridge and presented himself to Spock as "fit for duty." Uhura had expected Spock to have medics escort Sulu back to sickbay, but instead he had said, "Mister Sulu, you have the conn," and then he left the bridge for one final conference with the captain.

So much male posturing, Uhura thought with a small frown. *You can practically smell the testosterone on this ship.*

Needing a break from the constant stream of status updates and damage reports, Uhura ran a quick check of automated operations she had kept running on her console. Local subspace comm frequencies remained clear, which suggested there were no other starships in the vicinity. Various radio frequencies on Akiron had started to go dead, giving up their bandwidth to the ever-present static of cosmic background radiation. *That's not a good sign. It means the Kathikar are losing ground to the wights. They don't have much time left.*

Then she saw that her decryption program had finished unraveling the comm signals she had intercepted from Sarek and his aide, L'Nel. She skimmed through both of them, noting key details. The first transmission had been a conversation between Sarek and Admiral Deigaro; as the captain had suspected, Sarek had enlisted Deigaro's support in terminating the *Enterprise*'s mission to Akiron.

The second conversation had been initiated by L'Nel. She had contacted a Vulcan adept on Deneva to demand documentation of some kind of ancient ritual. It had been a tense exchange, and the gist of it seemed to be that the ceremony posed serious risks to its practitioner and its subject. Uhura knew enough about the Vulcan language to equate the word *katra* with the concept of a soul, but she was unfamiliar with the notion of *katric* arks or the specifics of the *fal-tor-pan*. Instead, the detail that had specifically caught her attention had been L'Nel's naked contempt for Uhura herself and for her relationship with Spock.

An internal hail lit up on Uhura's console, and she recognized the command code linked to it as Spock's. *Speak of the devil,* she mused as she opened the channel. "Bridge, this is Uhura."

Spock's tone was urgent. *"Have Sarek and his staff left the* Enterprise *yet?"*

She checked the latest mission-status report and blinked in surprise: not only was the shuttle still aboard, its pilot was issuing his third urgent summons for both L'Nel and Ambassador Sarek, neither of whom had reported to the shuttle or even contacted it to request a postponed departure. "No," Uhura said. "Their shuttle's still in its docking slip." Her answer was met by a long silence from Spock. She refreshed the status screen, hoping to see some change, but it remained the same.

What are they waiting for? She imagined the ambassador stowing away on the *Enterprise*, concocting some new scheme to undermine the captain. As for L'Nel, who knew what her obsessive interest in Spock might lead her to do?

Finally, Spock said, *"I need to ask a favor of you."*

"I'm not exactly in the mood to be granting you favors right now."

"Please, Nyota." Spock's use of Uhura's given name suggested this was a personal matter rather than an official one. *"It is important."*

Uhura suppressed her lingering anger from her most recent argument with Spock. "What is it?"

"I need you to make sure my father gets on that shuttle."

"Fine, I'll keep an eye on the shuttle's status until—"

"No. I want you to go to his quarters, find him, and take him to the shuttle."

She felt a new surge of fury. *"What?* No, Spock! That's not my job—this is why we have a security division."

"Nyota, my father is my only living relative—he and I are all that remain of our family. You have proved more than once that you can stand up to him. I need you to do it now, for his safety. And for me."

"Dammit, Spock! My place is on the *bridge*."

"There are many officers on the Enterprise *who I trust to monitor comm traffic. There is only one to whom I would entrust my father's life. Please, Nyota."*

Uhura sighed. "I'm on my way now."

"Thank you."

"Uhura out." She closed the channel, got up from her chair, and walked over to Ensign Megan Nesmith, who served as a relief communications officer. "Megan, I need you to take over at my station."

Nesmith looked up and brushed a lock of her dark hair from her face. "Why? Is something wrong?"

"No. At least, no more than usual. I'm needed belowdecks. Shouldn't be more than a few minutes, I promise."

"All right." Nesmith stood up and followed Uhura to the main communications console. She looked at Sulu. "Shouldn't we tell him first?"

Uhura gave the ensign a reassuring pat on the shoulder. "No, Hikaru has enough on his mind right now—like not passing out."

Spock stood near the back of the transporter room, behind the transparent safety partition, and watched Captain Kirk don a backpack that contained Mister Scott's miniaturized but still bulky—and no doubt heavy—subspace-pulse generator. The chief engineer was checking the straps on the pack and the settings on the device while the captain familiarized himself with the modified phaser rifle.

Kirk asked, "How many shots did you say this thing has in it?"

"A few dozen," Scott said, tightening the last loose strap on the pack. "Hard to be more precise since we've never tested a gray-dilithium weapon before."

"First time for everything." Kirk permitted himself an anxious grimace. He looked at his first officer. "Any last-second advice, Spock?"

"Send someone else to deploy the pulse weapon."

Kirk walked toward the transporter pads. "I'll take that under advisement." He grunted as he stepped up onto the platform. "Scotty, what's this thing made of, lead? I have to hunch forward just to keep from falling backward."

"You've got a miniature warp coil and matter/antimatter core on your back. We made it as light as we could. By the way, try not to bump it."

He cast a suspicious stare at the engineer. "Why not?"

"We cut most of the weight by yanking out the safety features."

"Great. Good thing we left all our gear behind when we beamed out of the mines. At least I don't have to haul rappelling gear and subspace boosters on top of all this. Have we confirmed that the boosters are still working?"

Scott nodded. "Aye, sir. Just pinged 'em. Good to go."

"Right. I'll maintain an open channel. Set the beam-down coordinates as close as possible to the entrance of the dilithium mine."

Spock stepped forward. "Belay that order, Mister Scott." To Kirk he added, "Captain, duty requires me to volunteer once again to take your place."

"No, it doesn't, Spock—but nice try."

Scott leaned sideways and poked his head around the partition. "Don't worry, Spock. These gizmos are top-notch, he'll be fine!"

"I admit that I harbor doubts regarding the efficacy of these weapons. However, I consider the greater danger to be one of simple numbers. You are only one man, Captain, with limited personal armament. The mines are infested with tens of thousands of wights. Even if your rifle had an infinite power supply, it is highly unlikely that you would be able to defend yourself from that many attackers at once. The wights will swarm and smother you long before you reach the intended deployment coordinates for the pulse bomb."

Kirk flashed a devilish smile. "Not necessarily." He nodded at Scott.

"Aye," the engineer said as Spock turned to look at him. "I had the same thought you did, Mister Spock—so I cooked up a wee distraction for the wights."

More concerned now than he had been before, Spock replied, "Dare I ask what manner of 'distraction' you've prepared?"

"A lure," Kirk said. "We'll use the *Enterprise* as bait."

"Precisely," Scott said. "The beasties like dilithium, and now we know their favorite energy frequencies. We'll use the ship's main sensor dish to send out a concentrated beam of signals we know they like. If I'm right, they'll swarm and follow the beam all the way back to its source—us."

Arching an eyebrow, Spock asked, "And if they do not take the bait?"

"Then I'm a dead man," Kirk said.

"And if the wights do take the bait . . . ?"

"In that case," Scott replied, "we can expect an attack on the ship that'll make the last one look like a spring cotillion."

Spock regarded the captain through narrowed eyes. "With all due respect, sir, your plan leaves much to be desired."

"We play the cards we're dealt, Spock. If you have a better idea that can be ready to go in the next sixty seconds, now's the time."

To Spock's profound regret, he had no superior alternative to the captain's plan. "I remain unconvinced that you are the best person to execute this mission. Why not send a security officer with tactical training into the mines?"

"We've been over this, Spock. My ship, my mess, my responsibility."

"So you have said. And yet I remain unconvinced."

"I really don't have time to debate this with you, Spock."

"Captain, if you are undertaking this mission for irrational reasons—"

Kirk cut off Spock's protest with a raised hand. "You're still paranoid that Gveter-ren planted some kind of posthypnotic suggestion in my head?"

"Not specifically. But you seem to have invested his opinion with a disproportionate measure of your trust."

The captain frowned as he stepped down off the transporter pad to stand in front of Spock. In a confidential tone, he said, "You think I've lost it, right? That I've bought into some kind of messiah fantasy, or been mind-controlled by some alien conspiracy?" He reached out with his right hand and clasped Spock's arm in a friendly way. "I'm fine, Spock. I'm not crazy. I'm doing this because it's the right thing to do." Perhaps sensing Spock's continued resistance, he added, "And yeah, I could send someone else in my place—and maybe if Starfleet had ordered this mission, I would. But on some level

I can *feel* that Gveter-ren was right—this is *my* mission, no one else's. I don't know if I believe what he said about me being 'a man of destiny,' but I know I have a job to do, Spock. And unless you plan on shooting me or relieving me of command, I'm going now." Kirk turned, stepped back up onto the platform, and positioned himself on one of the transporter pads.

Spock looked his captain in the eye. "Good luck, Jim."

Kirk smiled. "Thanks, Spock. Scotty—energize."

The chief engineer initiated the transport sequence, and in a swirl of light and a melodic rush of sound, the captain faded from sight.

29

Uhura arrived at the door to L'Nel's guest quarters and nearly walked face-first into it when it failed to open at her approach. She couldn't understand why the door would be locked. During a red alert, all doors were programmed to open for the ship's personnel in order to facilitate swift responses by damage-control teams, and to remain closed only to invaders or unauthorized persons.

She pressed the door's visitor signal once and waited impatiently while the red-alert siren wailed from overhead speakers and echoed through the corridors. *Come on,* she fumed, willing L'Nel to answer the door. After several seconds without a response, Uhura keyed her command code into the door's control panel and overrode the lock. The door hissed open, and she stepped inside the guest quarters, which were dimly lit, hot, and arid. With her second step over the threshold she felt the change in the artificial gravity beneath her feet; the room had been set to simulate the heavier gravity of Vulcan.

After taking a few wary steps forward, Uhura heard the door close behind her. It took a moment for her eyes to adjust to the faint red illumination and deep shadows that surrounded her. Then she discerned a feminine shape kneeling at the far end of the room, a weak silhouette by feeble candlelight. Mustering her courage, Uhura said, "Time's up, L'Nel. You and Sarek need to get on the evac shuttle."

Without turning to look at Uhura, L'Nel answered in a soft monotone, "I am not leaving, Lieutenant. Exit my quarters at once."

"Not until I find Sarek. He's not in his quarters. According to the ship's computer, he's in *yours*." Uhura stalked toward L'Nel. "I promised Spock I'd get his father on that shuttle, so if you're hiding him, tell me now." She stood behind the Vulcan woman, who continued to kneel in front of a makeshift altar, apparently meditating over an ancient baked-clay urn. The air was thick with fragrances of citrus and floral incense, and the candles' flames made it possible for Uhura to see the tenuous haze of smoke lingering around L'Nel. "Don't play games with me, L'Nel. I know you're hatching a scheme involving Spock and some kind of ancient ritual. I'm here to tell you it's over. Whatever you were planning, it stops now. So quit stalling and bring me to Ambassador Sarek."

L'Nel opened her eyes, stood, and turned her head to face Uhura. "Very well."

Then came a blur and a white flash of pain as a vicious

backhand strike sent Uhura sprawling and tumbling across the deck. She rolled to a halt against a chair, stunned and unable to focus on anything except the horrible, dull throbbing of her left cheek, where L'Nel's blow had made contact.

Footsteps drew near. Blinking to overcome the pain, Uhura saw another figure in the next room of the guest suite—it was Ambassador Sarek, lying unconscious on the deck. Realizing that whatever was going on had already spiraled out of control, Uhura sprang to her feet and scrambled away from L'Nel.

The Vulcan woman lunged at Uhura, who reacted by instinct, her Starfleet self-defense training taking over. Her arms snapped up to block one knifing blow and deflect an alarmingly fast punch. She tried to counterattack, but L'Nel swatted aside Uhura's kicks and punches with ease.

A snap-kick caught Uhura in the gut and sent her falling backward. She landed hard on a low table, which broke apart beneath her. She felt splinters of its top stab through her uniform into her back. As she tried to roll clear of the debris and get up, she felt L'Nel grab the back of her uniform. A moment later Uhura was airborne, tossed like a child's rag doll against the bulkhead. Her vision purpled as she made impact and dropped like deadweight to the deck.

"Pathetic," L'Nel said, prowling forward, her steps crunching on the table debris. "Slow and weak. In thrall to your emotions. What does Spock see in you?"

Uhura opened her mouth to respond, but as her lips parted she was rendered speechless by an outpouring of blood. L'Nel sprang forward and kicked Uhura in the ribs. A few of them cracked. Uhura cried out, then bit down on her pain.

L'Nel grabbed Uhura's ponytail, twisted it around her hand, and dragged her across the deck toward the room where Sarek lay. All Uhura could do was scream in agony and crawl as quickly as she could to keep up with L'Nel and reduce the strain on her scalp. Tears streamed from Uhura's eyes as L'Nel hurled her into the room. Uhura fell beside the battered, unconscious Sarek.

L'Nel stalked into the room, her visage emotionless but menacing. "It is not logical for Spock to choose one such as you. His people need him, and he needs a woman who can understand his needs as a Vulcan man."

Uhura spat blood at L'Nel's feet. "And you think that's *you*? Think again."

"Humans are so arrogant. You take what you want, and you never ask if it belongs to someone else: worlds, technologies, *mates*." She nodded at Sarek. "You seduce our best and our brightest with your irrational ways—with your promises that we can reap infinite rewards without making any sacrifices." She loomed over Uhura. "But sacrifice is *always* necessary."

Uhura tried to sweep L'Nel's legs out from under her with a scissor kick, but the Vulcan adroitly dodged the attack and then seized Uhura by her throat. "Predictable and clumsy." L'Nel tightened her grip. "You are not worthy to be the mate of a Vulcan man."

Uhura clawed at the woman's hands and arms to no avail. L'Nel plucked the communicator from the waist of Uhura's uniform, dropped it to the deck, and crushed it with a stomp of her foot. Then she lifted Uhura several inches off the deck. Desperate, Uhura punched at L'Nel's face. The Vulcan's head snapped from side to side with the force of the blows, but otherwise she seemed unaffected. L'Nel punched Uhura in the stomach and flung her at the nearest bulkhead.

As Uhura made impact, she thought she heard thunder.

T'Pring advanced on the stunned Lieutenant Uhura, ready to break the human woman's neck with a single sharp twist, when the ship lurched and deep concussions echoed through its hull. Struggling to keep her balance on the heaving deck, T'Pring watched loose objects tumble from shelves and shatter at her feet.

The katric *ark!*

T'Pring hurried back to the main room. Sarek's and Uhura's executions would have to wait. For now, all that mattered was the ark. Soon enough, Spock's body would belong to Stonn—and then Sarek and the human woman would die.

30

Kirk materialized on the rocky slope between the steaming mud plains and the plateau that led to the entrance of the dilithium mine. Through the darkness, he could see the tops of several abandoned large vehicles and massive ore-refining machines past the top of the slope ahead of him. He trudged forward, struggling to overcome Akiron's slightly stronger gravity and the region's muggy, sulfur-rich atmosphere. The weight on his back grew more oppressive with each forced uphill stride.

Heavy beads of sweat cascaded down his back as he pushed onward. By the time he reached the plateau at the top of the slope, his hair was wet with perspiration, the muscles in his thighs and calves ached, and every breath felt like a struggle. *Can't let up.* He began jogging past the scores of Kathikar dead who lay on the gravel. As he neared the fissure in the mountainside, he pulled his communicator from his belt and flipped open its cover with a flick of his wrist.

"Kirk to *Enterprise*," he said, his voice shaken by his running steps.

"Spock here, Captain."

"I'm nearing the mine's entrance now." Kirk cast wary glances in anticipation of an attack. "Have Scotty stand by to trigger the lure on my mark."

"The main deflector is charged and ready."

As he passed through the crooked opening in the mountain's face, Kirk stepped carefully over the small subspace signal booster on the ground. Even though he was moving quickly, he still found himself awed by the spectacle of the hollowed-out mountain peak and nauseated by the stench of ammonia, carbon fuels, and the odors of things burned or rotting. He reached the edge of the great pit and found the landing party's rappelling lines still in place, as he'd hoped.

Working quickly, Kirk gathered up several meters of slack from one of the lines and threaded it into the rappelling loops on his pack's five-point harness. He was about to inch his way over the edge when he felt a cold breeze pass over him.

He lifted his rifle as he pivoted in a full turn, and he pulled the trigger the moment he saw the stirring of shadows in the darkness. A beam of dark green energy shot from his rifle. It dissipated three wights on contact, scattering their smoky forms in a viridescent blaze. Twisting back and forth in search of another threat, Kirk froze as a gust of frigid air bellowed up from the yawning pit.

He slung his rifle and pulled out his communicator. "Kirk to *Enterprise*—fire up the lure! Now!" The next several seconds felt like forever as he waited to see what would happen next. Nothing in the cavern seemed to change—but then a legion of wights raced past him, straight up, obscuring the mountain's peak. Kirk scrambled away from the pit and took cover behind a boulder while he watched the wights surge upward like a black eruption.

All at once, it was over, and the thunder-rush of cold shadows vanished through the mountain's peak. Checking to make sure his communicator was still functioning, Kirk said, "Spock, you with me?"

"Affirmative, Captain. We have detected an approaching mass of wights."

"That's an understatement, Spock. You've got an army of those things coming at you. Do whatever you have to do, but protect my ship. Understood?"

"Acknowledged. Spock out."

The channel closed, and Kirk tucked his communicator back on his belt. Figuring that speed was his best bet for reaching the bottom of the mine shaft alive, he grabbed hold of the rappelling line, backed up to the edge, and pushed off. He made the fastest descent he could without letting himself slip into free fall. *If those things come after me now, I'm screwed.* He forced himself not to focus on worst-case scenarios. *Just get to the bottom.*

Whether by luck or by providence he reached the bottom of the shaft, and then he sprinted down the machine-drilled tunnel, whose chemical safety lamps continued to burn with a soft orange glow. Another telltale breath of chilled air washed over him, and he raised his rifle seconds before a pair of deadly shades emerged from the rocky ceiling. He snapped off two quick shots and dispersed the wights in brilliant emerald flashes. "So far, so good," he muttered, in a halfhearted attempt to bolster his courage as he pressed ahead, deeper into the darkness.

At the end of the machine-cut passageway, Kirk arrived at the natural gorge that spewed sulfuric fumes from the planet's fiery bowels, and the narrow rock bridge that traversed it to a cliff face honeycombed with caves. He moved on a straight path for the bridge—and then the ground quaked and knocked him onto his back. The impact sent a jolt of fear through him as he recalled Scotty's warning not to jostle the ponderous bomb. Lying supine and listening to the planet rumble, Kirk was grateful that at least he hadn't just exploded.

Then he heard the sharp crack of breaking stone, and suddenly he wasn't grateful anymore. He rolled over onto his stomach and pushed himself up onto his feet. Standing up on the trembling ground was hard enough; walking was a risk; running was all but impossible. But as Kirk had feared, the rock bridge was fracturing. Chunks of it were calving off into the abyss, leaving sections barely the width of a balance beam. Charging ahead onto the disintegrating bridge, Kirk wished he hadn't needed to haul the cumbersome bomb on his back.

He was halfway across the bridge when it started crumbling under his feet. Suspecting that sections of it were falling away behind him, Kirk made a point of not looking back. He had nearly reached the far side of the bridge when several meters of the path ahead of him broke apart. He leaped forward even as the ground beneath him turned to dust. If he'd been traveling light in normal gravity, it would have been an easy running broad jump to solid ground.

Instead his chest slammed against the rough edge of broken rock, and his hands clawed for purchase as he started sliding backward into the chasm. Seconds later he was dangling by his fingertips from the precipice. Against his better judgment, he stole a look down. All he saw was darkness. Wherever the pit beneath him ended, it was too far down for him to see. Above him, slabs of rock broke free of the cliff and smashed down like ten-ton hammers. The mouths of several cave openings began to vanish as the passages behind them collapsed.

Probing carefully with his foot, Kirk found a toehold and pushed himself upward. Fighting for every inch of ground, he got one hand back up over the edge of the bridge, then an elbow. His other hand followed. The pack felt as if it were growing heavier with each passing moment, but Kirk refused to give in to its inexorable pull. *I'm not gonna die here. Not like this.*

With both arms up on the bridge, salvation seemed so close, but he just couldn't heave himself and his burden any higher. He'd hit his limit.

Then a massive quake shook the cavern, and a fracture formed along the base of the cliff wall. As the ground near the cliff sank at a sharp angle, it lifted the remaining stub of the bridge—and suddenly Kirk found himself clinging to a small peak and staring at a downhill slope. Knowing a gift from the fates if ever he saw one, he scrambled up and over the edge, slid down the slope, and at the last second leaped clear to solid ground. He landed hard, but forced himself to get up and run.

He sprinted down the tunnel that led to the wights' cavern. Seconds later, a cave-in sealed the path behind him. *Less than two hundred fifty meters to ground zero. Almost there. Just keep going.*

It wasn't like Kirk to embrace pessimism, but as he listened to the rumbling echoes of the Underdark, he couldn't help but harbor a fearful thought: if a cave-in had blocked the route to his extraction point, this was going to be a one-way trip.

Spock circled the bridge to confirm that the crew's preparations for the coming battle were nearly complete. He nodded at Sulu as he took his place in the center seat. "Status report."

"Holding position in high orbit above the dilithium mine. We climbed to maximum range for the transporter to delay the incoming wight attack for as long as possible."

Nodding once, Spock said, "Well done. Mister Chekov, damage report."

"Shields still offline. Warp drive still offline."

Turning toward the science console, Spock asked Ensign sh'Vetha, "Are the wights continuing to respond to our lure?"

"Aye, sir. Better than we expected, actually." She pressed buttons on her console and relayed a computer-enhanced visual representation of her findings to the main viewscreen. It showed a massive dark surge rising from the planet's surface. "It looks like every wight in range of the signal is coming right at us. Time to intercept, three minutes."

Chekov grimaced and looked at Sulu. "Without shields, they'll swarm us." Looking back at Spock, he added, "We'll be sitting ducks."

Sulu swiveled his chair and asked Spock, "Should I plot an escape course to take us out of orbit? Just in case, I mean."

"Negative, Lieutenant. Hold your course."

"But if the wights reach us while our shields are down—"

"You have your orders, Lieutenant." Spock opened a channel to the engine room. "Bridge to Mister Scott. How long until shields are restored?"

Scott sounded flustered as he replied, *"At least twenty minutes!"*

"You have less than three minutes until the next wight assault."

"Best I can give you is quarter-power shields for five minutes, but after that we'll be a bloody all-you-can-eat buffet."

Chekov asked Spock, "Will quarter-power shields hold off the wights?"

"Perhaps—if we set their phase harmonics to match the frequency in the gray-dilithium weapon."

"Perfect. Any idea how I'm supposed to do that?"

"I suggest you improvise, Mister Scott. Bridge out."

The captain's voice squawked from the overhead speaker: *"Kirk to* Enterprise! *Do you read me, Spock?"*

"Affirmative, Captain. What is your status?"

"Almost at the drop zone. How's my ship?"

"Bracing for the next wight attack. Our best estimate is that we can hold our position for up to five minutes. We—" He was interrupted by the screeching of phaser fire over the channel. "Captain, are you okay?"

Sounding winded, Kirk replied, *"Still here, Spock."* More phaser shots. *"I've got a bit more company down here than I expected!"*

"We find ourselves in much the same predicament." Spock watched the updates on the main viewer as the ship's sensors tracked the imminent wight onslaught. "Lowering the shields to beam you up will pose a serious risk."

A few more short bursts of phaser fire preceded Kirk's reply. *"The pulse effect won't hurt me. Keep the shields up 'til I set off the bomb."*

"Captain, the pulse itself might not be harmful, but the shock wave it creates will almost certainly trigger widespread cave-ins. If those collapses obstruct the beam-out pathway, we will be unable—"

"Spock, I'm giving you an order: Keep the shields up until after I set off the bomb. Once you're in the clear, beam me up as fast as you can."

"And if you fail to trigger the device before our shields collapse?"

"Then you break orbit and leave me behind, Spock."

With great reluctance, Spock replied, "Acknowledged."

"Keep this channel open. I'm heading for the target."

Although Spock sometimes found his commanding officer's behavior less than completely rational, he had to admit that he felt a grudging respect for the man's valor and willingness to sacrifice himself for his ship and crew.

"Mister Chekov," Spock said, "has Ambassador Sarek's shuttle departed?"

"No, sir. The pilot says they are still waiting for two passengers."

"Order the pilot to lift off immediately."

Chekov directed a worried look at Spock. "Are you sure, sir?"

"If they do not leave the ship now, they will not reach safe distance before the wights arrive. This is a priority directive: order the shuttle to launch now."

"Aye, sir." Chekov relayed the orders via his console. Sotto voce, he added, "And what about the two passengers still on board the *Enterprise*?"

"There is nothing more we can do for them. We must save whom we can. Anyone still aboard this ship thirty seconds from now will have to take their chances with us."

31

Kirk charged out of the passage and into the wights' cavern, and immediately he was engulfed by pitch darkness and numbing cold. *The last mile is always the longest,* he thought, recalling a phrase his stepfather had been prone to utter.

He squeezed the trigger of his rifle a few times, laying down a field of suppressive fire to clear the path ahead of him. His only illumination came from the tiny tactical light attached to the barrel of his weapon; its narrow beam seemed overmatched by the great well of blackness into which Kirk had descended.

Just keep moving. He jogged forward. *Almost there.* Something rushed toward him from his left, a rippling of one shadow over another. Kirk pivoted and fired, dispersing another wight in a green blaze.

His footsteps echoed seemingly without end in the warren of caves hidden by the darkness, and his breaths were rushed and heavy, the product of exhaustion and fear. Atonal cries of wind resounded in the permanent night of the Underdark, like dogs howling a hymn out of key. Even as Kirk's imagination tried to paint pictures of what might be lurking beyond his sight, he kept his eyes on the ground in front of him, watching his step and the location tracker mounted on his rifle.

Ten meters to target. He sidestepped around a small crater roiling with black vapors. *Five meters and closing . . .*

He barely stopped in time to avoid tumbling headfirst over the edge of the great pit in the center of the wights' cavern. Arms windmilling to recover his balance, he stumbled backward, fell, and landed on his butt. *Touchdown!* He cracked a nervous smile as he shrugged off his backpack and opened it.

"Kirk to *Enterprise*," he said, trusting that the open channel was still being received. "I've reached the deployment zone. Priming the weapon now."

Spock replied, *"Acknowledged, Captain. The wights have begun their assault on the ship, and the shields are failing rapidly."*

"I hear you, Spock. I'm workin' as fast as I can." Kirk pulled the pulse bomb free of the pack and turned its control interface toward himself. He began keying in the final sequence to arm the device. When he tried to program in the five-minute delay, however, the display flickered and began showing gibberish.

A churning of darkness over shadows surrounded Kirk. He raised his rifle and harried the roiling shades with several shots while pivoting in a tight circle. Squinting against the nonstop emerald flashes erupting around him, he shouted, "Scotty, you listening? We've got a problem down here!"

"What sort of problem?" asked the chief engineer.

Kirk peppered the darkness with more defensive fire. "The countdown timer's busted! Must've been banged up on my way down. How do I fix it?" The status bar for the rifle's power cell dwindled at a fearsome rate.

"Well, if you've got a dynospanner handy—"

"Dammit, Scotty, I've got my hands full down here!" Another barrage yielded more lime-colored flares. "Isn't there a button I can push or something?"

Hesitantly, Scott replied, *"Well, you could try pressing the yellow button and the red button at the same time—"*

"That's what I'm saying." Kirk let go of his rifle. It fell to his side thanks to its strap, which was slung across his torso. He located the red and yellow buttons on the bomb's interface and held them down simultaneously. A moment later the flickering gibberish ceased and the screen read ARMED.

"That did it." Kirk lifted his rifle and turned to check behind him. "How do I reset the timer?"

"You don't."

"Come again?"

"You just bypassed the faulty circuit by setting the weapon to its default mode—detonation on impact."

Kirk rolled his eyes and bit down on his rising tide of anger. Keeping his vigil against the darkness, he grumbled, "You've gotta be *kidding* me."

"Afraid not, skipper. The good news is the pit behind you is

seven-point-four kilometers deep. If you can toss our little pres-
ent at least five meters from the edge, it ought to take at least two
minutes to make impact."

"I'll have two minutes to reach the extraction point? That's
the *good* news?"

"The alternative is manual detonation."

Kirk chortled in a sudden fit of gallows humor. "You know
that if I live, you'll pay for this, don't you, Scotty?"

"Aye, sir. In fact, I'm counting on it."

Spock held the armrests of the command chair as the wights'
attack shook the *Enterprise* from bow to stern. The irregular
percussion of their assaults on the ship's shields crackled the
comm channel with static and threatened to drown out what
little of the captain's signal actually broke through the interference.

At the forward console, Chekov looked across at Sulu and
asked, "Did I just hear Mister Scott tell the keptin to use *man-*
ual detonation?"

"No," Spock interjected, "he said that was the captain's
alternative to using the device's detonation-on-impact protocol." He opened an all-call channel. "Mister Scott," he said, his
voice reverberating from the overhead speaker on the bridge
and from the corridor outside, "report to the transporter room
immediately."

Scott replied over the comm, *"Already on my way, sir!"*

The lights flickered and went dark for a few seconds, and the consoles followed. As the bridge's command systems stuttered back to life, Chekov reported, "Shields down to ten percent, sir."

Sulu muttered, "Man, this is gonna be close."

Turning toward the communications console, Spock said, "Hail the ambassador's shuttle and confirm it is safely away."

"Aye, sir," Ensign Nesmith replied, opening the channel. As she conversed on a secure frequency with the shuttle's pilot, Spock got up and walked back to stand behind her shoulder. When she finished, she closed the channel, looked up, and said, "The shuttle confirms it's away and clear, sir."

Lowering his voice, Spock asked, "Ensign, has Lieutenant Uhura checked in regarding her search for Ambassador Sarek?"

"Not yet," Nesmith said.

Concern took root in Spock's mind. He reached past the young woman and called up activity logs from Uhura's console, reviewing all the files and tasks she had been working on immediately prior to her departure from the bridge.

Uhura had completed her analysis of Sarek's clandestine communication with Admiral Deigaro at Starfleet Command, the content of which was exactly as the captain and Spock had suspected. Another intercepted signal, however, caught Spock by surprise. He reviewed Uhura's annotations regarding L'Nel's subspace conversation with a Vulcan adept named Tokor. One term leaped out and filled Spock with alarm: L'Nel's invocation of the archaic ritual known as *fal-tor-pan*.

L'Nel must be mad if she plans to attempt such a ritual. Some-

one so disturbed would be capable of nearly anything. If Nyota tries to confront her, she will be in grave danger.

"Where is Lieutenant Uhura now?"

The ensign keyed some commands into her console and frowned. "I don't know, sir. I can't get a lock on her communicator."

"Scan the ambassador's guest quarters."

Nesmith called up an internal scan. "Empty, sir."

"Check his aide's quarters."

The ensign ran another internal sensor sweep. "Three life-forms: two Vulcan, one human."

Spock turned and moved at a quick step toward the exit. "Mister Sulu, you have the conn." Without waiting for the helmsman to confirm the order, Spock left the bridge and ran down the corridor to the nearest turbolift.

He pulled his communicator from his belt and flipped it open, speaking and sprinting at the same time. "Spock to security: meet me at guest quarters nine twenty-two alpha, immediately."

32

The hardest part of throwing the pulse bomb five meters past the edge of the pit, Kirk realized, would be not hurling himself in with it by accident. The bomb had been burdensome enough when loaded inside the pack, which had spread out the device's weight across his shoulders and hips. In his hands, it felt far heavier. Akiron's slightly higher gravity wasn't helping, either.

Kirk backed away from the pit, struggling to gauge how long a running start he would need in order to build the momentum to throw the bomb far enough to maximize its falling time. He took a few lumbering steps forward and realized a running start would be useless; a swinging motion was what he'd need.

Have to do this like a trapeze artist. He inched up to the pit's edge. *Gotta build up momentum with each swing.* He planted his feet, bent at the knees, and heaved the bomb away from the pit, then toward it. He continued the swinging motion, struggling to hang on to the device as the arc of his swing grew. When he reached the point where one more backswing might tear his arms from their sockets, he gave a final forward heave and released the bomb.

It soared on a shallow trajectory, tumbling slowly, then plummeted straight down into the abyssal depths, vanishing from Kirk's sight in the blink of an eye. He didn't know whether his toss had cleared five meters of lateral distance, but he knew he didn't want to stand there waiting to find out. With his rifle braced against his shoulder, Kirk sprinted away from the pit, dodging at a full run between vapor-spewing craters, following the path Spock had plotted for him.

He fired a bolt of green energy into one small crater and then hurdled over it, desperate to shave seconds off his exit. More shadows pressed in from all sides, and the floor started to come alive. Kirk set his rifle to emit a wide beam and started firing a steady barrage ahead of him, blanketing the ground and cutting a swath through the mass of wights threatening to seize him in an icy embrace.

The cavern bloomed with surges of green fire as wights dispersed, but each shot from Kirk's rifle seemed less potent than the one before. Its power was dwindling quickly and was all but depleted by the time he reached the labyrinth of passages that led to the extraction point. He decoupled the weapon's safety circuit and triggered a feedback loop in its prefire chamber. It emitted a low droning sound that grew louder and pitched upward to a piercing shriek. Kirk hurled his rifle backward and kept running.

He'd rounded two more bends in the tunnel when a massive explosion sent a tremor through the ground and flooded the subterranean maze with emerald light.

That oughta buy me a few seconds.

There was light ahead—not much, barely a glint of blue moonlight off fractured crystal, but enough that Kirk knew he was almost at the extraction point.

A crash of thunder rocked the ground and sent Kirk sprawling. Deep rumblings continued for several seconds, each bleeding into the next, as caves and tunnels imploded. Kirk pushed himself to his feet and scrambled out into the deep, narrow stone funnel that the *Enterprise*'s phasers had carved into Akiron's surface. Looking back anxiously for signs of pursuing wights, he pulled out his communicator and sent a recall signal. "Kirk to *Enterprise*, beam me up!"

Scott replied, *"Just a few more seconds, Cap'n! We have to wait for the pulse to disperse the wights that are knockin' on our door up here."*

Massive torrents of rock and dirt began breaking loose from the sides of the funnel above Kirk, and the passageway behind him caved in with such force that the shattered rocks and dirt moved like a fluid, rushing toward him.

"Time's a factor, Scotty."

"Wights are breakin' up now, Captain! Dropping shields—"

Great slabs of granite tumbled like dice down the sides of the funnel, kicking up clouds of dust that blotted out the distant sky and, with it, Kirk's hope of leaving the Underdark alive.

Scott exclaimed, *"Transporter lock in three . . . two."*

Darkness crashed down like a hammer of the gods, and all Kirk heard was the roar of the avalanche.

Spock darted inside L'Nel's quarters, ducking through the half-open doorway as the portal moved aside to let him pass. He was met by the familiar comforts of Vulcan habitation— low light, little humidity, higher gravity, warmer air. A haze of incense evoked buried memories—of the temple at Mount Seleya, of ancient rituals and childhood promises, of a world taken for granted until it was gone.

An impact shook the *Enterprise*, and the lights flickered and died in the corridor behind him. A crimson flash in the overhead betrayed the ignition of a plasma fire inside the guest quarters, most likely triggered by overloads in the ship's defensive grid. As Spock moved farther inside the room, the door slid closed and the red alert whooped.

Looking around, he saw candles burning but no sign of L'Nel—and then he turned and glimpsed two bodies lying on the deck in the next room. He rushed to them and saw they were his father and Uhura. Both appeared to have been severely beaten—they had swollen contusions and bloody abrasions on their faces, as well as other indications of blunt-force trauma. He checked his father first, pressing a finger to Sarek's throat in search of a pulse; it was weak but steady. Then Spock pivoted toward Uhura and touched her throat; he was relieved to find her pulse strong, despite her grievous injuries.

The room flared with blue light from a phaser beam that hit Spock in the back, and its high-pitched screech reverberated inside the close confines of the guest cabin. Spock's body tensed. His back arched, and his elbows pulled in against his ribs as he twisted and fell to his knees, still conscious but barely able to move.

L'Nel padded on bare feet into the compartment. She held her phaser in a steady grip and aimed squarely at Spock's chest. "I did not expect you to come to me so soon, but now that you have, I will not waste the opportunity."

"I do not understand." Spock forced words through his clenched jaw. "Why are you doing this, L'Nel?"

Circling him, L'Nel kept her gaze and her phaser fixed on Spock's chest. "My reasons are my own. But you brought this on yourself, by turning your back on your people at the moment when they need you most."

"I have done no such thing."

She sprang forward and kicked him in the gut. Pain bloomed in his abdomen as bile surged into his mouth. "Liar," she spat with a wrathful tone unbecoming a Vulcan. "Everyone sees! Everyone knows!"

Doubled over, Spock croaked, "Knows what?"

L'Nel nodded at Uhura. "Of your affair with that human whore!"

All of Spock's hard-won emotional control vanished, abandoning him to his rage, to his fury in defense of the woman he loved. As a child, he had been moved to violence in his mother's name; as a man, he would not suffer threats or slurs against Nyota. He fixed his murderous glare on L'Nel, and his voice took on a terrifying rasp. "You will not slander her—or I will kill you."

"Bold words from a man who cannot even stand." L'Nel adjusted her phaser's power setting, turned, and aimed at the controls for the door to her quarters. With a single, full-power shot she blasted the panel into sparking slag. After another adjustment to the phaser's power setting, she used it to begin welding the door to the edges of its threshold. "The *fal-tor-pan* will take some time, and I would prefer not to be disturbed until it is finished."

Watching her fuse the door into its tracks, Spock said, "You will not get away with this, L'Nel. That will not hold off my shipmates forever."

"I need only a few more minutes, Spock. After that, let them come. Another man's *katra* will live in your flesh and speak with your voice—and he will tell them whatever they need to hear."

"But Lieutenant Uhura and my father—"

"Will be dead. And for all practical purposes, so will you." She finished her sabotage of the door and pocketed her phaser. Moving quickly, she stepped past him, opened a drawer, and took from it a set of garments that resembled vestments once worn by the priests at Mount Seleya. L'Nel walked back to Spock, looked down, and said with contempt, "To think . . . I once consented to be your *wife*."

Before Spock could ask what she meant, she stomped on his face.

"The detonation in the mine has sealed the dimensional rift," Chekov reported. He turned and faced Sulu as he added, "The wights appear to have been dispelled—banished back to their own universe."

"Good," said Sulu, who clung desperately to the arms of the command chair to conceal the fact that he was barely able to function. "Helm, resume standard orbit. Lieutenant Nesmith, compile damage reports, all decks."

The communication officer confirmed the order with a nod, and then Chekov asked, "Secure from red alert, sir?"

"Not until we hear from Mister Spock or the captain." As far as Sulu was concerned, the crisis wasn't resolved until one of the ship's two most senior officers said so. He thumbed open a comm channel from his armrest. "Bridge to transporter room. Scotty, is the captain okay?"

Scott's response was fraught with tension. *I'll tell you in a minute!*

It wasn't supposed to be this bloody difficult! Scott had locked onto the captain's transport coordinates in what he'd thought was the blink of an eye, but by the time he'd started the beam-up sequence, the energy wave from the pulse bomb had turned all of Kirk's signal locks into an uglier hash than the one Scott's old aunt Patty had used to stuff her abominable haggis.

Every trick that Scott tried yielded nothing but more interference and less signal. *A few more of my bright ideas and there won't be anything left of the captain to save.*

He had one last trick up his figurative sleeve. Manipulating the transporter console's controls faster than he ever had before, he configured the system's annular confinement beam—a kind of energy tube that kept the signal from being scattered during the transport cycle—to work on an inverse harmonic of the pulse's wave frequency that the captain had unleashed against the wights.

All at once the interference dissipated, and he saw the captain's transport signal resolve into its normal pattern. Scott boosted the power past its rated maximum and initiated the process to shift Kirk from energy back to matter. A sparkling humanoid form appeared on the transporter pad, and Scott worked quickly to keep it stable and error free. Within the swirl of light and color, the familiar visage of Kirk took shape, and Scott flashed a grin of relief. Seconds later, the captain was solid and standing in front of him. "Welcome back, sir!"

Kirk blinked and shook his head, then he looked at Scott. "Was it just my imagination, or did that take longer than usual?"

"Aye," Scott admitted as the captain stepped down off the platform, "you gave me a wee scare for a minute or so, but I got you sorted, so no worries, eh?"

Slapping a hand on Scott's shoulder, Kirk smiled and said,

"Scotty, I just want to say . . . next time—don't cut it so damn close."

Scott's jubilant smile faded. "Aye, sir."

Kirk pulled off his tricorder and set it aside. "So what's the verdict? Did the bomb work or not?"

Scott nodded. "Aye, like a charm. Zapped those buggers back where they came from. And not a moment too soon—a few more seconds and they'd have been eating us for breakfast."

"Call today a victory for good timing, then." Kirk glanced at a nearby bulkhead, on which a ship's status panel was flashing crimson. "If the attack's over, why are we still at red alert?"

The chief engineer shrugged. "You'd have to ask Spock."

Kirk stepped over to the transporter console and opened a comm channel. "Kirk to bridge. Spock, report. Why are we still at red alert?"

"This is Sulu. I was waiting for you or Mister Spock to cancel the alert."

"Sulu?" Kirk gave Scott a confused look and then asked, "Where's Spock?"

"He went down to the VIP quarters to find Uhura."

As if on cue, an urgent-sounding announcement over the ship's PA echoed through the corridors: *"Security teams report to guest quarters nine twenty-two alpha—reports of phaser shots fired!"*

Kirk opened a small-arms locker behind the transporter console, grabbed a phaser, and left the transporter room at a full run.

33

Dazed and all but paralyzed from the neck down, Spock lay on his back and stared into the maniacal countenance of his father's aide, L'Nel. She was kneeling beside him, garbed in the robes of a priest, holding a *katric* ark in one hand and pressing the other against the side of his face as she forced a mind-meld upon him.

His lips parted, a trembling prelude to a feeble protest, but his mouth was dry and his tongue swollen. Not that it mattered—this woman was firmly in the grip of madness; she could no longer hear him, nor would she listen if she could.

He thought he heard voices shouting his name from the corridor, on the other side of the door L'Nel had phasered into an immobile barrier. They sounded muffled and distant, too muted for him to recognize, too far away to help him now.

"My mind to your mind." L'Nel's voice was a low chant, an

incantation backed up by the force of her psionic invasion of his innermost thoughts.

No! Spock tried in vain to marshal his telepathic defenses.

"Our thoughts are merging."

I reject you! My thoughts are my own. Despite Spock's passion, despite the vehemence of his silent resistance, L'Nel broke through his mental barriers with ease. Her thoughts flooded into his mind, washed through him like a cold wave of malice, merciless and unstoppable.

Then came the greatest horror, the revelation that filled Spock with dread. Once his attacker joined her thoughts to his, he saw her for who she really was.

T'Pring. Betrothed to him in a ceremony when they were only seven years old, she had stayed behind on Vulcan when Spock left to enroll in Starfleet Academy. He had not even seen her since their brief introduction at the Temple of Mount Seleya. Though he had been reminded many times that he would be expected to return to Vulcan to consummate his bond with T'Pring when his *Pon farr* began, Spock had disregarded such warnings. After all, once he obtained his Starfleet commission, he could hardly be compelled to honor a pledge of marriage that had been forced upon him during childhood. Sarek had sighed at Spock's reasoning. "You will understand only when the *Pon farr* comes," he had said.

Spock forced his dry, bitter-tasting mouth to form words. "T'Pring, please stop. I will honor our marriage bond or release you, as you wish."

"Your vow is irrelevant, as is your sanction." She continued breaking down his barriers and began plumbing his memories, forcing him to relive all his moments of torment and shame at the hands of other Vulcan children.

The emotional part of his mind wanted to lash out at her, to pummel her, throttle her. He raged at his impotent body—and only belatedly became aware of his degraded emotional control. "This is not right, T'Pring." He nearly choked on the words. "I see what you mean to do."

"It no longer matters. Cease your struggle and submit."

Spock felt his will crumbling. His strength was drained. All he wanted to do was sleep. He let his head loll to one side because it took too much effort to hold it steady and face T'Pring's unyielding stare.

Then he saw the bloodied face of his unconscious beloved, Nyota Uhura. A part of himself that he often denied and frequently denigrated, his human half, flared with defiance and strength.

He turned his head back toward T'Pring and focused his thoughts. *I will not roll over and die for one such as you.* He projected his thoughts through the mind-meld to T'Pring. *If you want my flesh, you will have to fight for it.*

She pushed her fingers harder against the side of his face. "Why persist when you know you will lose? Give yourself over, Spock. End this."

He hardened his stare. "Make me."

She laid siege to his mind and assaulted his psyche with images designed to provoke his emotions—only to discover too late the error of her tactics. Against a pure-blooded Vulcan, she could have turned his conscious and subconscious minds against each other with such an attack, but Spock was half human. Fueling his emotions weakened his Vulcan superego but strengthened his human id—which, as T'Pring learned to her detriment, was an all but inexhaustible wellspring of fury and darkness. It was amoral, illogical, boundless, and utterly beyond control.

Confronted with Spock's darker half, T'Pring recoiled.

"Surrender! It is the *logical* choice."

Unbowed, Spock unleashed his anger. "I assure you, T'Pring—it is *not*."

Kirk launched himself out of the turbolift as soon as the doors opened, and he was fairly certain he set some kind of speed record with his sprint to the door of the VIP guest quarters, where he nearly collided with a squad of burly security men.

"Someone start talking!" Kirk pointed at the door. "What the hell's going on in there, and why aren't you inside?"

A broad-shouldered lieutenant with a goatee replied, "The door's been welded shut from the inside. We tried forcing it, but it's solid."

"Okay, now what?" Kirk waited for a response, got none, and felt his temper rise. "Do you have a plan for getting in there or not?"

"We're working on it."

A trim and fresh-faced ensign added, "We might be able to

cut through the door or the bulkhead if we bring up a plasma torch from engineering."

"Do it," Kirk said. "What're you waiting for, an invitation?"

The huddle of security personnel dispersed, each of its members wearing a hangdog expression. The goateed lieutenant pulled out his communicator and began making a hushed request for someone to bring up a plasma torch. Kirk rolled his eyes. *If I wait for these clowns, Spock'll be dead by the time I get in there.*

He stepped away and pulled out his own communicator. "Kirk to Scott." Too impatient to wait for an answer, he added, "C'mon, Scotty, do you read me?"

"Aye, hold your horses."

"Lock on to my signal and beam me into the VIP guest quarters."

"What? Are you mad?"

"Scotty, just *do* it. It's gonna take these security goons twenty minutes to cut their way in, and I've got a hunch we don't have that kind of time."

"Tell them to wait, I can have you all inside in three—"

"Transporter. Now. That's an order."

"I don't think you appreciate how risky intraship beaming can be, Captain. One little fluctuation in the power grid and you could end up in a bulkhead."

Kirk found it difficult not to raise his voice. "Give me a break! We beamed across how many light-years onto this ship while it was moving at warp? Movin' me a few meters to the left oughta be a freakin' snap."

Scott turned defensive. *"Technically, it was your elderly Vulcan friend-who-shall-not-be-named who did the math on that little jump—I just came along for the ride. And it's not like he left me a step-by-step guide, did he?"*

"Are you saying you can't do this, Scotty? Because I can always go ask Chekov if he wants to take a stab at—"

"Hold on, now, no need to bring that gerbil into it."

"Time's a factor, Scotty."

"When isn't time a bloody factor?" Scott heaved a disgruntled sigh. *"Locking onto your signal now. Powerin' up the transporter."*

Kirk smiled. "Thanks, Scotty."

"Just don't blame me if you wind up part of the bloody furniture."

"I won't," Kirk lied. He flipped his communicator shut and braced himself for what he hoped would not prove to be a grave mistake.

No sooner had Kirk materialized inside the guest quarters than a sledgehammer punch snapped his head sideways and sent him reeling across the room. Blinded by the shock of impact, he tripped over a chair and crashed to the deck.

His phaser was kicked from his hand, and then he was picked up and thrown through the air. He slammed against a bulkhead and dropped to his knees.

Pushing himself up and back, Kirk looked over his shoulder to see who was beating the crap out of him. Sarek's aide

L'Nel stalked toward him. She snapped his phaser into pieces with her bare hands. He saw the Vulcan woman cock her arm; he didn't see the punch that followed, but he damn sure felt it. His lower lip split against his teeth, and he gagged on the sudden rush of blood inside his mouth.

Some small measure of Kirk's training asserted itself, and he lifted his arms to defend his head and face. Naturally, L'Nel's next blow was to his gut.

He was gasping and unable to breathe as L'Nel kneed him in the groin. She backhanded him as he doubled over. The next thing he felt was his face striking the deck. Barely conscious, wracked with pain and nausea, Kirk forced his eyes open—and saw an equally battered Sarek lying only centimeters away, looking at him.

"The urn," Sarek rasped in a feeble whisper. "Break the urn." Sarek shifted his gaze past Kirk, who turned his head and followed the ambassador's cue.

A small ceramic urn sat on a low altar at the far end of the room—past L'Nel, who was fixed upon Kirk and moving in for the kill. Kirk winced in anticipation of the thrashing he was about to endure. *This is gonna hurt.*

Kirk sprang to his feet, charged at L'Nel, and threw himself forward in an attempt to tackle her. As he hoped, she sidestepped him with ease, and he tumbled past her. Somersaulting and rolling across the deck, he regained his feet only a few strides shy of the altar. He lunged toward the urn—

—and crashed to the deck as L'Nel tackled him from behind, apparently wise to his intention. He kicked wildly, trying to free his legs, but she held on and clawed her way forward, pounced on him, and pummeled him with savage blows.

Kirk twisted and flailed, searching the deck for anything within reach that he could use as a weapon. His hand landed on the leg of a broken table. He seized it and swung it in one smooth stroke, hitting L'Nel in the head. She lost her balance for a moment, but even armed, Kirk knew he was fighting a losing battle.

Instead of taking another swing at L'Nel, he flung the table leg away.

It flew straight and true—and shattered the ceramic urn on impact.

A spectral flash of light filled the darkened compartment, and an unearthly mist erupted from the broken vessel on the altar. For a few seconds, Kirk thought he heard the whisper of a voice speaking in an alien tongue, and chords of a strange melody touched his thoughts like the echo of a memory.

L'Nel screamed. It was a sound deeper than anger, beyond anguish.

Roaring, she threw herself at Kirk and locked her hands around his throat. They rolled across the deck, entwined in a violent embrace.

Kirk clawed at her fingers but couldn't break her iron grip. He felt his esophagus collapsing, and he was certain his neck would snap at any second. *Please let it end quickly*, he prayed to whatever power might be listening.

L'Nel's head jerked backward and her eyes widened. Her grip loosened as her body went slack and slumped to one side.

She toppled over and fell to the deck, and Kirk saw Spock—bloodied and bruised, but with his hand clasped on the nerve cluster between L'Nel's neck and left shoulder. As soon as Spock seemed certain that L'Nel was unconscious, he let go of her and collapsed beside her.

Kirk coughed, cracked a pained and bloody smile, and drew the sweetest breath he'd ever tasted. In a hoarse whisper, he said, "Thanks, Spock."

An explosion disintegrated the door of the guest quarters in an orange flash. Before the smoke and dust had cleared, security men charged inside, phasers drawn, followed by Scotty and McCoy.

Kirk lifted his hand and declared in a shaky voice, "Over here." The security men rushed to his side and kneeled in a tight huddle. McCoy was right behind them. Kirk pointed at L'Nel. "Put her in the brig, get everyone else to sickbay."

"Aye, sir," said the goateed lieutenant. He snapped out orders to his men, who put the young Vulcan woman in restraints and hauled her away.

As they left, medical personnel hurried in, bearing medkits and stretchers. McCoy kneeled at Kirk's side, scanning him with a medical tricorder. The doctor frowned and laid a hand on Kirk's chest. "Time for your physical, Captain."

All Kirk could do was mumble, "Whatever you say, Bones."

72 HOURS LATER . . .

34

Spock arrived in the hangar only minutes before the scheduled departure of Sarek's shuttle to Akiron. His father stood at the gangplank to the small spacecraft, his hands laced in front of him, his countenance serene and dignified.

Spock halted in front of Sarek. "I apologize for my tardiness."

The ambassador raised one eyebrow. "Ship's business, I presume?"

"Yes." Spock glanced at the shuttle and saw his father's three advisers inside, looking back at him. He faced Sarek. "We have made arrangements with the Vulcan colony on Calidan III to provide T'Pring with psionic therapy during her incarceration."

A sage nod from Sarek. "That is for the best. Her crimes were serious, but her mind is greatly troubled. She owes us penance, but we owe her proper care."

"Indeed." Eager to change the subject, Spock asked, "I trust you have recovered adequately from your injuries?"

"I have. You and your shipmates also seem well."

"Yes. Doctor McCoy is a very capable physician."

Sarek reacted with a dubious tilt of his head. "For a human." He glanced at the shuttle, and for a moment he seemed pensive. "I must admit that I am surprised the Kathikar permitted Vellesh-ka to re-form his government and resume his office. When one considers the calamity they have suffered, and the fact that Vellesh-ka fled the planet and took asylum on the *Enterprise*, I expected he would face far more serious consequences upon his return."

"The Kathikar exhibit an unusually strong desire for security and continuity during times of crisis," Spock said. "Though I suspect that Captain Kirk's talent for persuasive argument might have been a factor in Vellesh-ka's reinstatement."

A fleeting twinge on Sarek's face hinted at a suppressed frown. "Yes. Your captain does have a way with words. Perhaps one day he will learn to use them *before* he resorts to swinging his fists."

"One can always hope."

"In any event, Kirk's verbal talents have kept you both from facing courts-martial, so I suppose I owe him a small measure of gratitude for that."

"I should think we both do."

At the end of the gangway, the shuttle's pilot leaned out the door and called to Sarek, "Ambassador? We're waiting on you, sir!" Sarek nodded to the pilot, who ducked back inside the craft and powered up the engines.

"Before I leave, my son, there are certain important matters that, regrettably, remain . . . *unresolved.*"

Spock met his father's stern gaze and intuited that Sarek was referring to Spock's relationship with Nyota Uhura, and how it might affect Spock's role in the continuation of the Vulcan species. He wondered what his father expected him to say. It was a complicated situation, and not one that lent itself to a swift or tidy resolution at a moment such as this. He gave Sarek the only honest answer he had.

"That is how *certain matters* are going to remain, Father . . . for now."

Sarek bowed his head, apparently accepting that the conversation was tabled for the time being. "Very well." He raised his hand in the Vulcan salute. "Live long and prosper, my son."

Spock reciprocated the gesture. "Peace and long life, Father."

With nothing left to say, Sarek turned, crossed the gangplank, and boarded the shuttle. Spock watched a crewman seal the craft's hatch.

Seconds later the shuttle eased out of its docking slip and made a smooth pivot to turn its nose aft. Then it accelerated and passed through an invisible force field as it left the *Enterprise*'s hangar.

Ever since Spock's childhood, Sarek had said many times that he simply did not understand his son. Watching his father's shuttle arc toward Akiron, Spock had to confess that, for once, the sentiment was mutual.

35

Kirk settled into his chair on the bridge of the *Enterprise* feeling rejuvenated. Despite the hardships of the past week, the crew was in good spirits. Their mood had been brightened by Doctor McCoy's discovery of a treatment to cure those who had been paralyzed by the wights, and morale had surged following their success in stopping the alien invaders. Reports of the Kathikar's spontaneous, global demonstrations of gratitude to them, as well as to Starfleet and the Federation, had made the victory that much sweeter.

For his own part, Kirk was just happy to hear that no one at Starfleet Command or the Federation Council would be pressing charges.

He swiveled his chair toward the science station. "Spock, what's our status?"

"All damage repaired, Captain. Ready to break orbit."

Kirk looked at Uhura. "Do we have new orders yet, Lieutenant?"

"Aye, sir. Admiral Perez directs us to continue ahead into unexplored space and make regular reports of our findings."

Smiling, Kirk turned his chair toward the main viewscreen. "My kind of mission. Sulu, plot a course for someplace no one's ever gone before."

"Aye, sir." Sulu keyed in coordinates with an enthusiastic grin.

As the bridge crew prepared for departure from Akiron, McCoy stepped through the starboard portal onto the bridge and sauntered down to stand beside Kirk's chair. "Aren't you looking like the cat that ate the canary."

"What're you saying? That I look happy?"

"Insufferably so."

"Well, why shouldn't I? After all, I did get a perfect bill of health on my physical fitness test."

McCoy frowned. "Don't remind me." He and Kirk watched the curve of Akiron's northern hemisphere sink out of sight on the main viewscreen. "So, Jim, I have to ask. Visions and hypnosis, past lives and all this talk of 'destiny' . . . are you going to start making command decisions based on faith now?"

Kirk responded with a good-natured chuckle. "Hardly."

"Not even a little bit?"

Kirk shrugged. "I'm not saying my mind hasn't been opened a little. It'd be fair to say I've gained a broader sense of what's possible in the universe—but let's not go labeling me a *believer* just yet."

Sporting a sly half smile, McCoy said, "If you don't believe in a higher power after all this, what *do* you believe in, Jim?"

Kirk looked over his shoulder, noted a discreetly tender moment transpiring between Spock and Uhura at the communications console, and had his answer.

"I believe in love, Bones. I believe in love."

ACKNOWLEDGMENTS

As ever, my first thanks go to my wife, Kara, for her unwavering love and support.

Beyond that . . . things get a bit strange this time around.

My first draft of this novel was written in 2010, roughly a year after the release of the feature film *Star Trek*. Mine was one of four novels planned as literary follow-ups to that movie. For various reasons unrelated to the contents of the books themselves, a decision was made by several parties to postpone the publication of those novels, perhaps indefinitely.

Years passed, and other projects came and went. I resigned myself to the idea that this story of Jim Kirk and his crew from J. J. Abrams's feature-film incarnation of *Star Trek* would never see publication. This saddened me just a bit, because I felt my tale had tapped into the unique characterizations and dramatic situations of that film, and that I had told a truly *Star Trek* story in the process.

Fast-forward to 2019 and a message from my editors telling me that they've decided to put my long-shelved novel back on the schedule. I was excited but also daunted. I knew there were continuity details in my original draft that had been superseded by the sequel film *Star Trek: Into Darkness*. Could my story be revised to comply with canon? The answer, as it happened, was yes.

As best as I was able, I've revised this nearly decade-old novel so that its style comports with my current expectations.

If it seems a tad short for a work published in this format, that's because it was written to be a light-and-fast mass-market paperback. A quick-and-breezy, pulp-style science-fiction adventure yarn, one that would feel true to the film that had inspired it. As such, it has a lighter style than many of my other books.

As for the work that went into bringing this novel to print after so long a hiatus in my computer's virtual trunk, I wish to extend my thanks to editors Margaret Clark and Ed Schlesinger, who patiently let me rewrite, revise, and re-edit the manuscript into something that I considered worthy of publication.

I'm also grateful to the fans who have so long clamored for the release of this novel, as well as the other three that were meant to be its shelf companions. Two of those other books— by Christopher L. Bennett and Greg Cox—have been revised into other tales. So it is that *More Beautiful Than Death* turned out to be one of the two left standing, along with Alan Dean Foster's *The Unsettling Stars*.

I also want to thank the powers that be at *Star Trek* for finally granting their consent to this book's publication. It's been a long time coming. Here's hoping that you, gentle readers, decide it has been worth the wait.

Live long and prosper, friends.

ABOUT THE AUTHOR

David Mack is the award-winning and *New York Times* best-selling author of nearly forty novels and numerous short works of science fiction, fantasy, and adventure, including the *Star Trek Destiny* and *Cold Equations* trilogies.

Mack's writing credits span television (for two episodes of *Star Trek: Deep Space Nine*), prose, and comic books. His latest work is his Dark Arts trilogy (*The Midnight Front, The Iron Codex,* and *The Shadow Commission*), a secret-history fantasy series published by Tor Books.

He currently works as a consultant on two animated *Star Trek* television series, *Lower Decks* and *Prodigy*. He lives in New York City with his wife, Kara.

Visit his official website, www.davidmack.pro, or follow him on Twitter @DavidAlanMack.